T0381110

HIDDEN END OF THE LINE

TESSA TUCKER

WESTBOW
PRESS®
A DIVISION OF THOMAS NELSON
& ZONDERVAN

WestBow Press books may be ordered through booksellers or by contacting:

WestBow Press
A Division of Thomas Nelson & Zondervan
1663 Liberty Drive
Bloomington, IN 47403
www.westbowpress.com
1 (866) 928-1240

Author Credits: Author of Altonian Summit and Indomitable Deaf Victorians.

ISBN: 978-1-9736-8212-7 (sc)
ISBN: 978-1-9736-8213-4 (e)

Print information available on the last page.

WestBow Press rev. date: 01/09/2020

Dedicated to my husband Ken, my daughter
Sharon, my son Caleb, and my brother Tim.

Contents

Author's Note

A few years ago, I asked my teenaged son what genre of books he liked. He responded that he liked adventure dystopian books, like *The Maze Runner.* I took his interest as my initial inspiration. Later, I toned down the thriller for a Christian audience. The other idea I fused with this approach for a story was "The Truman Show."

The locomotive theme developed when I read advice from authors to authors. The advice always suggests one should "write about what you know." I grew up with a railfan father who had us run a model railroad in our garage. If we ran the loco off the tracks, we got brownie points. Saturdays were spent watching my father take pictures of locomotives at the Santa Clara round house. Our vacations invariably involved riding behind steam. So, in my university California History class, what did I research? Theodore Judah, the man with the vision for the transcontinental railroad. More recently, in my Historiography course, what was my final project about? Of course, the transcontinental railroad. If there is one thing I know after all of that, it's trains.

Now, I need to add a special explanation about my noting. In the instances when the Deaf character signs, I include standard American Sign Language, ASL, notation. In the beginning of the book, the main character signs one sign,

I-L-Y, which means I love you. Notating a manual language like American Sign Language, ASL, proves difficult in print. ASL linguists and authors of ASL books use capital letters for a word that is a gloss. A gloss is the best approximation in English for the concept the sign conveys in the case when only one sign is used, such as PLEASE. Although there are two words in English, as with THOUGHT-of, the signed part is in all caps. When the characters sign phrases and conversations, as in the last chapter, the actual signs are in capital letters and the English words are lowercase due to the needs of a fiction novel.

The sign language used in this dystopian book of the future, takes the trajectory of ASL used now into the future. If you want to see the signs my fictional characters use, look at the real ASL of today. Check out the YouTube videos of NAD vlogs (National Association of the Deaf video logs), and other Deaf people's vlogs on YouTube. This list gives a sample of Deaf of Deaf signers of modern ASL.

Prologue

THE SUN WAS more luminous, but cooler through the smoggy atmosphere. The moon hid its reflective face. Not a grey cloud in the sky. Not even a warning breeze to reach the siblings. But an ominous white cloud formed, pale as the bleached bones in the desert. Two hundred years ago, Old Denver was founded in the high desert. Fortunately, the government protected pine forests as close as ten miles away. Unfortunately, they used them for their terrifying purposes.

Tekka, Ty and Trini stood on the asphalt of a narrow alley bordered with tall brick apartments. The summer heat penetrated through the cracks in their sneakers. It smelled of discarded week-old chicken bones and cat excrement that littered the alley. The siblings grew up in the neighborhood. Ty still wrinkled up his nose in disgust.

On all four sides, the tenements stood decades old and untouched by the War and Transformation. The people in the "Liberty Square" community scoffed at this name as the only thing to change about their lives were two things. One was the change in name to Liberty Square and Liberty alley. The other change was worse and would start on this day.

The preschool-aged brother was tall for his age, coming up to his brother's chin. He stood between his siblings, his sister on his right and his older brother on his left. His reddish-brown hair fell in his eyes and he brushed it back. The sleeve of his hand-me-down synthetic shirt was too short. He tugged at the bottom to cover his exposed belly button. The BB-8 image stretched so that its bottom sphere wasn't a circle but more of an oval. He stroked his chin with the cleft in it. Then, he lifted the middle metal cup, showing that the tiny white ball was located under this cup. Two identical cups sat on opposite sides of the cup with the ball. The reddish-brown-haired sibling moved the three cups over a smoothed heavily lacquered portable little table. In fact, it was an old discarded TV tray. The younger siblings and the short man barely stood a head above the table.

The player, a short man with a red nose and six days-old growth of whiskers, stood on the other side of the little table. His watchful grey eyes glanced to the pale cloud only for a moment and then looked from the kid's right hand to his left hand and back again.

Ty knew exactly which cup hid the spherical toy beneath its covering. The tan boy kept his eyes on all three cups, like a watchful cat. His small tan hands moved quicker than a racoon's paws, looking like a tan blur. His younger sister, Trini with her eagle eye tracked the cup the ball was under. She stared at it until the toddler formed an "O" with her lips remembering something and suddenly switched her stare to the wrong shell. Her face changed instantly as a performer takes off one mask and fits on a new one, as a Greek performer would take off one mask and replace it with another. Her eyes widened. Every muscle of her face tensed with effort like a child trying to control the urge to tell a secret.

"Trini," Mrs. Davis called, "I want to speak with your mother about a new hat. Come with me." Mrs. Davis, a plump older woman stood about ten meters away on the street that led to the Lib. Her right foot tapped as she impatiently waited for the little girl.

"Not now." Trini's curt reply was followed by pursed lips.

The sweaty palmed player nervously weaved his 10 Intermountain coin between the fingers of his right hand. When the copper-haired brother brought his lightning fast shuffling to a halt, the player nodded with a half-smile. He wiped his sweaty palms on his oil-stained pants never taking his eyes off the metal cup. The same one Trini stared at. The player placed his 10 coin in front of the cup on the right now nodding his head up and down. His gaze then met the copper-haired kid's brown eyes with gold specks. The kid betrayed nothing.

"Trini, now!" Mrs. Davis yelled.

The little girl's head whipped around. Her dark brown hair loose and wild like ornamental grass. Peeking between the tussle of hair, she looked at the portly woman. "We're busy. Five more minutes."

The elderly woman shaded her eyes with her hand like a visor. Looking at the street ahead of her where rays of the morning struck her face, the woman said something to herself. Trini couldn't read lips and dismissed it. The woman slung her bag onto her shoulder and walked towards the Lib.

Trini turned her attention back to the game.

As Ty maneuvered the cups, he felt the smooth cold metal against his fingertips. When he let go of the cups, the player shot his right hand to the metal cup on his right, turning it over. Nothing. Just a vacant space that mocked him.

With a Cheshire Cat smile, the kid lifted the metal cup to the man's left. He spoke the first word since the player approached the table, "Tada."

Tekka, the teen brother, said, "A lead bet has a perfect chance to score big." He bent over to collect the bet.

The middle sibling was perfectly quiet with a confident gaze at the player.

Trini looked up at the taller people with her big brown eyes, pumped her arm, and said, "Yes!"

The player's mouth gaped open.

The siblings gambled and won, as they had hundreds of times, with their Whizkid middle sibling moving the cups and youngest sibling conning with her innocent-looking stare. The oldest sibling, quickly scooped up the money from the small table. They collapsed the table and stood shoulder to shoulder. The player shook his head and with a shrug of his shoulders, turned to walk the way he had entered the apartment lined alley. As he went, he muttered, "Little Wayfield brats. Young things should be in a nursery."

Eagerly, the younger two stood on their toes to see their big brother count out —

"One hundred ten dollars," the middle sibling said before his brother separated the last three coins. Ty smiled broadly showing all his baby teeth. He liked his teeth. They were small, but straight and neatly spaced, as opposed to his brother with crooked teeth. Everyone in the Lib and apartments surrounding it had teeth that looked like an aged fence with planks leaning one way or another.

Tekka shook his head while looking down at him. The teen's shoulder-length brown hair danced. One strand got caught in a protruding tooth. The teen pulled the hair and tucked it behind his ear, then turned and gave him an approving sock to the arm.

Ty was feeling proud of himself and smiled broadly. Sadly, it was gone when the excited sister stepped on his toe as she jumped with delight.

"Hey, watch it, Trini," he said. "And aren't you supposed to interpret for Mrs. Davis?"

"Mrs. Jabba the Hutt," Tekka said. The teen laughed while he moved his fingers among the coins in his right pocket.

Ty shook his head in disgust at his big brother's lack of respect. Emphasizing the title, Ty said, "Mrs. Davis wants Trini to interpret." The older brother stared at Trini, "Go on with you."

"Why can't you do it, Ty? You're older," Trini said. She pouted.

"I don't know many signs," Ty said. "Remember last week when Mr. Garcia's trash can was knocked over and mother called me over to them. And, I tried to remember the sign for racoon, but I signed ugly?" Ty repeated the sign in which his two hands moved in opposite directions. The young boy used only one instead of two fingers over his face. The other difference was that he drew each straight index finger into a crook.

Trini and Tekka were laughing.

Ty threw his hands out at his sides, "I'm no good at signing."

Next, Trini looked up at her oldest brother with her big brown eyes.

Tekka rubbed his lip back and forth on one of his crooked teeth. His sister's eyes on him stopped his nervous habit. "No. I don't interpret. You know I mostly fingerspell to mother," he said. Then, the teen fingerspelled, "HA-HA." The teen grinned. "After I put our money away, I have to meet some guys. You go on. Mother and Mrs. Davis have business to discuss and you're needed."

"This is the fourth time. I don't like having to listen so much. It's hard." Trini crossed her arms.

"They're going to make it hard for you to sit if you don't hurry up," Tekka said.

Trini rolled her eyes and signed. Her little body slumped.

Tekka turned and gave Ty a half smile, He amiably socked him in the arm again. "Ty, you're a whiz—"

"Kid," a new player said, holding out a 10 Intermountain coin in his outstretched palm. He was a short pale man in old clothes with holes between the soles and the sides of the shoes. He could have been any one who lived in this large ghetto.

"Sorry, we're closed for the day," the older boy lifted his square chin and shoved the folding table under his arm.

While the siblings' attention was on the short man, the strong arms of three men grabbed them from behind.

The siblings twisted in the iron grip of each man holding them, shouting their protest.

Ty felt their strong grip on his arms like a dog on a bone. They wouldn't let go.

"Settle down, kids," a new voice said.

The oldest sibling shouted, "Let go, or our father will be looking out that window any minute and shoot you," glaring at the speaker for the group. He had a uniform on that the kids had never seen before. It was neither the fern green of the Intermountain Rangers, nor the grey-clad police. The man wore a tan khaki uniform with a patch embroidered with, NFLS on it. On his head was a felt Stratton hat. Although clean-shaven, an old scar ran down his chin looking like a single ghastly whisker.

"Liar," Scar jaw said. "Your father died in a fire. Your mother sits at Liberty Square selling her baskets and hats." The cold stare of the man's icy pale eyes dared Tekka to contradict him. They stood like that in their "stare down." After rocking his weight from foot to foot for a minute, Tekka looked down at the ground. At this, the preschooler spoke up, "Hey Mister, I know you're here for me." The preschool-aged kid lifted his cleft chin with no hint of fear.

"Ty," the man said, "we've noticed your genius. I have half a million Intermountains to give your mother in exchange for you." The man nodded.

While the lackeys still held the other two siblings' arms, Scar jaw scooped up the preschool Whizkid.

1

Justin

HE HAD A huge smile on his face. The cowboy thought about all his blessings as he met the new day.

"I know you can hear me," his mother said. "Eat, shower and comb that mop." Mrs. Wayne wore her platinum-blonde hair teased in a poof around her head like a fountain. She kept up with the newest trends.

The clean-shaven teen rubbed his eye as he sat up in his bed. Justin enjoyed the life of a contented sixteen-year-old, soon to be seventeen, more than contented - blissful. His life in Hidden Valley could be envied by any of his peers. Today his family and girlfriend were celebrating his birthday a day early. Tomorrow they would be busy at Justin's big competition. Ignoring his eggs and bacon on a breakfast in bed tray, Justin looked out his door and observed his mother as she went a step into the hallway. She stopped in front of a mirror and smoothed her strawberry-blonde hair. The lipstick she wore reflected the same color as his cherry-red car. The other ranch wives in the valley envied Mrs. Wayne's beauty. He had heard them say so. Justin always wondered why appearances were so important to her. In actuality, both Mr. and Mrs. Wayne always wanted to look their best. His father, Mr. Wayne, went for a haircut every week. Justin could care less how he looked when he first woke up. Still, his mother lectured him every morning, and especially this morning, chiding him to groom.

They had a cook who prepared the breakfast that sat on his tray. Laying still in bed, his stomach was almost even with his mouth. He scooted his way to a more upright position and straightened his torso so he wouldn't push on his stomach. He made quick work of the breakfast, keeping the apple for later. His mother had laid out the outfit she wanted him to wear; a new brown, gold and white calico western shirt, which matched his eyes, bootcut jeans, rattlesnake skin boots, a bolo with a cow skull clasp, all new. He topped his outfit with his white Stetson on his day-old haircut. Dressed to the teeth, the cowboy stepped out onto the deck. The apple rested in his palm. He planned to play catch with it, as he did with every apple since he could remember.

"Justin," Vanessa called. She balanced from one foot to the other.

His parents and Vanessa, his girlfriend, stood waiting and shouted, "Happy Birthday!"

Justin looked to the right and left. Looking back to the three he held dearest, he said, "Sorry, you've got the wrong cowboy. Today's... not my birthday." He had a twinkle in his eyes.

"Oh, very funny, dear," his mother said. She, like Vanessa and his father, all spoke funny. It wasn't how he spoke, not exactly. When the three of them, really, everyone in Hidden Valley spoke, it was like the people in the 1950s westerns he watched with his parents.

His father, tall dark and handsome with bright turquoise eyes, could be a movie star. As Justin shook his father's hand, he thought again how he didn't look like either of his parents. When he remarked on it, his parents would recount all the family members who *were* auburn-haired and brown-eyed.

Like a vision, Vanessa walked tall with her long blonde tresses hanging down her back to Justin. She put delicate fingers on his cheek and kissed him briefly on the lips. She smelled like springtime and he inhaled her scent. His girlfriend looked up to him with large sapphire eyes and batted her long lashes a couple of times. Smiling, Justin stared at her face and thought, *I love this girl.*

"Come and get your presents, Babe." She took his hand in hers and led him to the patio table. Two presents sat on the surface like twins. "I got two things for you." She went on her tippy toes while tilting her head then went back to her sophisticated stance.

Justin's forehead wrinkled slightly. He thought there should be a big present from his parents as usual. Last year, they gave him a wonderful surprise - a new convertible mustang; red like he wished for. How could anything top that? He shouldn't expect too much this year, he knew. At the back of his mind he remained disappointed. He would only be getting two gifts both from Vanessa. He decided to focus on the gifts his girlfriend was excited for him to open. He set the apple down just as the groom snuck up behind him. Sky his dark chestnut horse had a leather strap attached to the present from his parents in her mouth. Justin whirled around when he felt her muzzle and the slightly rectangular cardboard box touch his back.

"Sky, what do you have there?" the cowboy stroked his horses' head affectionately. "Thank you, Sky." It was the size of a hat box. Justin placed the box on the table and opened the top. A new white Stetson hat with a braided leather band sat in Styrofoam and a clear bag. He lifted it and smiled broadly. "Thank you Mom and Dad."

His mother smiled with her perfect white teeth.

His father said, "Put it on, son."

Justin placed the Stetson on his head. A perfect fit. "It's perfect." He turned, threw his shoulders back and modeled the new hat for his girlfriend.

Vanessa gave Justin her dazzling white smile, then drew his face to his and kissed him full on the mouth.

His parents stood up and went to pet Sky, leaving the two love birds for the remaining gifts from Vanessa.

Justin broke off the kiss. It went against his natural inclination, but this was a family event. "Just practicing for the Prom," he said. "Mom and Dad, sorry, come back here." It was prom season and the

3

two teens planned on going. In fact, Justin was so excited, like a bull rider anticipating a rodeo.

His parents came back to the table, still standing.

The birthday boy picked up the gift bag, but he didn't bring out the gift. Instead, his face went dark and his mouth twisted in horror. "Augh, it bit me." Justin wrestled it with the hand in the bag, finally yanking it out and broke into laughter. When his parents saw it, they hooted. The leather belt lay in his hand with both ends hanging down.

"Funny, son," his father said.

"Very funny Justin. You had me going," his mother smiled.

"Justin, the belt is made of the finest Italian leather," Vanessa beamed.

He measured the belt around his waist. It will fit perfectly but he stared at the end where something was missing - the belt buckle.

"Open the other present, Justin," Vanessa said.

The love-struck teen obeyed. Putting the belt on the table, he picked up the bag. It sagged with something heavy within. Justin pulled the present out. This time without joking around. He held onto a rectangular silver belt buckle with an eight-pointed gold star that stood out. It was 3D. And looked like the pointed wheel of a cowboy's horse spur. He spun the gold star a round and around.

"Wow, Vanessa. It's terrific. Thank you!" he said. His eyes, lips and being smiled at the love of his life. He hoped nothing would ever come between them.

2

Justin's Shock

THE FIRST OF the disappearances burned in Justin's mind, like a hot iron brand on a steer. The teen kidnappings started eighteen days ago. He and his friend, Leo were competing that day in the Model Railroading Competition.

The Union Pacific Big Boy 4000 chugged from the station. The huge black steam engine picked up speed to climb the grade. The mighty steam engine easily surmounted the summit. As the locomotive sped down the opposite grade, it picked up speed, too much speed. Justin used the on/off switches to prepare the track ahead. He made key strokes on a conventional transformer control box. His deft hands pushed the throttle for the Big Boy to increase its speed.

Leo pushed a handheld remote unit of his digital command control operating switches, setting four different trains on their courses. The intense grades and train trestles, acceleration and deceleration on curves, the perfect stops in front of the evenly spaced stations, and the impeccable timing of an engine going over a bridge while another locomotive went under, impressed Justin. Leo orchestrated his trains in a harmonious symphony. Never once had Leo derailed. Justin liked to watch the best Whizkid at each International event, and when it came to model railway engineering, he had to admit that Leo stood above the rest. Justin realized with a start, that he had sped around a curve, derailing his train.

"Five brownies, mate," Leo said.

Too bad for me, Justin thought. Leo is the better operator. He'd never heard of Leo and brownies spoken of in the same breath. Brownie points were demerit points for speeding, unsafe operation and derailment, in other words, negative marks against the model railroad engineer that could cost them the contest. Today, Justin and Leo competed against the best of them.

The new Intermountain Expo Center had been finished two years ago, east of the airport and west of the Capitol, Intermountain City. The enormous expo center, with its high ceilings and concrete floor, echoed with the electronic sounds of tiny train whistles. Puffs of white grey smoke could be seen trailing above the trains. Flashing red lights blinked from tiny railroad crossing signals. The layouts had everything from dollhouse sized gas street lights to miniature working switches. Eight high school boys and two girls stood in the center of eight of their train layouts. The boy or girl controlled every locomotive and switch, as if he or she were a dispatcher controlling the flow of traffic. No one wore engineer caps. These teens were too old for that. Besides, this was a serious competition, and these elite competitors were fighters.

The floor held the eight model railroad engineers and their layouts, like Greek gods, manipulating their domains with the flip of a switch.

Justin maneuvered his first train over his layout. The loco bolted down the straight track. The sharp whistle of a knock-off model Silverstream steam locomotive reverberated. He ran the train on the track in front of him. He expertly parked the engine right in front of him. He grabbed the container of steam oil and squeezed a few drops in the smokestack. He looked over at Leo, also in the middle of his railway layout. He watched as his friend first rubbed his index finger over his square jaw while looking at the array of scented oils in front of him. The golden-blonde teen selected one and squeezed steam oil into the smokestack of his prize Lionel Empire State Hudson diecast steam locomotive with its sleek streamlined tender. Justin nodded as he admired Leo's expensive engine. He would have to ask his parents for one. There was always a birthday or government celebration when they gave him gifts. *That's wrong, I should be grateful for what I have.*

Puffs of the smoke lifted out of his smokestack into the air. The smells wafted to Justin's nose. Justin's stomach growled. *I can't wait to eat and I gotta get some of that scented smoke oil,* Justin thought.

Leo brushed his golden-blonde bangs to the side, "Look at the speed of this loco!"

Leo's Mikado ripped over the tracks, like lightning across the sky. He used the toggle on his control box and pushed the deceleration button with uncanny timing. His locomotive stopped right at the miniature station.

Justin tipped his cowboy hat, "Nice piece of work par'ner."

"Did you check out my competition?" Leo asked loudly. He looked expectantly into Justin's intelligent brown eyes with the flakes of gold color.

Justin knew each competitor's strengths and weaknesses.

He strained over the cacophony in the room, "Yup. Dylan's layout is elaborate, but slow." Dylan designed elaborate layouts, but it slowed down his trains.

Then, Justin motioned with his head toward Lydia's area, "As usual, she had every train and scene on the layout historically accurate within five years! But, she had simple and straight rail lines with only two engines running."

Leo nodded in agreement.

Justin added, "Now, Lydia has only one train running."

He looked over at Zach, groaning when his locomotive came off the tracks. He had just derailed for the second time in under five minutes. All morning Zach's trains jumped the tracks, and he derailed the locomotives while speeding on curves. When Zach's three trains were on the tracks, they were lightning fast.

"Zach can't keep his locomotive on the tracks, the speed demon," Justin crossed his arms.

Leo questioned, "Are you sure about Zach?"

"Of course. You have nothing to worry about." Justin reassured his friend.

On the other side of Leo's layout, Justin saw Gary. Gary had an innovative track layout and at least three fast trains running simultaneously. But, he overshot train stations and often backed up his trains.

"You know how Gary can't stop a train on a dime? He keeps overshooting stations and backing up his locomotives," Justin said. He immediately squeezed his lips together. He knew not to gloat and gossip. *Where did that come from?* Justin wondered. His parents, the Waynes didn't teach him that. They let him say anything.

Leo grinned, "He'll lose points for that. That's a relief, because I saw the amazing layout he designed. Good thing he can't park."

This time, Justin grinned back, not at Gary's weakness. Justin smiled in admiration of his amazing friend with the engineering skills of a master. Of course, Leo designed, built and ran his rail lines with clockwork efficiency. Justin couldn't think of a weakness in Leo's model railroading. Sure, when he was younger, he made mistakes; but, he was seventeen now. Over the years, Leo had honed his skills.

At this level of competition, operators aimed for zero brownies. The rules were taken from the Brown system, which is traced back to George R. Brown, during the 19th Century. He invented a system of demerit marks for when men broke the rules. If a railroad man received too many Brownies from the superintendent in a given period, it resulted in dismissal.

Justin didn't hear ordinary people use the term "brownies," except for the dessert they ate. Then, there were ancient legends of sprite brownies. Also, he'd heard of a long-dissolved troupe called the Girl Scouts that had Brownies. Justin's brain swirled with such factoids. But, what annoyed him to anger, was how people declared you'd get brownie points, if you did something good. That made no sense. When a model railroader derails his train, it is something bad; thus, he gets brownies. Justin shook his head at people's misuse of a perfectly good railroading term.

"I *saw* that Justin," chuckled Leo giving his friend some good-natured ribbing.

Justin gave a smile back, weak, but still a smile.

"I saw you watching my trains, mate. You've got to focus on your own," Leo advised and tipped his rabbit fur felt bush hat.

Justin tipped his leather cowboy hat in return, then finished aligning the metal wheels of his locomotive on the O-gauge tracks.

Television cameras hovered over them with their robotic technicians on tall poles. Television was a big deal in The North American Union. No one went to movie theaters any longer, too risky with all the terrorism. The North American War was over, but terrorism was back. In the mid twenty-first century, even the government made television programs and movies for TV. The National Forest Service, became the National Film Location Service, NFLS, that preserved National Film Parks. Other boys told him that there are TV programs running non-stop everyplace one looks in Continental Square downtown Intermountain. Most families had projections of one program or another in every room of their dwelling! Justin's parents didn't allow this. They had one televised projection in the family room that only they controlled. He could almost hear his father say that program viewing and television has become our culture's god, instead of worshipping Heavenly Father. *Still, I wouldn't mind knowing what was going on in the world, watch the news, view a football game-but no. We have to live in the stone age on our ranch.*

The footage of today's model railroading competition would show from five to seven p.m. that night on one of the 950 channels.

Justin's parents, Sam and Winona Wayne, obsessively hovered over him. They never left his side. Did he catch a bored look on his mother's face? When he turned to look at her, she quickly put on a big smile. Sometimes Justin wondered if she wore a mask of caring for him, that would peel to reveal her disdain for him. Was she tired of taking him to his many competitions, railroading, even baseball?

His father quickly said, "Son, you're doing great! Keep up the good work." He enjoyed all the attention from his father. His father played catch, taught him games, and rode horses with him. They were engaged in constant activity.

Standing directly across from him with her eyes glued to his face was Vanessa, his girlfriend. He took in her beauty. Long blonde silky hair, sapphire blue eyes and great curves in her slender frame, she could be a model. With a big toothy white smile, she said, "Babe, you're so good at this. I know you'll place." He loved when she called him "Babe." And her breathy voice drove him crazy. She chewed her gum with a couple smacking noises.

Justin turned his focus to the timing of his locomotives, while Vanessa and his parents quietly watched. He had to get this model O scale Mikado steam engine started now. Then, start the diesel rolling thirty seconds later. They would just miss each other, when he triggered the switch, which turned the diesel locomotive west. It was Justin's best maneuver. At the end of the allotted thirty minutes, Justin only derailed his locomotives two times... each. He had a bit of a lead foot.

When the scores were tallied, Leo won. Justin came in fourth, to his chagrin. The Whizkid wished he would be getting a trophy, but he just missed third place. His skills hadn't kept up with the other competitors and he knew it. Sure, he had plenty of other skills; but it was apparent that he wasn't competitive enough in any one game to take first, except baseball. Besides, trains were for fun. He turned to congratulate his friend. Leo was already at the steps ready to go on the stage.

Last year's winners were on the stage to present the awards, Jack O'Neill and Akio Mineta. On the left stood a young man with wavy hair. Standing to his left stood a teen with Asian features, who shook the winner's hand.

Then, the first young man spoke, "These three represent the best youth model railroaders. Their layouts were sick! Mad cool! I mean really awesome, Dude!" He gave a fist bump towards them.

The young man with Asian features, Akio, added, "And, Man, they showed innovation with awesome new electric cars, switches and controllers." Gary held up his free hand high in the air.

After the award ceremony, Justin went to the platform steps to congratulate his good friend Leo. First, a teen boy wearing glasses, carrying paper and pencil approached Justin between the seats and the stairs to the platform.

"Hey Justin. Can I have your autograph, please? I never miss your-" His words were cut off by his parents and Vanessa dashing between Justin and the boy wearing glasses. Justin wondered what was going on. Some adults escorted the boy with glasses out of the building. Justin couldn't help thinking how odd for the boy to ask for his autograph. Maybe he thought he was Leo. *No, he called me Justin,* he thought. *Leo, I need to talk to him.*

Then, he saw the second and third place winners chatting at the bottom of the steps.

"Where's Leo?"

"He was just here," Akio looked left and right. He's a happy one. Sure, I'd be happy, if I won second place.

"Hey, congratulations!"

"Thanks."

The third-place winner, Dylan, jived with jealousy, "Man, Leo went with the photographer, somewhere over there." He pointed to the bench near the restrooms.

Justin followed his gaze. A heavyset photographer, black hair in a man-bun, walked towards the boys.

"Excuse me," Justin started asking, "Where is-"

"No, not him. The photographer that Leo went with had short brown hair," Zach wagged his finger.

Justin looked around, squinting his eyes, straining to spot his friend Leo. Dads walked with their young sons or a daughter, the judges talked, the contestants' parents gathered trains, ...but no Leo. Leo's parents approached Justin.

"Hey Justin. You did well. I liked your Old West layout and steam locomotive."

"Thank you."

"Have you seen my son? We can't find him anywhere."

"Me neither," said Justin.

His dad asked, "When was the last time you saw Leo?"

"Yup, five minutes ago, when Jack O'Neill and Akio Mineta awarded Leo first place on this stage." Justin pointed to his left at the platform.

Justin frowned, knowing that Leo loved nothing more than to show off. Nor was it like him not to gloat about his victory. Leo savored his bragging rights. Strange. For Leo to miss the opportunity to rush up and flaunt his first-place trophy, for Leo not to jump at the opportunity to rub in how he trounced his less skilled friend, wasn't like the brash Whizkid. Still, Leo remained missing.

Leo's parents wrinkled their brows. A tear streaked his mother's face. They heard the announcer squawked on the PA system, "Would Leo Smith, please come to the stage for a picture?" After twenty more minutes of waiting, a stocky security guard approached Leo's parents and said, "I'm sorry. He's not anywhere in the building or close by outside."

His father said flatly, "It's not like him to leave his trains unattended for so long. Those, and his first-place trophies, are his pride and joy."

Justin remembered the image of Leo's parents, his mother crying, and his father massaging his forehead. For the first time he noted the color of the room, pale as bone. He still remembered the smell of fried bacon smoke oil and hot metal, the sharp odor and faint burnt taste of the air, and the moment the realization dawned on him. Leo was gone.

He had been kidnapped —the first of many disappearances.

3

Trini's Disgust

LIGHTNING FLASHED TO the South. It lit the surrounding area making it pale, like bones. The sunbaked earth craved precipitation, like one sickened with dehydrated. A dark cloud blew down over the dry landscape. On the desert floor were tracks - train tracks.

Narrow-gauge railroad tracks three feet, three and three-eighths inches extended for miles through the high desert. A dark train—a diminishing distant speck on the horizon— rolled towards the sunset. A shadow followed it. Something out of place lay behind in this barren wilderness. Between the tracks, a dark stain soiled the gravel.

The relentless sun baked the ground on that, the longest day of summer. Hot rays bore down on the tops of broken arches, red rocks, canyon walls, the desert floor and everything on it. A scarlet puddle dried out. It and the train were gone with the next breeze.

"The only things left were train tracks, basked in the sunlight in the middle of the high desert in a place called The Plateau," the TV show's narrator in a metallic grey suit said. An electric blue shimmer disappeared over the large base where the TV image had projected. Next, a commercial played on the same TV in the window front.

"That's revolting. I can't believe that show is for entertainment,"

14

Trini said to her older brother. She picked up the next empty plastic bottle on the sidewalk.

"Yep, hard to believe a reality show, would do that kind of thing," Tekka added. He picked up a sticky mostly empty container that used to hold a purple sports drink and dropped in in the bag. His eyes moved from one container to the other, counting their haul.

Trini walked holding one end of the bag while talking and gesturing with her other hand. "That's so disgusting. The producers are reprehensible but so are the advertisers. Then there are the viewers who tune in and raise the show's ratings. They all should be ashamed for producing that show," Trini said. She leaned over to pick up the next empty bottle. When she tried to pick up the bag, she noticed how heavy it had become.

"What was the name of that show?" Tekka asked. He counted the few new plastic containers.

"I don't know. It must have been up on the screen before we walked past." They dragged the bag. Tekka hefted it up to miss a stray rock on the sidewalk.

"Oh well. So, I counted what we've collected. We have one hundred ninety-four now. Just six more and Buck will give us 50 Intermountain coin." His smile faded when he looked at Trini's face. Sweat dripped down Trini's face and she wiped her cheeks on each sleeve of her worn grey T-shirt. She sighed.

"Let's get busy and finish this," Tekka's voice was soft but concerned. The sister and brother hastily collected the rest of the discarded plastic they needed, shoved it into the bag they held between them and hurried home.

4

Justin is Kidnapped

HE OPENED HIS eyes to slits. Light glared in them. Gusts from the helicopter's blades flapped his shirt tail. His muscles tightened, squeezing the rope as he braced himself. Attempting to wake from this deep sleep, felt like trying to swim through a pool of honey to the surface. He broke that surface by opening his eyes. The light which glared in his eyes, hurt them. He gazed down and could now see that he and his seat hung from a red rope far above a moving train car. Justin yelped. Then, the frightened teen looked up. Canvas straps on the rope held his hands. Only these and a seat harness seat held him up in the air.

Circling, bobbling, and lowering, the seat harness moved. The dizzy teen's brown eyes bulging under his reddish-brown bangs, he hugged himself closer to the rope. Heart pounding, breath quickening, he could barely breath. He wasn't a big fan of heights. He swallowed down bile.

My chest is collapsing, and I'm going to have a heart attack, he thought. Justin didn't look down. Instead, he closed his eyes tightly. *Where am I?* Swallowing, he shot his eyes wide open to face the terror. *Wow, were up high!* Above the opening in the ceiling of the boxcar, Justin saw a glowing blue light sparked, like electrical pulse. Opening his eyes and looking up, he saw the underside of the white helicopter. Should he climb up the cable? Could he do it? His alternative was shrouded in darkness below, like a black hole. The winch lowered him down on a cable attached to his harness seat until he was now two feet above the floor of the boxcar. Before Justin could grip the cable, it detached. The shadowy form in the helicopter door had dropped him. He fell the remaining couple feet, landing in a squat position, absorbing the shock. His knees ached as they usually did. He balanced with his hands straight in front. The ceiling opening now shut with a loud clang, like a jail cell shutting. Then, the sparkling blue flickered. A forcefield closed above the boxcar. Justin was squatting. He moved with the motion of the speeding train. No sound, except the clackety, clack. The darkness hung thick like fog at night.

In total darkness, Justin sprang to his feet. Now what? Don't want to be trapped. But it was better than dangling high in the air and being dropped. His heartbeat slowed to its usual rhythm. The rope, coiled around his head, fell easily when he pulled. His mind went back to the last person he was with—Vanessa. He and his girlfriend, had stood at his red mustang in the parking lot of the diner. She excused herself to go back inside to use the restroom when a figure stabbed him from behind with a hypodermic needle. It was coming back to him as the drug wore off. Where was Vanessa? Was she in the boxcar below? Or, did they have her in the helicopter?

He searched walking slowly and moving his hands in front of him. Nothing in the boxcar and he slumped. Would he be left here alone? Was he the only person on this train? If he was the sole person, how would he get out of this box car?

Justin realized the train sped him away from his home. Where was the train taking him? All he knew was that sick people tore him away from Vanessa. And, the train took him away from his loved ones, his mother, his father, the Waynes, and Vanessa. As he sweated in the hot boxcar, he longed to be riding horses with them. Well, he'd be happy just to see them. A thought burned in his mind, like a bug zapper, his senior prom. He had to get out of here and get fitted for the tux. He had to take Vanessa to the prom in four days. They must be worried about him. Picturing his family, he imagined the police telling his parents. His mother would have cried. They would find his father rounding up steers with his ranch hands. His father would have told his mother everything was going to be alright; then, set his jaw tightly. Justin was concerned that they would be sick with worry and his eyes ached under the tension. He pictured his beautiful girlfriend with her luxurious blonde crown. He longed to see her beautiful smile again. How was he going to get back to her? Vanessa probably called the police to get help. Maybe they followed the helicopter and are going to rescue him.

The scent of wood and dust wafted from the floor. Justin stuck his tongue between his lips again and again. He tasted plastic dust. *Strange*, he thought.

"Hello. Anybody here?" The genius listened in the darkness for the sound of another person, and hopefully, not a creature. Nothing. He scanned the pitch-black boxcar, on his left, the outline of faint light through the space around a door came into focus. As he stared, he saw no flicker of movement outside the door. All was still. When he reached the door, he felt for a knob or latch. The smooth metal door cooled his warm, slightly swollen hands.

"Somebody open the door." Still, no response. His hands searched the door. No handle. He pushed. The door didn't budge. Trapped. As he groped in the dark, his hand finally felt door hinges. *So, the door would swing into the boxcar.* He put his mouth close to the door until his lips touched the door paneling. In his loudest voice he again screamed, "Somebody, open the door!" He pounded his fist against it for a few seconds; then, stopped. The sweaty boy listened while his cold sore hand ached. Still no voices in response. He heard only the sound of the train wheels on the tracks. *I wonder if this is what happened to Leo*, he thought. Justin closed his eyes and opened them again, hoping it would be lighter when he opened them. The darkness hung thick around him. He reached out his hands again, searching. He held out his left hand as he walked groping in the blackness. His right hand moved in a circle on his shirt front. He suddenly knew he was signing PLEASE.

"Please God, help me," Justin prayed. At that moment, the frightened teen remembered the lighter in his pocket. It was the lighter he used to burn leaves around his family's ranch. First, his fingers ran over the symbol etched in the lighter —A Circle W, their family brand. He rolled his thumb on the spark wheel. Nothing. Biting his lip, he tried again. Still nothing. He thought, three strikes, you're out. With a deep breath, he steadied his hand and ran his thumb pushing the wheel and igniting the lighter. The flame cast a yellow glow. Justin turned up the gas on it and it grew. With more light, he looked around. Just as when he used his hands and feet, there was nothing in the boxcar. Placing the lighter in the middle of the boxcar, he unbuttoned his dress shirt, keeping on his white t-shirt. Finding a small slit, he tore the shirt at its side seam. He planned to just use the small strip. But after rolling it up, he decided to use the whole shirt. What an amazing blaze he would get with the whole shirt. Next, he took out some note paper from his pocket. On the paper, he had written his to do list: buy the prom ticket, get fitted for the tuxedo, and buy Vanessa's corsage. No sweat. He could remember those. So, he rolled up the list and a blank piece of note paper for kindling. First, he had a small fire going. When he added the small piece for the shirt, it kept the fire going. Finally, when he added the rest of the shirt, he had a good fire. He sat cross legged in front of the fire, sweating beads of moisture and breathing rising smoke, admiring the way the flames flickered back and forth. He understood why even on hot nights, lone cowboys sat at a fire. Fire kept the cowboy company. But for Justin, fire was an obsession.

All of a sudden, the door to the vestibule flew open with a gust of wind and several boys pushing on the door until the hinges stopped it. The gust put out Justin's fire.

"Hey! What did you do that for?" Justin stood up, a grimace on his tan face. He half stepped, half lunged forward through the now open door.

A teen with golden-blonde hair and a square jaw stood just inside the door. He looked at the burnt ashes and smoke, then coughed. "Justin, let's get you out of here." The golden boy grabbed Justin's hand, pulling him towards the door. By the time he was in the doorway, Justin came out of his pyromaniac trance. Justin ran his hand over his eyes, now in the brighter space. With his brow furrowed, Justin pondered his predicament and the jargon these boys used, like Newb. He hadn't heard that before. Justin took in an astonished breath, followed by a flood of relief. He could not believe his eyes. A smile spread over Justin's tan face. Standing before him was a tall boy greeting him.

"G'day, mate," Leo said.

Justin couldn't believe Leo, of all people, opened the door to let him out. *Thank you, God,* Justin prayed. Justin had just been thinking about Leo and his disappearance and then praying for his own rescue.

"Leo, it's you. Where are we?" Justin asked. Then, the teen coughed.

A friendly crooked smile over a square chin greeting Justin. Leo hugged his friend. "I'm so glad to see you, mate." Leo led him through the vestibule and into the dining car of the train. The narrow-gauge train car's narrowness meant the boys had to back into the dining car to let the tall boys through. Leo patted him on the back. "Now you understand what it's like being kidnapped, Newb." A twinkle danced in the golden boy's eyes.

Justin patted his good friend on the back and smiled. "I'm so glad to see you safe," Justin paused. "...It ... it is good to see you alive, Leo."

Leo nodded and then, gestured around the dining car. Four more faces smiled at Justin. He took a deep breath and exhaled. Relief washed over him. He wasn't alone. Justin surveyed these five of the ten whiz kids who had disappeared. Warmth spread in his chest. Justin spread his hand up his shirt stopping at his heart. He swallowed and blinked. But, they couldn't just sit around. His thoughts turned to getting off the train. "Let's get off this train!" He shouted as he sprang towards the opposite door of the dining car.

"Easy Mate," Leo said. He put an arm out, blocking Justin's path, "We can't get off of this train."

5

Justin's Orientation to The Beast

"OF COURSE, WE can get off, we just jum—,"

"There's a forcefield eight feet around us at all times, Leo announced.

"A forcefield, of course," Justin said. His arms were limp at his sides. He tightened his lips into a line.

Then, a younger kid with large brown eyes walked right up into Justin's space, "Hello. I am Kofi. The younger kid took Justin's limp hand and shook it. Our friend in the corner there, is Nick,"

Justin felt a bit dizzy. He still hadn't gotten used to the movement of the train. Or, was he just overwhelmed at being entrapped on the train.

Suddenly, Justin heard a voice with a Cajun accent. "Where y'at?" Nick stared at the new boy.

Justin stared back, studying a slightly overweight young man with brown hair and a goatee sitting in a chair in the corner. Justin didn't understand the young man's speech, but wanted to be friendly. "Howdy, Nick," Justin greeted him. Still, Nick just sat, shuffling a deck of cards, not offering his hand. A gambler's cane leaned against the table at his right hand. The cane seemed a necessity, within easy grasp. Justin had seen gamblers at the tournaments with their gambler's canes. His curiosity peaked. Did it have a sword hidden within? He could see that clear glass sealed the bulbous top and contained two green objects, one with two white dots and the other with five white dots. Dice. Maybe lady luck was with this feller.

Another boy approached on his other side. A short teen with exceptionally intelligent brown eyes under bushy eyebrows.

"Hello Newb," Tej ribbed.

Again, they called him this strange name. Justin understood what they meant. He decided to go along with them.

"Yes. I'm the Newb." Justin said smiling. He took the ribbing good-naturedly.

"I'm Tej." The short boy said in an accent from India. "I won the championship in Mahjong in the East. What are you good at?" Tej especially liked to call the new boys who were Dropped since him, Newbie or Newb.

Justin's head hurt. This guy talked too much, Justin thought. Justin just wanted to lay down, but he took the bait.

"Good at what?" Justin said with a puzzled expression.

"Kofi won the chess championship; Nick, the pinnacle championship; Leo, the model train engineering championship. We're all whiz kids. What is your skill?" Tej rephrased this time.

Justin's mind now caught up with him, suddenly feeling alert. Leo stood right in front of him now. A shocked Justin's mouth dropped open. Of course, he had been worried about his friend Leo from their last model railroading competition. "Leo. What are you doing here?"

"We're stuck on a speeding locomotive. I would say it's ironic, but I hate irony," Leo said.

Justin looked around at the faces of the next boy, Kofi. Something about the African boy seemed familiar. It dawned on Justin of the last time he competed in chess, but it seemed like ages ago. He looked at Kofi square in the face and remembered him as that boy who kept beating him. Justin felt better now that his memory was back.

"Right. Kofi, the chess champion. You checkmated my king

for the 2062 chess master title. That was … what … five years ago?! Wow, time flies while—" you're sheltered from the outside in a fortress of a valley, like where I grew up. "Hidden Valley lies beyond those hills." He pointed to the West and they looked. "But I didn't get any news. So, I didn't keep track of you, Kofi. Good to see you again, partner," Justin said. Kofi smiled, "Same here."

As relieved as Justin felt, the fact that he and these whiz kids had been kidnapped grated on him. Why were these geniuses put together with him? So, some horrible kidnapper, put champions in: chess, pinochle, poker and Mahjong and model railroading, with… what was Justin the champion of? He searched his memory, the last time he placed second was in model railroading, three years ago. His parents took him and the champion Leo out to a fancy dinner to celebrate. It was then that his parents let him drive a truck on the ranch. Then, they bought the red mustang to drive on the ranch, until he turned sixteen last fall. Since then, it has been room service only. For the last three years, his passion has been baseball. His team won nationals the last two years. But his parents didn't say much about it. His father had said, "Good job, son." His mother sounded so stiff with her, "Good boy, Justin." Why had his mother sound so stiff? He knew in his core that mothers should affectionately hug tightly and praise sincerely. Even his coach could do those two things genuinely. Once, Justin overheard his mother telling his father that *his* son wasn't living up to his full potential. So, he guessed that when he stopped getting second places when he competed individually, his parents grew disappointed in him. That's all I am, he thought, a disappointment.

Justin noticed Tej, head tilted and eyes trained on Justin, still waiting for an answer.

"Oh, yeah. Well, I stopped chess to focus on, well, … train engineering and baseball." Justin put his hands on his hips.

"Baseball, seriously?!" Tej crosses his arms.

Justin was proud of his leadership with his baseball team and his performance on the field. *Hum baby! I'm the team catcher. Our comp team won the national title the last two years straight, and this year we will—* Justin ached with disappointment. He pounded his fist into his palm. He would miss spring practices. He had to get off this train.

"Welcome to the Beast," Tej said.

Justin didn't want to be welcomed to the train, Beast, whatever. He refused to think he would be here more than 24 hours. He was determined to find a way off and get his life back. Vanessa and his parents were waiting for him in Hidden Valley.

Justin raked his eyes over the inside of the dining car. The windows on his left had been painted over with black paint. The windows on the opposite side had shades, but were clear. Most of the window shades were up, letting in the maximum light. Between the windows, sconce electric lights were attached. Booths sat at the far end on both sides. On his right, a kitchen and customer counter took up more than a fourth of the car, and last, to his left were round tables and curved-backed chairs like you found in an ice cream parlor. He kicked one of the chairs over.

"The Beast is a prison like no other," said Leo.

"The Beast, what in-" Justin asked while leaning forward.

"This train. Let me tell you how it is on the Beast," Leo said.

"The walls close in. You lose track of direction. You try to get your balance. The noise is constant. *Clickity Clack and Huff, Huff.* You can't sleep. Once the nausea settles, you go outside for fresh air, and you almost get knocked over by the gust created by the high speeds. If you stay out during the daytime, the Screakers come after you," Leo said.

The frightened Kofi, with arms crossed, moved his hands up and down his crossed arms.

"The Screakers?" Justin said. He had heard stories about monsters around the campfire. The cowboy could play along. "What are the Screakers?"

Kofi cast his eyes downward and visibly shivered.

"See, they're like nothing we've ever seen before. Not until we were dropped on the Beast." Kofi fell silent and shivered.

Tej whispered, "Fresh meat." Snickering.

Winking, Leo continued, "I've been here the longest, understand," rising up to his full height, "Let's see, the last time I saw you, I proved to you," his voice rose with energy and in pitch, "I was the best model railroad design engineer." Leo crossed his arms.

"Yeah, something like that. So-" Justin glared at Kofi's shivering body. Annoyance etched on Justin's forehead. He wondered, how bad a train ride could it be? "Go on."

"So, there was another whiz kid, Aiden. We called him BBQ. One day, he went out in daylight. Several of the monster Screakers cornered him. The Screaker's buzz saw arm had cut BBQ's hand. BBQ had jumped right over them and ran in here. Kofi doctored him up by soldering it with a hot poker. At that time, BBQ was still alive!" said Leo.

Justin doubted them and knit his eyebrows together. This all sounded fantastic. *What did Leo say? At that time, BBQ was still alive! They didn't introduce me to him. So, BBQ must be gone for good.* As disturbing as that information was, Justin thought about how Kofi healed a severed limb. He expressed awe, "Kofi, -"

Tej interrupted, "I have to warn you. If you hit the force field that surrounds this train eight feet around, a shock of electricity courses through you, throwing you backwards under the train wheels, honestly it happened to BBQ, um, Aiden, in the end. Poor fellow." Tej bowed his head.

"I know what force fields will do to someone who touches it. You don't have to tell me." Justin crossed his arms. "Don't go on the outside of the train. Nasty Screakers, mate!" Leo exclaimed, always putting in his two cents, Leo stood with his hands on his hips.

Always putting in his two cents, Justin thought. "I get the picture," he said. Grim as it was, Justin wasn't about to give up. He watched out the windows. He snuck peeks out the opening between the cars, and made a hole in the plastic vestibule to look through. Justin could only see about five feet through the eye-sized hole. He noted the position of the sun and the distant mountains. The train passed a switch. The sight triggered a memory from Justin's days competing with model railroads.

Justin took big strides, looking for Kofi. The smaller boy was sitting in the next train car.

"I want some paper and a pencil," the taller boy said. He itched to find the solution to this puzzle. With the track and switch that he saw, he grabbed the paper and pencil to jot the information down. He drew lines and the switch with the pencil at the table. He drew the track in front of Hidden Valley Station and the switch at the cut off. If only he could see the whole Colorado Plateau from a bird's eye view. Justin's view was blocked on one side of the train's windows, and there were the metal monsters, the Screakers. The heat, the heat felt like they were in an oven. How was he going to put the map together? He slammed his fist on the table.

That night, Justin thought of his home. At dusk on horseback, his father would turn his horse towards their stables first. Justin like to linger watching the cows in their corral. His dad would say, "We're burning daylight, son. Pronto." He thought how his father sounded like John Wayne. Coincidence that they had the same last name. At his father's reminder, Justin would turn back, walking his horse. His mother wrote articles for women's magazines, so she was often away at a writer's weekend or conference. When his mother was home, she would fuss over him every minute. He'd have to clean himself up before dinner, help her carry casserole dishes to the table and help with the dishes. After the dishes were put away, they would watch an old movie on the flat screen slightly recessed in the wall. His mom passed out popcorn and his dad went to the digital play list and picked the flick. Justin loved westerns.

He remembered early one Saturday morning, about two weeks ago, when he turned his horse sharply as a cow stomped in the corral. It spooked his horse a bit so that she reared up. Justin tumbled and the horse tipped over with him, laying on his chest. Of course, his dad came quickly pulling the horse off of him. Surprisingly, he had no broken bones. Many cowpokes had tumbles. He was grateful his hadn't been serious. He finally fell asleep this first night on the Beast.

The next day, Justin rose before the other boys. Dark bags hung under his eyes and his disheveled hair stuck out in wisps. He wanted to get more information for the map. Facing forward, he watched the landscape flash by him through the left clear windows. The whiz kid made notes of the direction they were going and the time of day as "sunrise." Then he recorded on the map the tracks since the last time he looked out these windows, which was sunset. Now he figured maybe he could walk on the iron breezeway on the right side facing forward. His plan was to get to the front of the engine and take a look.

Justin walked on the walkway between the two train cars. Coppery wisps fluttered in front of his eyes.

"What are you doing, Justin?" Kofi closed the door behind him.

Justin jumped and then licked his fingers to wet his bangs to one side. "I have to know what's out there."

"Please don't go out there. It's crazy," Kofi pleaded.

Justin was full of confidence in himself. He scanned the opening between the cars.

"I'm quick. I can do this," Justin said.

"You'll get maimed and I'll have to doctor you up." The small teen tried to get height by balancing on tip toes and looking right into Justin's face.

"I'll be right back." With that, Justin held on to the hand holds and placed his feet on a very small breezeway that had been welded to the side of the train. Hands gripping and feet moving sideways, he felt good about his progress. He could look in each window. Soon, he had an audience of Tej, Leo and Kofi who were waving him to come in.

He thought he read their lips as saying, "Come back in." The wind blew in his face, making his eyes water. Was it so different riding his horse in Hidden Valley? He set his face towards the front of the locomotive, stepping along the breezeway along the coal car, he could see the curve of the engine ahead.

The breezeway was wider here and he stepped on to it. Just as his second foot stepped up, he heard it. *Tap, Tap, Tap, Scrrreak.* His palms felt sweaty. He reached to grab hold of the rail, but his hand slipped. When he righted himself, he saw two black metal legs, bent at an upside-down V. *Tap, Tap, Tap, Scrrreak.* Another Screaker appeared coming around the other side of the locomotive on the walkway.

With the deadly monsters so close, Justin didn't have time to survey the tracks. He turned once to look around the front. Movement. *Tap, Tap, Tap, Scrrreak. Tap, Tap, Tap, Scrrreak.* The two moved towards him. He wanted to stay in this position as the next switch was coming up. The Screakers raised their trailing buzz saws. Justin turned towards the steps, a Screaker purchased on the rail. Forgetting the blur of ground as they sped along, he grabbed the rail on his side and swung himself around to the walkway. The second Screaker landed on his foot at the same time. It's hinged black foreleg pierced his foot. A shock of sharp pain shot through his foot. He bent over and reached with his left hand and automatically said and signed with his right hand, "OUCH."

His eyes darted to his foot in his cowboy boot.

6

Trini's Phantom Pain

THE FEVERISH TRINI sat in an old stuffed chair in the space next to her mother's. She insisted she didn't need to lie in her bed. This way she could watch all the happenings in the square. Her mother tucked the last soaked reed into the rim finishing the basket. A bitter willowy smell lingered that Trini had always enjoyed.

Her mother set the partially finished basket on her work table and rubbed her callous and cracked fingers. She was feeling for slivers and brushed them off. At a mile high, the temperature at the Lib, where her mother sold her baskets and squash, went from cold to freezing in the winter. But on this summer afternoon, Trini was under a moth eaten blanket and her mother only needed her one threadbare sweater. The crisp air carried a scent and slight taste of fish. They were miles from a river. The merchant next to her served fish soup today. Trini wrinkled her nose. Her mother brushed her cracked dry hands on her tattered shirt. Her hands were always dark tan, but a light tan band remained on her left ring finger. The accessory adorning her plain clothes was just a memory. Trini watched her mother rubbing the spot, out of habit, as if turning an invisible ring.

The sick girl lay back in the curves of the overstuffed chair. The cushions had gone so soft that it seemed to envelop and swallow her.

He gaze lazily fell on a scene on the other side of the square. Their landlord Mr. MacGoon handed money to a teen girl. Trini sat up and recognized the shapely teen Kitty. It seemed Mr. MacGoon had just descended the stairs of the madam's place where Kitty "worked." *Hmm, Mrs. MacGoon wouldn't like her husband visiting Kitty and that place,* Trini thought.

On her plot of land in the marketplace they called, the Smub, she rented, she made her baskets. Behind her small crates of different squash that she sold: zucchini, yellow, spaghetti and summer squash were her other businesses. She sold her baskets. And she cut hair. Being five foot seven inches, she didn't have to have a raised barber chair. At the back was her garden of squash and beans.

Last, in the park strip, she had a tree. Each plot renter had to take care of the one tree on the plot because no one else would. The tree Around the bottom of the almond tree she had planted Lamb Quarter wildflowers. As a girl, the community center took her and the other children on a trip to a meadow on the Continental Divide. As she admired the colorful wildflowers, another Deaf child, a boy, likened the green of the Lamb Quarter wildflowers to her bright green eyes. She gathered a pocketful of seeds to bring home. Years later, she married that attentive boy. She planted the green flowering stalk-like plant seeds around the almond tree which was on her mother's plot. One day, when the family had nothing left to eat, she made a Lamb Quarter soup. She roasted the soft stems, leaves and flowers before boiling them. Turns out that it makes a delicious soup. Now, the plants on the rented plot belonged to her, she kept the wildflowers and tree watered. She wouldn't get ripe nuts to harvest for four more months.

The rectangular shaped Lib had been closed off to vehicles, save one street, New Liberty Highway. After the Transformation, a new capitol rose west of the airport, Intermountain City. Our city of Denver became the Hood and the Juliet Street was changed to Liberty Street. *Liberty, that was a joke. The Intermountain Government only gives true liberty to those in positions of power and wealth who run things. The rest of us aren't allowed to move, to attend higher education or get good paying jobs. Some kind of "liberty."*

Tenement apartments stood around the Lib like a wall her family couldn't climb. They depended on the locals who shopped at the covered outdoor market for two generations. People like her family, the Wayfields and the Godfreys weren't educated. It was the children and grandchildren of the ruling party who went to school beyond middle school and got white collar jobs.

Trini's mother, Saunia Wayfield worked at the Lib selling her goods, as her mother before her. Her grandfather, a musician, played his tenor sax for the customers. When Old Jazz lovers ventured to the lounge closest to the Lib to hear him play, they once threw a silver dollar in his basket.

Trini had a pile of aluminum cans that she was smashing in the middle of her mother's space. To the right of her mother's space, the Godfreys sold bread and rabbit or fish soup, depending on what her husband caught that morning.

The fifty-something Mrs. Jessica Godfrey was also Deaf. Shuffling in her stained brown dress and water-stained brown shoes, Jessica got Saunia's attention by waving her hand up and down. Then, Trini moved her hand even closer to her mother's face to get her attention for Mrs. Godfrey. Her mother looked at her and Trini pointed at Mrs. Godfrey.

When her mother saw Mrs. Godfrey, she smiled and the crows-feet at her eyes wrinkled.

"Saunia, any news about an extension on your rent?"

"No, Mr. McMann said he needed to pay his bills with my rent money."

"That mean old McMann. He has enough money to own a single-family house. You think he would give you another day," Jessica signed. Her signs were quick and smooth having learned from both of her Deaf parents and she was second generation Deaf. "It's a good thing the fish have been plentiful. We paid our space rent yesterday. With the festival tomorrow, Mr. Godfrey is off hunting to bring in extra. At the end of today, whatever soup I have left is yours to feed your children."

"That is so kind of you, Jessica," signed Saunia, "but I'll only take half, and insist you take some squash and Lambs Quarter plant from my garden."

"That would be great. I'll put it in tomorrow's soup." She winked and chuckled.

Saunia nodded. She appreciated Jessica's help, but she rather make fair trades and not take advantage of the Godfrey's kindness to her.

Trini looked at the edge of her mother's business lot where she grew her plants. There were a meager four or five plants. But, it was like her mother to give to others. Trini didn't really mind because she preferred fast food and sandwiches.

"Can I get a haircut now?" Mrs. Godfrey came around Trini. She squeezed the teens' shoulder gently as she passed. She smelled of roses, but underneath that ... fish soup.

"I insist the trim is at no cost," Saunia signed.

The stout woman shook her head. "I insist on paying."

Trini noted the strained look, wrinkled brow and her mother's downcast brown eyes. She knew how her mother worried about how she would feed her family. Trini worried about her mother. The week after McMann collected rent, the shop owners didn't have money for a haircuts, baskets, or even fish soup. McMann, and the mob boss Sterling, not to mention his biker gang, had money. But they always went uptown for their haircuts. Trini trusted that there would be enough to feed the three of them, but she was impatient for this interchange to end.

"Mother, you could give Mrs. Godfrey a forty percent discount. Now that is done, why don't the two of you catch up on news." Trini gave Mrs. Godfrey a wink.

With all the cans crushed and put back in the bag. Her mother was thanking Mrs. Godfrey for the 4 Intermountain coin she received and put in her pocket.

Now Mr. MacGoon appeared on the opposite of the square that he had been on that morning. Trini watched the blonde landlord in the tailored suit walk towards her mother's booth. Her mother was busy sweeping the discarded cut hair on the blacktop. Trini tried to get her mother's attention by waving, her arm fully extended to no use.

The next second, he was in the booth. He waved and got Trini's mother's attention. Saunia was pinning her loose braid back in place looped at the back of her head. Trini thought the hair style of the women her mother's age looked like a spoon handle hanging down from their heads.

All of a sudden, Mr. MacGoon stood in front of her mother. He moved fast for a fat man. *Rotund, I should think of him as a rotund man. That's more respectful,* she thought. *Her mother had always taught her children to think respectful, so you act respectful. Too bad it didn't work with Tekka.*

"Saunia, where's your plot space rent? It was due yesterday, and you weren't at the Lib," the man said in signed. The pink faced tall man with expressionless black eyes leaned with one elephantine foot on a low table holding her baskets. He had knocked several to the ground when his foot took its place. The landlord tapped his monstrosity of a shoe. A fly buzzed near his head and he swatted at it.

"My daughter has been very sick-" She signed with deft hands and gestured towards Trini.

"I don't care. Where is your rent?" The KODA signed. The kid of Deaf adult(s) spent his whole life in the Lib. When his father passed on, he took over collecting rent for the mob boss, MacGoon. Saunia never hung out with him and his crowd.

"I have it here, but I won't have anything left. I had to buy medicine for Trini."

"Where is that boy of yours? Why doesn't he get a job at the factory like the other boys?"

"The mindless work would drive him crazy."

"So instead he's a street performer? That's mad."

Tekka wasn't one of the musician street performers. He had always gambled. He would set up his portable table with a game of chance and take bets. The twenty-six-year-old could calculate the probability in his head quicker than you could blink. Trini thought, *Tekka always said, "A lead bet has a perfect chance to score big."*

"Can I give you half now, and half at the end of tomorrow? With The Treystar Festival Day business, I'll have enough. But right now, I need to buy ice and spring water or my daughter. . ."

"No, you're already a day late." He knocked another basket off the low table. "Give it to me now." He held out a dirty hand.

Saunia reached into her pants pocket, retrieving the money. She looked at it with her tired eyes, placing it into Tremblay MacGoon's awaiting hand. Immediately he counted the silver coins. The broke woman gave a forlorn look at the greedy landlord, then back at her empty hands. What would she feed her sick daughter and son? More bean soup. Trini had a hard time digesting beans. She had her squashes that she grew on her plot. But if she used those, she wouldn't have them to sell during tomorrow's festival day. Surely, they would make due. They always did with the Creator's help.

Trini looked up at the sky. This was the place with the most sky showing and although the city lights overpowered their light, she saw a few of the brighter ones. Focusing on the brightest one, she said a prayer, as she always did. She prayed that her mother, older brother and especially her lost brother would be healthy and at peace. As she opened her eyes, she saw her mother, head bowed, eyes closed and hands interlaced.

In that instant, Trini felt a sharp pain through her right foot, as if someone had taken a spike and driven through it. She gave a sharp cry. For her Deaf mother's sake, she signed, "OUCH," with her index and middle fingers closing on her thumb at her nose. She cast her eyes at her throbbing foot expecting to see a spike through it. Nothing. How odd. She stood up and took a couple steps. Her foot worked fine, but throbbed.

It was a good thing she followed Deaf etiquette because her mother did notice her look of pain.

"Did you hurt yourself? You were fine a minute ago," her mother signed.

It wasn't the first time Trini experienced this strange phenomenon.

7

Justin and the Screaker

JUSTIN PULLED AT the Screaker's forearm with his left hand, then both hands. Finally, the spiky limb came out of his foot. Justin winced and bolted along the locomotive catwalk. He slowed down as he walked between their two train cars to the door. Justin limped.

He couldn't get a break. He tried to go out on the locomotive and the train knew to send the Screakers. It was like they were herding him back into the train cars. He shook his head, then, took his time now that he was back in the dining car. Well, that didn't work. This train, the Beast, blocked his plan every time, it seemed almost alive.

Justin spread out on top of a booth stuffed bench.

"First Aid kit," Justin yelled. He grimaced at the pain.

Kofi sprang up and grabbed the kit.

The next morning, Justin watched out the windows. He snuck peeks out the opening between the cars, and made a hole in the plastic vestibule to look through. With the track and switches that he saw, he grabbed paper and pencil to jot the information down. As he drew lines and switches with the pencil at the table, a map of the tracks emerged. *I have to find a way for us to get off. Tomorrow is my prom.*

That day would throw them for another curve. They thought they knew how things were on the train, the Beast. They didn't expect the worst.

Kofi was in a chatty mood. "How are you, friend?"

"Fine."

"Weren't you afraid of that Screaker?"

"Of course, but I'm safe in here now," Justin's voice lacked energy. "I don't want to talk."

"I can talk for both of us. Did you know that I beat that tall Russian kid in Chess last year? Well, in the last match, it only took me three moves—"

"Can we talk about anything else?" Justin rolled his eyes.

"Sure, um. Do you know the nine points of loading a percussion musket?" Without waiting for Justin to respond, Kofi went on, "You get the command, 'Load.' You place the musket between your feet. The first point is 'Handle Cartridge.' You flip the paper tail of the cartridge with your thumb and tear it with your teeth, exposing the gun powder. At the command, 'Load Cartridge,' you pour it into the muzzle of the musket."

Justin was now concentrating on what he was hearing —a whirling of metal above the train.

"Do you hear something?" He asked Kofi.

Kofi stopped mid-sentence with his mouth agape. He squeezed his eyes shut.

"What is it? What's wrong?" Justin started with his questions when he heard an additional noise and it dawned on him. The roof door to the Entry Car was opening.

The boys with their perplexed looks and arms crossed stood outside the Entry Car when the door opened. All their mouths dropped open. Leo recovered first and extended hospitality to the unexpected Newbie. "Hi. Welcome. Um, come this way." Leo's cheeks were red. Of course, they were red, like all the previous times he had talked to a girl.

Inside the club/dining car they watched her.

Justin noticed she looked at everything, surveying the inside of the car with her large brown eyes as if it would give her the answers to her new predicament. Trini, with her full smooth cheeks and petite nose looked to him to be about a year, not more than two younger than himself. Her brunette hair the color of his horse Sky and pulled back in a green rubber band. Inside her pants pocket he saw yellow. Her tennis shoes had holes in them.

"I know this all must be new to you, and, oh, I'm Leo," the Aussie tilted his head and smiled. "I am almost the one who has been here the longest. And don't you worry about anything. I'll help you. Your shirt has 'Liz' on it." They could see a beautifully embroidered Liz in pink on the right side of her periwinkle T-shirt.

"Liz. That's the name the mean kidnappers called me." She scrunched up her right eye looking down at the embroidered name. "It's a weird name and I hate the color pink." She reached down with both arms crossed as if to take off her shirt. Everyone stared at the girl.

8

Trini's Sudden Appearance

TRINI CHANGED HER mind and flung her arms down. What would her mother say/sign? Her mother signed to her since she became a teen, "Keep the window closed, daughter." Her mother was not talking about a part of a building.

"Well, that's what the kidnappers are, MEAN!" Trini shouted.

"No, I mean yes, they are, well ...," stammered Leo.

"Cool, you saw the kidnappers." Kofi said.

"What's your name, gal?" an impatient Justin inquired.

She whirled around to face the cowboy, her ponytail whipping behind her. "It's not gal or honey. It's Trini, pronounced tree-knee." Trini stared at Justin waiting for an apology or for him to at least say her name as she had pronounced it. Instead he looked towards the side the way people do when they are remembering something they heard. She knew because when it was something you saw, you looked up to remember.

"And what are your names?" She asked. She put her hands on her hips. They told her their names, except Justin. He was still looking to the side with his mind far away.

Trini snapped right in his face. "You, hey, wake up." She put her hands back on her hips.

Justin took a step back and looked down at her. "Justin. So, we are all in the same boat—"

"Actually, we're on a train," Tej interjected.

Justin glared at Tej. Then back to the group, "You know what I mean. None of us chose to be here. So, let's just —"

"Let's not," Trini said as she rose from the bench seat. She turned abruptly toward the door. The end of her dark chestnut ponytail slapped Justin's nose. She peered back to see him brush his nose as if a bug had flown too close to it. He narrowed his eyes at if ray beams were hitting her and burning her.

Her hand began to turn pull on the door when she heard, "Cher, listen to me, you do not want to go outside."

Her hand dropped and as she faced Nick, she said, "This is a replica 1923 Pullman passenger combine car with a .." she looked through the forward windows, "J-3a Dreyfuss locomotive," she looked through the window downward, "on a narrow-gauge track. So, I already know plenty about trains."

"Listen Cher, you shouldn't go outside."

"And why shouldn't I?" she snarked.

In an equally snarky tone Justin said, "Maybe we should let her go ahead and learn her lesson the hard way." Justin stood with legs shoulder width apart, thumbs tucked in his belt.

Trini walked around Justin and stood in front of Nick where he was seated at his table. "Nick, please tell me what I need to know."

Justin tilted his head back, closely watching Trini, his brow wrinkled.

"There are these metal robotic like guard dogs. They're all black with beady little black sensors that look like shark eyes. The points of their spider like legs are deadly sharp. They make this screaking sound."

"So, we call them The Screakers," Leo threw in.

"So," Nick stared at Leo.

Trini knew it was Nick's way of warning Leo to not bud in again.

"If you go outside during the day, they sense you and crawl out from under the trucks of the train cars and locomotive," Nick put a palm up towards Leo before he opened his mouth, "So, they screak and then their metal legs make a tapping sound…" Nick continued to fill Trini in on the dangers of The Screakers and the forcefield. Occasionally the others took turns annoying him by interrupting with tidbits they threw into the talk.

Justin ignored Trini and worked on the map shading in landscape with his pencil. Trini decided to ignore the boorish cowboy in turn. Sitting down, Trini fixed her eyes on the hands of the Cajun. Nick held up a straw and told her, to pull an invisible thread connected to the straw in the air. She was a good sport and pretended to pull the straw with a string that couldn't be seen. The straw bent with her pulling. "Now let go," Nick said.

She pretended to let go. The straw snapped back up straight. Trini launched into a smile and giggled in amusement.

The illusionist said, "Cher, good job. Take a bow." The straw slowly bent forward and slowly raised upright.

"Nap time, Cher," Nick whispered to the straw. The straw bent into his shirt pocket and then straightened.

The illusion was good. Trini wondered, *What is this guy, illusionist, magician, gambler, or cardWhiz?*

"Cher, how about a game of pinochle?" Nick asked while shuffling the cards.

"That is a game I learned and love to play. So, … sure," Trini nodded.

"Are you a Whizkid too? What is your thing?"

"Whizkid? My thing? I don't know what you're talking about," she said and then gave a great sigh. "All I know is the kidnappers drugged me, put this shirt on me and when I awoke in the helicopter, called me Liz. They said, 'Have a nice trip down, Liz.' That's when I was lowered into that boxcar back there." She stood up so quickly her chair fell over, "I don't want to be here. I want to go back home." Trini picked up the chair. She turned to Nick and said, "Thank you for the magic tricks, but I don't have time for any more games." Trini looked at each boy, looking for something, anything that would help her get back home.

Justin only lifted his eyes from the map, "I have to figure out how to get us off of this train."

"No worries. Any minute now, my parents will fly their private jet here to get me. If not them, then my New Vegas agent will find me and bring me home," Nick said with confidence.

Trini thought, *This guy must be delusional.* She had heard Nick's story and knew it had been over two weeks that Nick had been on the Beast. Thinking that just because he's a big shot in New Vegas, he's going to be miraculously rescued ... *Nuts!*

Nick went back to shuffling his deck of cards.

Losing the snarky tone, Trini said in a conciliatory voice, "Could you please explain your map to me?"

As Justin carefully explained all he saw on the one side of the train was in one fifth of the map. "It's still not enough to see the hidden parts of the line."

She listened to his voice while studying the map.

Then Justin said, "It is extremely dangerous outside. No one wanted to say it, but one rider already died."

Trini studied the area of the map that was blank to the east. She ran her fingers along Justin's drawing of tracks going through the Rockies, "Here, the tracks go through GJ."

"GJ?"

"It used to be called Grand Junction," Trini said. She looked at him like he came from another planet. One of her eye brows was still raised and mouth crooked as she stared at the cowboy.

"You didn't get out much, did you?"

"Nah. I grew up in Hidden Valley riding my horse, Sky."

"Of course, you did." Trini nodded several times.

"What about you? You seem like a, um, a cosmopolitan ga-, girl," Justin measured his words.

"Old Denver."

"But you're so smart. How did you get an education there?"

"I went to school early every morning, read in the library and checked out books."

"How do you know so much about the physical workings of trains?"

"Old Denver, remember. I used to watch every kind of train. I would walk far to see old narrow-gauge steam engines like the one we're riding on. Except this one is a plastic replica."

"See what I mean. You're definitely a whiz kid." Justin smiled and his eyes sparkled.

Trini expected Justin to mock her. She surveyed his face and realized that he was sincere.

The cowboy pulled his right hand out of his pocket, placing it on the map and a scrap of paper fell onto it.

Trini didn't notice at first, as she batted her long eyelashes. Then, she reached out her hand to his tan hand and interlaced her fingers in his. He gently squeezed it. It felt like electricity tickling her hand and running up her arm. Why did this happen? When she looked back up into his face, his attention was totally on her.

Oh, he has the cutest smile and the whitest teeth. Why was she so attracted to him? She never liked the cowboy type. For some reason, he hid something inside. She was realizing that he would have to be peeled like an onion. But would he even know who he was when it was all peeled away?

His bangs fell in his face. He yanked his free hand out of his pocket and swept them back. "Aw, I need a good haircut." He looked up at his bangs with an annoyed look.

She was going to say how it made him even handsomer, but the scrap that landed on the map now grabbed her attention. A picture of a blonde bombshell with blue eyes. The adoring words died on her lips.

Suddenly, she jerked back her hand. She saw the look of hurt on his face now.

"Trini, what's the m—"

She had already turned walking towards the passenger car.

She sat on her padded seat in the passenger car. The coil still protruded on the right back cushion of the bench seat. She lay across the hot surface of the seat. The vinyl stuck to the back of her arms. Her legs bent at the knee and feet almost touch the floor. Not comfortable, but at least she could rest and think. The electricity could have been static electricity traveling from Justin to her. The floor did have carpeting and could have caused static electricity. Still, it wasn't until she looked into his brown eyes. *What was it about his eyes?*

9

Justin Faces the Newbie

THE BOYS LIVED on the train, prisoners to its forcefield. Three days had passed since Trini had been dropped in. A frustrated Justin resented missing his prom and grimaced. He thought, today should be the day of another Drop. The windows on his left side were all painted over in black paint. He tried scratching at the blackened window. Nothing. Think, the paint is on the outside. He stared out of the half opened clear window on one side of the right side of the train. The musty odor of the light rain, mixture of sage and sand, wafted to Justin. He sneezed. The usual dry heat, bright sunlight, and surreal orangish-red reflection of the red rocks pained his eyes. So, he placed his hand like a visor over his eyes.

On this day, Justin heard the hum of the hovercraft approaching the train. The whirling sound over the last car of the train increased. A hot gust blew. He remembered from his experience that a new kid was being dropped into the Entry Car.

Justin felt hopeful. He smiled and said, "I think they are dropping a New kid! But keep your eyes alert!"

Trini and the boys, except Nick, stood in anticipation. Five pair of eyes focused on the last train car door. When they released the door lock and a figure scrambled through, their mouths fell open.

A tall red-headed boy, about their age stepped through. His

black leather studded jacket hung at an angle, showing the insignia of a biker gang, Silver Thunder. Not only did his black T-shirt have the silver lightning bolt over windswept clouds on a blood-red sky, but the large round patch on his back was prominently displayed.

"Not you!" Said the new kid in black, frozen in shock. Then, he thrusted an accusing finger toward Justin.

Justin, with a furrowed brow said, "I don't know you." He shook his head slightly.

An angry expression came across the new kid's face. Shoving Justin aside with one muscular arm, he walked past the boys who separated to clear a path. Striding with a clear purpose, the new kid went through the door into the dining car.

Justin welled up with righteous indignation. What had he done wrong? Nothing. *The red-head thinks he can push me.* Justin strode after him.

The curious teens tore after the two tall boys. The new teen, with the boys following him, reached the breeze way on the coal car to the locomotive. In the locomotive cab, nothing the new kid pulled or pushed budged.

Leo yelled from the porch on the front of the passenger car, "Mate, we've tried that!"

They peaked around the coal car and heard a clank. Red pulled one more lever.

"Nothing," Red shouted.

Justin leapt into the engineer's compartment. He pulled with Red. They finally succumbed to defeat. "Snap! Won't budge," Justin said weakly.

Red glowered at him.

Justin especially hated being belittled unjustifiably. Okay, he had to admit that he always hated being belittled. What was with this Newbie?! They both climbed back to the porch of the passenger car.

"What did I do?" Justin asked in his defense, while standing near the door to the train car.

"Nothing. Absolutely nothing," Red said.

Leo stepped closer to the two tall boys. "Mate, are you hungry?" Leo said with hands gesturing back to the other car. "Let me get something for you, eh?"

Trini and the boys held their collective breath. The big new kid, swooped his long red bangs to the side and looked down on everyone except Justin. He stared at Justin, eye to eye. He clenched his teeth. A furious red vein on his neck looked about ready to burst.

"Oh snap!" said Leo, who jumped in front of the new kid blocking him from Justin. Leo led Red to the dining car. Justin followed, thinking that Leo just wanted to avoid trouble.

Justin leaned his head into his thumb and right index finger. His irritation rose. Then he looked up, searching Red's features. Justin knew he had never seen this boy before and shook his head. "Do you know me? Justin asked.

Red bumped Justin's shoulder going into the train car.

Kofi remained with Justin walking behind the others.

"What was that about?" Kofi asked.

"Wish I knew," Justin replied shrugging his shoulders. He stopped just outside the dining car door.

In the dining car, Leo shifted in his seat in a failed effort to maintain self-control. He took in the new kid's biker attire and wanted to ask him for a favor. But the biker's whole attention focused on shoveling food in his face. the biker finished off his third sandwich, while Leo sat across from him at the booth. Leo looked from the new kid, to the windows to Trini and back to Red. Leo kept the pattern of watchfulness as he ticked off the seconds. Justin and Kofi hadn't come into the dining car yet.

When the last drops of mayo and mustard were licked off the plate, Leo asked, "So, what's it like being in a biker gang?"

At the same time, Tej sat down across from the biker and asked, "Newbie. What's your name?"

"Red." The biker motioned his hand in a curt turn.

"Yeah, I can see that." Tej said while admiring Red's hair, long in the front. "I've never seen you competing."

"Where do you live? Who's your family?" asked Tej.

The new kid answered Tej, "New Vegas. My biker gang is my family."

Leo's eyes grew large and he sat up straight. "Harleys too?" He tried to hide his excitement.

Red nodded.

"Cool," said Leo, "I've always wanted to ride a Harley."

Red swooped the hair to the side and looked at Nick. "How do I get off of this thing? Nick, why, of all high schoolers, are we," he looked around at the boys surrounding them, "stuck together on this, this-"

"We call it the Beast," Tej said.

Red, looked irritated and said, "Yeah, I already heard that."

"Clyde, or pardon me, Red, welcome to the Beast. Wud ya' like a pop?"

"Nick, come one! We've gotta stop the locomotive!" The biker walked towards the front.

"You can't, Newbie. It's rigged, so we can't work it." Leo said coming up behind him.

"I'm getting off the Beast now!" Red ran towards the door. The boys near the door blocked him.

Leo, having seen what happened to BBQ first hand, panicked. He put his hands up, palms out. "Stop! Mate. You'll never make it!" Leo yelled behind him.

Turning around, Red said, "And why is that?"

"For one thing, we didn't get off. You know we're all the smartest of the smart," Leo replied. He was relieved that he got Red talking. He chewed his bottom lip.

"Whiz kids!" Tej put in.

"Yeah, so?" Red said.

Red walked to look for more food in the refrigerator. Justin was already leaning into the refrigerator taking out a small frozen cheesecake, but Red yanked it from Justin. The perturbed Justin, reached around the cheesecake, but Red elbowed him.

"Hey, Newbie! Watch it!" Justin exclaimed. He watched Red walk to a booth and placed the cheesecake on the table, then proceeded to devour it. The courteous Justin let it go and got a bag of Zinger chips, sat at a booth and ate.

All the boys now sat in the dining car.

"Err, Red," Leo said, "I can help you. Let me tell you everything, since I'm the first one to come on this train."

Red nodded.

"After I came on the train and couldn't get off, another kid Aden came on. He told me to call him BBQ, like everyone else did. This kid BBQ talked on and on about his memories. At last, BBQ said, 'I got a hankerin' for a fresh pulled pork sandwich. Yum, our homemade BBQ sauce makes a body's mouth water. I can't stand this packaged food any longer.' His eyes were wide and wild. Then he shouted, "I'M GOING HOME!!!" Poor guy. He jumped off the train."

"When BBQ came in contact with the forcefield, it sparked with a sudden zap and he was suddenly thrown in the opposite direction," Tej emphasized with a smack of his hands.

Red nodded, "Gotcha."

Leo clapped his two hands together, "Whiz-SMACK! The forcefield zapped him. The poor guy was blown under the wheels and nulled." Leo said, "It left tracks." Leo smiled at Red.

Justin grew angry and his stomach tightened. *He's sticking to the facts this time When told to me, he coated it with drama. Wonder why he's different with Red, Justin* thought to himself.

Justin stood up with a sober expression.

Kofi sniffled, fighting back tears.

"How do you know a train was there? It left its tracks, ha, ha, ha," Tej laughed.

"Not funny Tej," Leo scolded.

Tej put his head down in embarrassment, like a puppy with ears down and tail between his legs. Justin briefly put a comforting hand on Kofi's shoulder, all the while keeping his eyes on Red. Justin just couldn't place Red.

Leo coughed and croaked, "Justin, *ack*. . . you fill in *ack*. . . the rest." While Leo went to the sink to get water, Justin stepped to the middle of the car.

Justin noticed how Leo had forgotten their friendship and wanted to refuse doing anything Leo requested. "I was the person to arrive before you, Red," Justin explained while Red scowled at him, "I woke up from a sleeping drug the Villains had their lackey give me, finding myself trapped in the Entry Car."

Red asked in confusion, "Who are the Villains?"

"Unknown powerful people who put us in here. They obviously have money and resources. So, since I don't know any more about them, I just call them, the Villains. Anyway, what I was saying about my first day on the Beast is that the opening in the roof was halfway closed. As I stood up, I saw the tail of a hovercraft as it was speeding away. I spotted letters on the craft, NFLS."

"What does NFLS stand for?" Red inquired.

"I don't know," Justin said, "But, I opened the one-way door into the vestibule to the passenger car. Then, I met these gents here. I had already competed with Leo and Kofi. Tej is good at Mahjong."

"Good? I'd say better than good. I am the reigning world Mahjong champion-" Tej said.

"We know," Justin said sighing with exasperation, "Let me finish my story. So, I saw Tej playing Mahjong on this handheld game device. It was the first time I've seen a game device. Then, I saw that Kofi played his chess against a miniature computer on his handheld device, as well. I'm telling you, I have never seen this kind of technology before, which they say is common in the world. I have been kept so isolated. That made me suspicious. Something is going on."

"We had this technology in New Vegas, but not in Hidden Valley," Red stated.

Justin glowered at him.

Raising a hand between the two tall teens, Leo continued his story, "Red, since you now know there is a forcefield, you see that the Villains can turn it off above the Entry Car. Each of us was dropped in it, three days apart. We tried to get in the door of the Entry Car, but it only opens from the inside." Leo looked up at the roof remembering something, "Yes. The NFLS."

"What's the NFLS?" Trini asked no one in particular.

"National Film Location Service," Leo said. "The NFLS took over the former National Parks that are in The Redlands with their headquarters in the capital, Intermountain City." Leo went on to explain how the NFLS used the Parks as filming sites for their popular reality shows with top name sponsors and advertisers. Leo, as usual, was long-winded.

Meanwhile, Red took advantage of Leo's gabbing. While the riders were gathered around Leo, the biker picked up the map. "I see the switches are positioned so the train goes over and around, snakes back around and under then to this blank spot. We need this part of the map." He pointed at the middle and eastern part of the completed part of the map. He seemed to be talking to himself.

Justin, being protective of the map, walked over to Red. "Leave the map on the table."

Looking at Justin, Red said, "So, can you-"

"Hey, Hidden Valley Station!" Tej exclaimed as he ran to the clear window right side of the car. Justin and Red walked to the best place to get a view, the opening between the first two train cars. As their speeding train neared, it began to slow. The *cush, cush* sound slowed and then the locomotive spit water and steam. Through the windows, they saw the people who were standing on the platform.

An attractive blonde stood on the station platform. She held a sign in her hands. Justin held up his right hand with the I-L-Y sign. He learned it, well... when he was little and always has signed it to Vanessa, meaning I love you. She and her poster came into view. She blew a kiss. The Beast accelerated. Whoosh. The station became a smaller rectangle and Vanessa a speck.

Both Justin and Red longingly peered as far as they could see around the outside of the car. When the station was out of sight, they straightened.

Justin knit his brow and pursed his lips. Anger rose when he thought of the message on Vanessa's sign. Justin kicked the outer wall and the black surface broke. The train car was made of plastic, but he didn't give it a thought. He glared at Red. "You stole my girl!" Justin yelled on his toes, body tense like a spring.

Irked by Justin's accusation, Red scrunched up his brow. "You left, cowboy."

The inflamed Justin squinted his eyes. Heat rose in him until he ranted, "I didn't leave! I...was....kidnapped! Those Villains took me away from my girlfriend. It seems you made a move on my girl!"

At the same time, hearing the escalating accusations, the boys came to watch. Kofi asked Leo, "What did her sign say?"

"*I love you, Red!*" Leo said in a girly voice with an Australian accent.

"Not good. The first time the Beast passed Hidden Valley Station and Justin saw Vanessa blowing him a kiss, he told us that she was *his* girlfriend."

"I know. There's gonna be trouble, Mate." Leo stayed close to the two love-struck opponents.

Red heated, his face crimson. "Can I help it if she's beautiful and went for me?" Outrage in his voice, he spewed, "Back off, Pyro."

Bam! Justin punched Red in the face. He raged, "That's for Vanessa!"

"Ahhhh!" Red screamed.

While cupping his hand under his nose, he grabbed his handkerchief. Riled, Red took in a deep breath and lunged at Justin. The biker grabbed Justin by the shirt and swung him around. He ran Justin into the door. Then, the biker slammed his fist into Justin's nose.

"Ow!" Justin held his nose.

"How does that feel?"

The train lurched. Red let go with one hand to balance. When he regained his footing, he finally opened the door. Justin was still off balance. The biker grabbed Justin with both hands again, throwing him at the ladder. Justin hit his head against the steel ladder. The side of his face throbbed in pain He held his hand at the spot.

"Climb! We need the rest of that map." Red leaned into the doorway as Leo approached. "Hey man, get me a hot poker from the engine."

Leo squinted his eyes, saying, "Why should I?"

Red whispered, "Do you remember when you said that you wanted to ride my new one? I got two. You and me man. What do you say we get a hot poker to motivate this scaredy cat to finish surveying the map?"

"Mate. Sure!" Leo said impulsively and walked towards the locomotive.

Justin, still catching his breath and gathering his wits, wondered what those two were talking about.

Red still held him in a choke hold. "You shouldn't have punched me."

"You did something to my girl, while I was stuck on this prison of a train. Why should I be punished?"

"You can see she loves me."

"That's impossible. You're not her type."

"Oh, she know a real man. Not some scaredy cat who won't go out in the daylight."

"You're crazy. The Screakers are deadly. It's reckless," Justin spat at Red.

Leo came back a couple of minutes later with the hot poker and leaned it against the door. The hot iron made a scorch mark on the wood.

Justin blinked, trying to focus his eyes.

But, Red had kept Justin cornered just where he wanted him, near the ladder.

Justin and Red looked at Leo. Red lifted his chin to his new "friend." Leo handed the hot poker to Red, and at that moment, their eyes met. Shock in Justin's green eyes and numbness in the Aussie's eyes.

Besides his physical wounds, his heart ached. He rubbed his hand over his eyes. Until now, he and Leo were friends drawn by mutual interest. Justin first met him when he had entered the Middle Schooler's Model Railroad Engineer's contest that year in Chicago.

Sadness gripped him. He should be with his baseball team, the Diamondbacks, practicing for their next game. Justin blew away the competition as catcher for his competitive baseball team. His team, yet again, would compete for nationals. Justin grieved and rued the day when the Villains took him from his life. The catcher wondered what they were doing without him. He missed them. His old friend, Leo, shared entrapment on the train. Leo had been friendly to him. Justin saw no connection between the engineering Aussie and the sadistic biker. And why was Red so hostile towards him when he had never seen Red before in his life? Justin worried about what the biker would do to him.

"Let's see the brave young man that you say Vanessa was interested in. Go on!" Leo shoved him upward on the ladder.

The cowboy didn't budge. Leo stood where he was, but crossed his arms. All of a sudden, Red approached Justin on the cowboy's left side with the hot poker.

"Ow!" Justin screamed. Another involuntary reaction was his hands going to the place of the wound. "Owwwwwwww!" And again, but longer. He breathed heavily and looked at the wound. The edges of his over shirt and undershirts were black and singed with a faint ember dying out on one side. The hot iron poked and left a red third degree burn about the size of a quarter. He turned to walk back inside when Red shoved Justin against the iron ladder which led to the top of the train car.

"Climb up." Red's callousness should have alarmed the unarmed boy.

"No," Justin said.

Red grabbed Justin's collar then held the hot iron poker a foot away from the cowboy's face. "If you don't climb up the ladder by the time I count to three, you'll again feel what a log of wood experiences in the boiler. One." Red's voice was cool, showing no emotion.

Justin had no doubt Red would do it … again. Reluctantly Justin placed his hands on the iron rails of the ladder.

10

Trini's Connection

TRINI SAT IN the dining car at one of the tables with Nick and took a drink of ice water. She pulled her elbow away from the window, heated by the noon day sun. Used to living a mile high, this desert plateau was too hot for her. She shoved another mouthful of the microwaved meal into her dainty mouth.

Nick wrinkled his nose at the smell of Salisbury steak. "Whoa Cher, take it slow."

Still chewing her food, Trini responded. "Um, mm, but I'm famished."

"I can see that," Nick said, "I used to eat like a hog, um, I'm not calling you a hog."

Nick put out his hand and shrugged apologetically.

"I know." Trini filled her mouth with her meat and mashed potatoes.

"When I was a boy in New Orleans, whenever I could get foot, I shoveled it in. It took a long time to counter that habit." Nick's gaze drifted out the right-side window. He had that far away and long time ago look on his face.

Trini was good at reading expressions. She spent her life reading Deaf people's facial expressions. Nick's expression told her he felt regret for something in the past. "Do you want to talk about it?" She looked up at the Cajun.

Nick sighed and shook his head. He took another sip of his Apex soda. "Grape. You would think a train would stock more than grape." He rocked the half full can gently.

"It's a clue," Trini said, "Why did the Villains only stock grape soda on the train?"

Nick momentarily narrowed his eyes at the girl, saying nothing. His face returned to his usual cocky half-smile.

Trini filed Nick's reaction away in her God-given filing cabinet and sat up, "Maybe it's the color." She looked around, "Is there anything purple in here."

Nick lifted his grape soda.

"Other than the soda can." She rolled her eyes. "Hmm, nope."

"I think the kidnappers are just lazy and stocked only one kind of drink."

"Yeah," she said. She squeezed more of the small lemon that she had in her pocket and cut up in the kitchenette into her plastic grey cup of water. There were more plastic grey cups on the next table over.

"Wait," she said. The girl stacked three of the cups and brought a tiny white ball out of her pocket and set it on their white topped table. She set the cups from left to right in front of her. Then she put the ball under the right cup. She shuffled the cups around then looked up at Nick.

He was smiling his snarky and nodding. "The old ball in cup game. I used to do it when I was like, two years old."

Trini quickly up righted the cup with the ball under it, grabbed her ball and shoved it in her pocket. Her cheeks felt warm. She quickly changed the subject. "You know I've been thinking about my life in the tenements," said Trini. "I never travelled far. The farthest we went was to the train tracks to watch the trains pass by and roll out of sight behind the tenements. But my whole world was there. I collected—"

The sound of arguing voices reached them.

"Justin and Red are arguing," Trini said. A puzzled expression came across her face, "I wonder what that's about."

Nick brushed his hand towards the door, like he was swatting away a fly. "Let them argue about Justin's girl. I am sitting with the prettiest girl in the West." He reached his hand to Trini's side of the table and placed his hand gently on it.

Trini blushed, looked around, seeing her napkin, released her hand and picked up her napkin. She dabbed her mouth, although she knew it was already clean. She kept looking at her napkin to avoid meeting Nick's eyes. *Why did Nick do that? Had she given him mixed messages? No, she didn't think she had.*

"So, does Justin have a girl?" She asked.

Nick tilted his head, then suddenly said, "Yes, yes, he told me about her. Pretty blonde, Jole Blon." Nick bit his lower lip, then suddenly looked up, "Did I tell you about New Orleans already? A group of us would stand at night outside the window of "The Cajun Cabin," a club and dance joint on Bourbon Street. We would listen to the sweet sound of the fiddle and lively tune of the accordion. They would call a customer who came the greatest distance to come up and put the rubboard on. They gave him two metal spoons and taught him to play along dragging those spoons up and down the rubboard."

Trini closed her eyes and Justin's face appeared with those brown eyes. *What was it about his eyes. She couldn't place it.* She opened her eyes and had been half listening to Nick. But she had been watching him and he had an expression of pure joy on his face, with no effort to entertain.

"I especially loved the beautiful waltz, Jole Blon. Did you know it's the National Anthem of the Cajuns?"

"No, but I ...," Trini almost said she would like to dance to it, but changed her mind. She definitely did not want to give him the impression she would do anything with him. "I ... don't listen to music. My mother is Deaf. .. I used to listen to my grandfather play

Jazz on his tenor sax." Trini touched upon one of the few joyful memories of her childhood and smiled with a light from her eyes like the growing brightness from a fire flaring up.

"I love Jazz, especially the Zy'aire Ross Jazz band."

"I don't know any jazz bands. Just my late grandfather," Trini said. "Why do you like that band?"

"Well, I like many Jazz bands. The Zy'aire Ross Jazz band as a few others play the traditional roots Jazz. They do use stored solar amplification. This band stands out because of their skill and how they anticipate each other. They're just so good. When we get off ..."

"I don't want to talk about when we get off this train," Trini said. She was used to taking one day at a time. As she knew, she couldn't even predict what would happen in even an hour. "Lord willing, we get off this train, they we can think about ... well, I would be thinking about the next book that I'm going to read."

"I know you don't want to talk about the future, so what book did you just finish reading?" Nick leaned forward.

"Oh, I can tell you about that. It was a book called, Ahead of her Time: The Story of Anna Pierce Judah." Trini looked at him expecting he knew the book.

Nick shook his head. "No, Cher. Haven't heard of it."

"Of course, you have heard of Theodore Judah, right?" Trini's face shined with enthusiasm.

Nick again shook his head, then, his eyes got really big, "Oh, you mean in ancient history, how that Cat, ... um ..." After a pause, Nick snapped his fingers. "Yes, they called him Crazy Judah because of the railroad he wanted to build over the Sierra mountains." Nick sat up straighter.

"Exactly. His wife assisted him. Anna Pierce from the leading family in New England.

"Franklin Pierce was president."

"Anna Pierce was his second cousin twice removed. Theodore Judah married this educated refined active woman. When Judah took her past Dutch Flat on the slope of the Sierra Nevada to survey the railroad route, she painted watercolors, made drawings and collected wildflowers. When Judah put up his surveys and map of his transcontinental railroad at the San Francisco convention, she organized, compiled and help display them. Seeing the success of the exhibit in San Francisco, this intuitive woman suggestion they put up more exhibits and make a Transcontinental Railroad Museum in Washington DC to get more support. His maps went on the walls and her beautiful Sierra watercolors, drawings and dried wildflowers were on the tables. A general came to listen to her promote the Sierra route of the transcontinental railroad. She was an enthusiastic supporter of it, and Sierra nature and of their museum exhibits. The general told Judah how he found Mrs. Judah to be as enthusiastic for the transcontinental railroad as Judah was himself," Trini said. Her voice rose to a higher pitch with zest … and she was running out of breath.

When she took a break to take a deep breath, Nick asked a question. "Who was the general?" His normally lazy eyes were now wide with interest.

"Attorney Thomas Ewing and future Union General," Trini stated.

"What year was the museum opened?"

"Early 1862."

"During the Civil War. I seem to remember from my ancient history that the Northerners wanted the transcontinental railroad route to follow their central route through to California."

"Yes. And the museum was temporary. The Judahs traveled back and forth between San Francisco and New York." She held her head up high.

"You certainly know your train history. Isn't this," Nick looked around the train car, "and the trains running ancient history too? I mean, we fly anywhere we need to go."

"Those of you with money fly," she said. "I have only ridden a bicycle, or I walk."

"Except for your plane ride and don't forget, helicopter ride to this train," Nick gestured with his hand out and then in.

Trini narrowed her eyes and leaned forward. "Ya, but do I remember that? No, because I was drugged by some crazy kidnappers." She pounded her fist on the table.

Nick startled. He picked up his empty glass which had fallen over.

Trini picked up her glass, but was still cross.

"Um, ... ya. So, there are seven us on board now. That has to be lucky." Nick tilted his head with a placating half smile.

"I don't believe in luck. I relieve in connections."

"What do you mean?"

"For example, yesterday I saw Justin make a sign, the sign for CANDY. The connection excited me." *Justin excited me. And he's very expressive.* "Anyway, I considered the possibility that Justin knew sign language, like I do with my mother and neighbors ... but ... well ... then, I concluded it was a coincidence and he had just made a gesture."

Nick shook his head, "I didn't notice. I would just say it is a coincidence."

Without warning, Trini doubled over with pain on her left side. "Owwwww."

"What is it?" Nick inquired. "I hear a scream outside, too." Nick turned from her to look at the door.

Trini's pain went away after the initial feeling of being stabbed with a hot, *what? Knife, poker, cane?*

Nick leaned in closer. "You're frightening me, Cher." Nick scrunched up his face as Trini lifted the left side of her shirt.

Nothing.

"Humph," she said. "It felt like a hot pain." She knit her brows while looking at her smooth light brown skin.

"Maybe you need to lie down," Nick suggested. He frowned.

"Huh, I don't feel anything now, that's funny," Trini said. Her brows were still knitted.

She reached for her glass and took a long drink of her water with lemon.

Concern was still etched on Nick's face. He had moved his cane closer to him and was rubbing the bulbous top, which contained his dice.

Trini noticed his unease. "Don't worry. I'm fine." She sat up straight. "But there was the scream outside." She thought of Justin. He and Red had been arguing. What became of the two? She rose and saw Nick pushing on his cane and the table to get to his feet. They should look in on Justin and Red.

The had taken four or five steps when they were thrown by a sudden turn of the train. Trini had been thrown into the nearest booth laying on her right arm. She looked at Nick who had been thrown into the table. The plates and glasses they had left had fallen over and clattered in piles against the window. The whole train was making a U-turn.

Trini's heart beat fast.

Nick's hand was pulling her up by her left arm. She brought herself up the rest of the way and looked out the clear window. They were headed directly East.

11

Justin and the Recalcitrant Red

RED PINNED JUSTIN to the top of the speeding train. Justin lay on his back pressed down. The hot metal roof burned the skin on his right cheek and right arm. He felt the weight of Red on top of him, breath like onions. His eyes watered. The roof stretched only eight and a half feet wide. They struggled, like wrestlers, only on more limited space. Red shoved the right side of Justin's head into the roof. Justin's ears rang and all he could think was how much his head hurt, as if a vice was crushing it. He knew Red was strong enough to kill him. Sweat ran down his copper-colored bangs. He shut his eyes as the salty sweat burned them. The height above the blurry ground made Justin dizzy. His vision blurred as his whole head ached. The copper-haired teen closed his eyes to avoid seeing the distant sunbaked ground far below. Sweat dripped from both teens.

The constant rumble of the wheels filled the air. Wind whipped around them. Justin grew nauseous at the dizzying height. The teen's stomach swirled. Bile rose. Head spun. The hot poker burned the Justin's left side below the ribs on his pale skin where his shirt lifted.

"Ughhhhhhhh," Justin screamed. Burning pain seared through him. He let out a terrible scream.

"Look at the tracks and switches," Red yelled, "Justin hurry, there isn't much time. Look at the train tracks!" Red's eyes darted between the distant end of the train car and Justin's face. "Hurry. Look! What can you make out?" The heavier boy didn't let up on the railroad whiz. Justin clenched his teeth, and felt his left leg spasming. He couldn't even open his eyes, let alone lift his body to get a view of the layout of the tracks as Red wanted. But he still sensed the great distance to the ground, not to mention the deadly speed. Justin froze, terrified of heights.

The train rushed on with the two teens still on top. Finally, Justin fixed his eyes on Red's face. It was the only spot not swirling. Again, Red's attention was divided between watching the end of the roof and the boy he pinned down. Justin watched as Red bit his lip. A tiny drop of scarlet trickled down on to the pale boy's chin. *He's afraid of something.*

Adrenaline pumping, Justin's throat thundered, "No, not for one like you!" He spit the words out at Red. With anger and adrenaline coursing through him, Justin pushed against Red trying to flip him, but Red had all of his weight on him. Red, eyes steeled and focused, still looked at Justin's face.

The train traveled southwest, climbing slightly in elevation. The boys rolled a quarter turn and both planted their palms on the hot roof, ignoring the hot surface. Red had dropped the hot poker in the process.

An old road ran along the left side of the train. Then, Red could see a great canyon, which the Colorado River ran through. The great canyon had tertiary canyons off of it. From a bird's eye view, the plateau looked like an arrowhead with notched edges. The train came near to an edge which dropped off a thousand feet into a canyon directly to the left of the road. Red looked down and saw a trail crisscrossing the tertiary canyon. Now, he could no longer see it as the train speed on. Justin and Red continued to struggle on the roof, like wrestlers, Red still dominating Justin.

Red punched the same spot on Justin's side where the poker burn was he had given the railroad whiz to get him to climb the ladder onto the roof.

Justin's eyes bolted wide open and he let out a short scream, while a distant sound also reached their ears. Could it be an echo from the scream? A thin high *screak* from the back side of the train car reached their ears. There was nothing out here on this "island in the sky," on this high plateau. *Probably a bird*, Justin thought. The train continued to slowly rise in elevation through a secluded grassy pasture.

The verdant pasture grew in his mind and Justin went to his happy spot, remembering his family's pasture at home. He loved the evenings, when the sun just set, casting a golden shower of light on the serene pasture. His soft horse, Sky under him. He would pet the soft luxurious dark brown coat on her neck. He loved how her neigh sounded, as if to say, "Ah, that's the right spot. Don't stop." The irrigated pasture ground and grass cushioned the steps of her prancing hooves. He chewed on mustard grass and smacked his tongue against his lips, enjoying the sour taste. The smell of grass drew his attention. The cat lurked in the grass and held a field mouse in its mouth. The soft mooing of the cows in the distant corral brought home memories of his parents' ranch. Squawks of the mockingbirds on the hurricane fence around the yard echoed. Penned in the yard, the dogs wouldn't bother them. Justin rode for hours in the pasture before this— before the nightmare on the train.

Higher on this mesa the two teens rolled. Justin could see the canyon now, not three yards on their left. Since the train had been traveling straight before he couldn't tell that the train rode on a trestle now over the end of a tertiary canyon. He averted his eyes from the ground, his body trembling. Red's mouth dropped open as he looked down a thousand feet below to the old trail at the bottom of this canyon.

The train descended into a small eroded bowl. *Ugh*. Justin felt his stomach rise into his throat. Now, Justin could see an approaching white and red sandstone arch spanning the locomotive. The arch was almost over them, with only two feet of clearance.

"Duck!" Justin yelled up at Red and dropped his head and hands flat against the scalding roof.

Justin watched the arch against the sky as he pancaked himself to the train roof sped under it. Exhausted, Justin continued to lay flat on his back looking up at the sky. It looked like the train was flying in the air over the canyon from this view. He wondered why Red hadn't gone back to wrestling him. *Did Red ignore the warning to duck? Maybe this battle of will and fear ended with the arch taking out Red.* Then, he felt hands on his knees and Red between his legs. The pressure of Red's pink and freckled hands increased on Justin's tan arms. Once again, Red pinned him. Red in his cut-off biker jacket, biceps bulging was too strong for Justin. He wondered how this was going to end. Was Red going to beat him up, throw him off the roof, get them both knocked out by the next arch or tunnel? Again, Justin focused on Red's face to avoid looking at the height.

The sound was louder this second time, more metallic and closer. It registered with Justin— The sound was being made by The Screakers. *Scrrreak, Tap, Tap, Tap. Scrrreak, Tap, Tap, Tap.* Justin swallowed. *They're coming.*

They cast glances down toward the front sides of the train car. It was blurry as the train sped under them. Justin felt dizzy from the height and speed. *I never liked heights. Wonder if I would break my legs falling from here down there?* he thought, looking left and right for the source of the terrifying sound. He couldn't jump.

The hot pain drove Justin to open his eyes. As he did, he caught the fearful look in Red's wild eyes.

"You're crazy Clyde!" Justin screamed into his face.

"Don't call me that name!" Red spat at him.

"You snake! You're lying about Vanessa!" Justin yelled, struggling.

"Jealous, aren't ya?!" Red gloated, putting more pressure on Justin.

"You're lying, that she's your girlfriend. We've been together for the last three years." Justin said as loudly as he could, trying to be heard above the chuffing of the locomotive.

"And how long have you been away on this train, huh?" Red questioned.

"Only four days." Justin answered.

"A lot of love making can happen in four days," Red said with a sly grin.

"Liar!" Justin shouted as he tried to free his right hand from under Red's left knee and his left hand from under Red's right hand.

Soon the Screakers would get to them. Justin didn't have time to contemplate, which he would rather face. Red lifted the hot poker above Justin's chest. Focusing just on his attacker, Justin used his athletic legs, and kicked Red. Red slid toward the front of the train car. The biker rolled partially off the front side, but grabbed onto the ladder, white knuckled. The hot poker, where was it? Justin looked at Red's hand and saw the weapon.

Then, they heard what they dreaded, *Scrrreak, Tap, Tap, Tap, Scrrreak, Tap, Tap, Tap,* from the back of the train car. *Snap! The things* were getting closer. Red's eyes widened in terror. Then, in a blink, he vanished down the ladder. Justin lay on his back in the same spot. He thought that he heard the Screakers approaching up the rear and sides now. Metal scraped on metal, *Scrrreak,* and three metal legged *Tap, Tap, Tap. Scrrreak, Tap, Tap, Tap.* Justin flipped over. Looked up. Took a deep breath. With every hair standing on end, he crawled flat bellied to the ladder. The train wheels bumped over some small thing on the tracks, but enough to jostle him over the front of the car. He tried to grab hold of something, scraping the sides of his hands on the rot iron railing. But he fell. He landed with a thud on the metal breezeway, one leg dangling over the coupler. Yikes! Ouch! Pain riveted through every part of his body. His leg felt heavy and began to droop a tiny fraction of an inch closer to the wheels. A dangling string on his pants threatened to catch. Looking between the two train cars, he saw the tracks and reddish ground whistling by. If his foot or pant string got even an inch closer, he would have been pulled under the wheels.

Heart pounding, he noticed the annoying sound getting louder. They were coming. *Scrrreak, Tap, Tap, Tap, Scrrreack, Tap, Tap, Tap.* Justin found one last ounce of inner strength and managed to pull his leg onto the metal breezeway. He winced. Moving his limbs hurt too much. So, he just lay there.

His mind went to the place everyone in his right mind knows he should not have let it go. He thought that dying would be so easy. *Just give up; that's what I should do,* he thought. The exhaustion, pain and shock were eating away at his lucidity. Happy memories of his childhood occupied the forefront of his mind. Game competitions, since he could remember, model railroading, rodeos, winning chess tournaments, and then baseball tournaments. His father told him stories of how his grandfather used to play an ancient game, Yu-Gi-Oh! He too was a tournament winner. The whizkid never met his grandfather-died before he was born.

His favorite animals came to mind- horses. He envisioned them running in the corral.

Three years ago, Justin got a new filly. A long legged dark, muscular, fine horse standing one foot behind the blindfolded Justin. His father gave the lead rein some slack and the pet nuzzled against the hood of Justin's jacket.

"Whoa -?" He exclaimed with a start.

Sky found a hidden apple in the hood and took it out with a crunch, right next to Justin's ear.

His parents busted up laughing to see him jump at the sound.

Justin grew tired of their joke. Itching to see his new horse, not just with his inner eye that told him that he was going to love his horse, but with his natural eyes too. He wasn't disappointed. She stood tall and lean. Her fur shined. He didn't miss the mischief in her eyes. He kept with the first name that came to mind - Sky. The name suited her. He climbed up in the saddle, but she bucked him off. In doing so, her back hoof just caught him in the left hip. He fell hard to the ground. Feeling like all the nerves in his body pulsed in pain, he kept his eyes shut. Justin felt like he never wanted to get up. That's how he felt now, aching, withdrawn, and sleepy.

Mostly, Justin saw two faces throughout it all- his parents. A seventeen-year-old boy couldn't love a mom and dad, like he loved his parents. He admired his dad who had taught him so much. His dad would have lost his one son today. He thought he heard his Dad's gruff rancher's voice now, "Now son, mind you keep the present taking up the largest part of your vision." He said this with one hand on Justin's shoulder.

Justin looked up, keeping the present as the largest part of his vision.

The door to the passenger car loomed less than two feet away. *Tap, Tap, Tap, Scrrreak. Tap, Tap, Tap, Scrrreak.* He look at the door one last time, then closed his eyes, still hearing the menacing *Tap, Tap, Tap, Scrrreak* growing dangerously close.

12

The Screakers Attack

WITH HIS EYES closed, he saw his coach's tan face, crows' feet at the corners of the bright amber eyes, and remembered his coach saying, "reach deep down inside for something extra, 'cuz others are depending on you." Justin also recalled how his father encouraged him after Sky's kick to "power through it."

With determination to rise to responsibility, as his coach taught him, and to power through it, as his father instructed, Justin opened his eyes. He took a big breath and on the exhale lifted his whole head with a stab of pain. He groaned. Finally bringing his eyes to focus, he saw Kofi, dark skinned big white smile, on the other side of the window of the door witnessing Justin's resurrection. *How long had he lain there?*

Scrrreak, Tap, Tap, Tap. Scrrreak, Tap, Tap, Tap.

Getting up to his hands and knees, he crawled to the door that Kofi opened. *Slam!* The door shut behind him. The first Screaker scraped up to it. *Clank!* Its metal bulbous body slammed into the door. The second one stopped short of careening into the first. The Screacker, with its ratchet arm, spike legs, and buzz saw arm out through opposite slits looked ghastly. Their six appendages, gave them a likeness to a spider, minus two limbs. They turned around and walked back, if you could call it that. These metal monsters, with their round bodies and three legs, now scuttled back to their hiding places.

Justin had heard about the Screakers on his first day on the Beast.

"G'day mate," Leo patted him on the back, "Now you understand what it's like being kidnapped."

Then a tall kid with glasses walked right up into Justin's space, "Hello. I am Kofi. Our friend in the corner there, is Nick," Kofi shook Justin's hand.

"Where y'at?" Said Nick. Justin briefly noted a slightly overweight young man with brown hair and a goatee sitting in a chair that looked uncomfortable. Still, Nick just sat, shuffling a deck of cards, not offering his hand in greeting. A gambler's cane was leaning against the table at his right hand. The cane seemed a necessity, within easy grasp. Justin had seen gamblers at the tournaments with their gambler's canes. His curiosity peaked. Did it have a sword hidden within? He could see that clear glass sealed the bulbous top and contained two green objects, one with two white dots and the other with five white dots. Dice. Maybe lady luck was with this feller.

Then, Justin eyes looked down to someone who came into his view on his other side. A short medium dark teen with exceptionally intelligent eyes.

"I'm Tej." Tej said in an accent from India. "I won the championship in Mahjong in the East. What are you good at?"

"Good at?" Justin said with a puzzled expression.

"Kofi won the chess championship; Nick, the pinnacle championship; Leo, the model train engineering championship. We're all whiz kids. What is your skill?" Tej rephrased this time.

Justin looked around at the faces of each boy. He knew Leo from their model railroading competitions. But, the last time he competed in chess seemed like ages ago. He looked at Kofi square in the face and remembered him as that boy who kept beating him.

"Right. Kofi, the chess champion. You checkmated my king for the 2062 chess master title. That was … what...five years ago?! Wow, time flies while you're sheltered from the outside in a fortress of a valley, like where I grew up. Actually, Hidden Valley lies beyond those hills," he pointed to the West and they looked, "But I didn't get any news. So, I didn't keep track of you Kofi. Good to see you again, partner" Justin said. Kofi smiled, "Same here."

Then Justin noticed Tej still waiting for an answer.

"Oh, yeah. Well, I stopped competing in chess to focus on, well, … train engineering and baseball," Justin put his hands on his hips.

"Baseball, seriously?!" Tej crossed his arms.

"Yeah, I'm the team catcher. Our comp team won the national title the last five years straight."

"Welcome to the Beast," Tej finishes.

Justin rakes his eyes over the inside of the train. It wasn't much.

Kofi explained, "The Beast is a prison like no other. The walls close in. You lose track of direction. You try to get your balance. The noise is constant. *Clickity Clack and Huff, Huff.* You can't sleep. Once the nausea settles, you go outside for fresh air, and you almost get knocked over by the gust created by the high speeds. If you stay out during the daytime, the Scrrreak come after you." Kofi, his arms crossed, moves his hands up and down his arms.

"The Scrrreak?" Justin said either just curious or in disbelief or both.

Kofi cast his eyes downward and visibly shivered.

"The Scrrreakers … well, they're like nothing we've ever seen before." Kofi fell silent and shivered.

"The Beast, what in-" Justin asked curiously.

"This train. Let me tell you how it is on the Beast," Leo said.

Tej whispered, "Fresh meat." Snickering.

Winking, Leo continued, "I've been here the longest, understand," rising up to his full height, "Good to see you mate. Let's see, last time I saw you, I proved to you," his voice rises with energy and in pitch, "I was the best model railroad design engineer." Leo crosses his arms.

"Yeah, something like that. So-" He glared at Kofi's shivering body. Annoyance etched on Justin's forehead.

a deep voice with an accent reached him.

"Justin, isn't it? Let me show you something," Nick smiled a broad grin sandwiched with dimples.

Justin looked between the map and the Cajun shuffling the cards. Then, he looked at Nick's club feet, really his special shoes. He also noted the gambler's cane leaning against the table. *He's such a cheerful friendly guy, that you wouldn't know that he had a disability.* So, Justin figured he could spend a short time at Nick's table. The poor guy obviously isn't going anywhere. Justin walked over.

Nick just finished making a ribbon with the playing cards. He quickly started shuffling them with his fingers. His fingers deftly rotated the cards in opposite directions .

He watched Nick fan the cards, carefully remembering the bottom card that he put in the center.

"Touch a card," he stated the imperative.

Justin tapped the middle card in the fanned deck.

Nick turned the card over, which revealed the eight of spades. He slid the card in the deck and continues his shuffling. Justin knew the trick involves a slight of hand. He tried to focus on Nick's hands, but nothing looked out of the ordinary.

Nick told Justin, "Look in your right pocket."

Ah. Couldn't hurt. Justin pulled the eight of spades from his pocket. *Wait a minute, how DID Nick do that? Tricky Nicky indeed.*

"So, BBQ was cornered by several of the monsters. A Screacker's buzz saw hurt BBQ's hand, Kofi doctored him up. He was still alive!"

Justin expressed awe, "Really?! Kofi, -"ofi waved it off. "There's more," he said and turned as Tej started speaking.

13

An Injured Justin

THE INJURED JUSTIN, sprawled on a vinyl passenger seat, opened his eyes to see Trini and Kofi leaning over him.

"Justin, are you alright?" Trini lifted his shirt on his left side. An angry red burn marred the skin under his ribcage. She took out a tube from the first aid kit.

Kofi asked, "Man, do you have a death wish, or what?" Kofi leaned his weight on his one right hand on his friend's right side.

"Ow!" Justin and Trini said at the same time.

"What?!" Kofi exclaimed as he looked at Justin's and Trini's expression of pain.

Justin continuing to pull back his shirt and revealed not one but two angry hot poker burns. "Man, Red did that to you?" Kofi said.

"Red's gone off the rails," Justin whispered. "Kofi, first aid kit. Give it here."

Kofi picked up the kit and held it out.

The tube of burn cream was handed over by Trini. Concern shown in her kind brown eyes.

Justin brushed the two riders aside. He would do it himself.

"There's this one blistering spot you can't reach on the back of your burn. You're going to need my help. I'll hold the back part of the gauze," Kofi said.

"I'll do it," Trini offered.

"My father is a doctor. I know what to do," said Kofi.

Justin winced as the doctor's son touched the gauze to his burns, especially the third degree burn in the middle of it. He saw the girl contract her muscles in pain, putting her left hand protectively on her left side. *Wow, she's really sensitive to other people's pain,* Kofi thought.

Kofi's deft hands held the gauze in one hand and helped wrap it around Justin's back with the other.

Trini handed the scissors to Kofi. He cut the end of the gauze.

The girl timidly spoke up, "Um, Justin, why is Cyde, I mean Red, so mean to you?"

Shrugged his shoulders, while looking down at the gauze, Justin said, "Beats me."

Trini and Kofi looked at each other.

"He does beat you, literally. There has to be a reason for it," Trini put her face directly above Justin's. She smelled like lemons.

"I can't talk now ... weak ..." Justin settled more into the seat.

"Justin ..." said Trini. She frowned and sat back.

He closed his eyes, hoping the nightmares wouldn't return.

A while later, something startled Justin. He awoke to Trini standing over him and speaking to him.

"Hot soup." She set the soup down before the recovering Justin. The wounded teen remembered how his mother used to serve him the same, chicken noodle soup, not only when he had a cold, but anytime he was aching. He couldn't think about his mother and father, the Waynes right now. When he did, his emotions threatened to choke off his breathing. Justin left thoughts of home behind and looked forward. He looked down at his shirt as he pulled it down. He grimaced, sick of being stuck in this train, not able to go out for fear of the Screakers. It was dim in the train car and tight, like he was swallowed whole by an enormous creature. The thought sent goosebumps down his arms. He noticed his arm and hand that held the soup cup. Huge bumps. He had to get a grip.

Kofi entered, "So, the cowboy is awake."

"Justin—"

Kofi spoke at the same time, "What did you see on top of the train?"

"If it's not too nauseating for you," Trini said. She frowned and leaned in with concern. *I feel like a train hit me, but all this attention is nice.* He lingered on her full face, perfect hairline, petite nose and those large brown doe eyes. *Her eyes remind me of someone. Who else has eyes like those?*

"Well, did you see anything that you can use for the map?" Kofi said.

"Well, I barely saw anything. But what I did see were the closest switches changed all of a sudden. Red and I each went to the opposite sides of the roof and hung on to the edges. I saw that we hadn't yet come to the edge of the, uh, I guess I'll call it the peninsula with canyons all below. We were prematurely diverted in an almost U-turn."

Kofi looked around and noticed Red and Leo playing cards at the far end of the car, ignoring Justin.

Kofi gave his full attention to him, "Uh, Justin, I'm listening."

A half smile crossed Justin's face, like a summer sprinkle crosses the plateau, "Thanks."

"And me, as well," Trini said.

"Thank you, Trini," Justin said. He took her hand and squeezed it. Her presence comforted him. He began to wish they were alone. He shook his head and thought, *I have to focus on getting us off this train.*

"So," Justin spoke to Kofi, "since you've been on the Beast, has anyone, BBQ or anyone noticed the switches changing?"

"No." Kofi stated flatly. The faithful friend shook his head and looked around the car. "But, don't you have an urgent problem right here with those two?" nodding towards the far end of the car.

Justin, took a moment to find his self-control, "What I can't figure out, is why Leo has become Red's partner in crime."

Trini and Kofi shrugged.

Justin sat up a little more. Looking at the space created on the bench, Trini sat next to him, smiling. From inside Justin, a joyous warmth flowed to the surface of his skin. He took small breaths trying not to move his shoulder any closer to her. He kept his gaze looking at the far end of the car.

It was there Red was seated with Leo, leaning in. He whispered to Leo then they rose and sat down at Nick's table . Red took out a deck of poker cards and a bag of hard candy from his pockets. Red shuffled the cards. They coax Taj off of his handheld Mahjong game to play with them.

Justin sighed and said out loud to no one in particular, "I guess they're just going to play games the rest of our captivity. We'll run out of food and starve on the Beast. We may go mad and start fighting. We may end each other."

Finally, Justin asked Kofi, "Where did he put the hot poker?"

"Back in the locomotive, why?" Kofi raised an eyebrow.

Justin responded, "Just, well, I want to make sure it isn't here. I mean, I could be sleeping and I wouldn't want Red attacking me with the weapon."

Trini said, "He's a violent one!"

Kofi nodded his head vigorously.

"Yeah, you can say that again!" Justin winced. His burned flesh stung and his fractured rib and bruises hurt. The athletic boy knew the pain of injuries, but the added burn added to his agony.

Trini sat next to him smiling pleasantly.

Kofi chided, "Just lie down and stop stirring. Here." He handed Justin the Sudoku pages and a pencil, "Stay, and don't get up."

"Yes, nurse Kofi," Justin mimicked a female's voice.

Rolling his eyes, the chess player picked up his handheld.

On his half of the bench, Justin looked at the Sudoku puzzle on the top sheet of the game book. He noticed Trini reach for something from the pile of games on the table, an alphabetic cypher wheel. With the cypher sheet and pencil, she worked on cyphering the first code on the paper. In a minute, he finished the first Sudoku puzzle, filling in the correct numbers, in under three and a half minutes.

After the 20th Sudoku puzzle, Justin sat straight up and attempted to rise.

"You must stay still, if you want to heal properly," Trini said. She patted his shoulder and removed her hand as Kofi approached and put both his hands-on Justin's shoulders.

But Justin muscled his way, too strong for Kofi to push around and he stood up.

So, Kofi took another tack.

"Please, sit back down, friend," Kofi pleaded. His eyes had bags under them and he bit his lip. He quickly looked from Red across the room at cards up to Justin towering above him.

Justin nodded, "Alright friend." He sat back down. He leaned his head against the clear window.

Trini got up, took another worksheet from the Cypher pile and sat opposite Justin in the booth. She stuck her tongue out a tiny bit as she worked on the cypher. She was enthralled in her challenge, like a cowboy practicing rope knots took joy in his challenge.

Justin looked out his window at an Australian shepherd dog running along the tracks. The sight of it evoked an image of his father's old dog, Clownie. As Justin recalled Clownie's intelligent eyes scanning the livestock, Justin's eyes got a little teary. He blinked them away in frustration. Justin led an isolated life on the ranch, and he missed spending time with this parents, the hands, and the animals, but especially his dog, who kept the ranch running.

As Justin lay with his head back on the train car booth, he dozed off. In a short time, he started dreaming. He squatted in an ally of an old city with tall apartment buildings, dark alleys, and garbage in the streets, like a concrete jungle. It was dark. He could barely see any sky and barely any stars with all the city lights. Faint moonlight and an odd orangish-brown glow shone from the west.

A distant street light barely illuminated the grimy alley. Years of inner-city decay, a war and decades of neglect left old automobile grease, a thick layer of dust and refuge. He looked a second time down the alley. Beneath the fire escape, a Ford truck stood. It was less than five years old, but unusual. No one on this block owned a vehicle. He thought that the truck must belong to an important visitor. Trash littered the asphalt around the trashcans on this corner of the alley. No one would see him here. With dirty hands, he struck a match. Then, he lit another, then four. One matchstick finally caught. It's warm glow spread as it ignited the handful of papers next to it. He lit one and held it to a crumpled piece of paper. A warm glow grew. It blazed into a fire. The fire burned his index and thumb. He dropped the flaming paper before it singed his whole hand. Ignoring the burn on his fingers, he stared into the fire, mesmerized. The fire moved like a living thing, swaying, breathing and playing. The now, three-foot-high fire, seemed to speak a silent language straight to his being. He was transfixed on the ephemeral glowing fire. It was something that he had made, and yet it possessed him, like an addiction to a drug. He didn't move when the sound of the growing fire crackled. He didn't move when the flames spread throughout the apartment building and consumed it. Nor did he turn and look or he would have seen the people running out the front and scrambling down the fire escape.

A man struggled to the open door, his mouth open screaming. His back was on fire. Justin walked to the front of the building to where the screams were coming from. The man handed a child to the mother who ran to the curb. He was back lit by flames, then they engulfed him in a fireball. Justin saw what he had caused, the inferno that consumed this apartment and a man.

Justin woke up with a start, with terror flowing through his chest. It was a familiar nightmare. His clothes were soaked with perspiration. His heart was pounding with an animal terror. He felt pursued, but not by something animate. It was always the same: he's lighting paper on fire, he was captivated while it blazed out of control, people ran out of the blazing apartment building, then he saw the screaming burning man. Justin knew that he had an unusual fascination with fire. But why this nightmare of the burning man of the apartment building? It seemed so real, even the second after he woke up. It wasn't like his dream about Mr. Woodburn, the butcher. He knew that really happened. Well, he didn't want to think about that real nightmare. But, could the burning man in the apartment building be real? Something long ago? No, it was just a nightmare. He shook it off while getting up to go to the toilet.

The toilet was a three foot by three-foot bathroom. After Justin splashed his face with cold water, he looked in the mirror.

Justin read, Do not flush while train is in the station, on a vintage sign hung above the toilet. He used to have a model O gauge sleeper car with a sign on the door to the restroom that had the same saying in tiny letters. Brushing his hands over his face, he couldn't shake how he felt manipulated. The Villains controlled his life now, and left him impotent. He was powerless to stop this train. He wondered if someone from the train competition was doing this to him. Could it be Gary, the second-place winner, or Dylan, the number three guy? No way that it was those train nerds. They were very one minded about their train layouts and didn't venture out.

Justin tried to lay down and get some sleep on the uncomfortable bench seat. His troubled thoughts kept him from rest. Who was doing this to them? How were they going to get off this speeding train?

Justin decided to get up and stretch his muscles. Kofi rushed over to let Justin lean on him for support. Kofi didn't know that Justin had gotten up already. While they walked around past the open area in the passenger car, Justin noticed things. There were blankets, an extra chair and table, an empty tool box, a broom and dust pan, a tenor saxophone and his cowboy hat. Justin grabbed his cowboy hat and marched through the train car, his side tender and his foot throbbing. *If I don't get us working on a solution, who will?* "I want some paper and pencil," Justin explained to Kofi. At that moment, he heard Red arguing with Leo at the corner table with Nick.

"Someone has to go up on the roof and finish the map!" Red raised his voice

Nick pointed a finger at him, "Why don't you do it?"

Bam! Red jumped up knocking over his chair. All eyes were rivetted on Red, who turned the game into fifty-two card pick up saying, "Yeah. Well, you're forgetting one thing."

"Well, what's that?" Leo stood up, cards falling around him.

"I'm smarter than you, losers," Red bounded to the opening and leaped off the train.

14

Justin Tries to Unite the Riders

RED JUMPED IN midair, his knees bent. His feet hit the dirt. At first, he ran at a slower pace than the train. Then, he kept pace. Finally, the boys saw Red overtake the train. With adrenaline and his hair flowing, he jumped upon the switch. The switch moved and the train took the new direction. Red's pace slowed. He now ran behind the opening between train cars now. His shoulders rose and fell over and over as he puffed.

"Come on!" The boys shouted.

Red picked up his pace again. At the opening, he grabbed at the handrail. He gripped both hands tightly, but his feet dragged, wearing off patches on the bottom of his shoes. He tried to lift each leg, but failed to get higher. As his strength waned, Justin stood on the bottom step, secured Red by the belt and hauled him up. Leo held onto Justin, Tej held onto Leo and last, Kofi held on to Tej. They all heaved as Justin hauled Red up. Then, they fell back onto the platform between the cars. Nick didn't join them. From inside they hear, "What y'at?"

Once up, Red stumbled into the dining car, to a booth and laid down.

Nick said loud enough to be heard, "Join me for a game of cards or, watch Cher and I perform some magic?"

Trini moved her left palm gesturing. "No time to care about Magic now that we know more clues to help us get off this rolling prison," Trini said. She threw her hands in her lap.

Nick fanned his cards. "Pick a card, please." He looked at Trini imploring her to play.

Leo ran straight to Red and stood over him.

"We haven't gotten off this train in *all* the time we've been on it," Leo gestured with his two hands, while Red looked at the ceiling, "and you know we're the smartest of the smart in the world, mate." Leo slaps his bush hat on his leg in exasperation.

Tej says, "whiz kids." Tej struts back and forth with his chest out and head bobbing like a rooster.

Kofi rolled his eyes at Tej, then placed French fries in the toaster oven. As he sat down with oven baked French fries and ketchup. Tej snuck one, so that fry disappeared before Kofi even sat down. Kofi eyed him, "Hey, it took me a long time to make those." The taller boy wagged his finger.

"You didn't make those. You baked them, goofball," Tej said. Tej razzed him.

"So, you can bake your own," Kofi scolded.

"Check it out. You know when you drive up to a bank, how you put withdrawal slips in a tube?" After Kofi nodded while stuffing his mouth with French fries, Tej continues, "We need to get those on this train, but for food. Push a button, and have your food delivered right to ya."

"I'd like to see your smoothie arrive in that!" Kofi teased.

"Or shoestring French fries shooting out of it and I try to catch them in my mouth, *pew, pew, pew*." At the same time, Tej gestured with his hands like projectiles darting and hitting his mouth, tongue and face.

Trini threw her hands out at her sides. "I already told you the clues are more important than cards," she said. "What do you think about the end segment that I saw on TV with BBQ jumping into the forcefield and getting thrown back under the wheels?"

"You heard the others talking about it and now you're making it up you saw it on TV," Nick said. He dealt out cards to the two of them.

Trini pushed the cards away from her. Nick scooped them up and continued shuffling.

Meanwhile, Justin stepped right in Red's face and exclaimed, "What was that stunt?! You could have been killed. We all could have died saving you," Justin put his hands on his hips, "Stop acting like you're better than we are, like you're a big deal. No one person can find a way off."

Red crossed his arms, staring at Justin.

Justin grunted. A saying came to him, light the fire within. Every time his parents saw him discouraged, they would tell him this saying. His parents knew they had picked an ironic phrase to use with him- the pyro. The Waynes never called him "Pyro." It was the kids at school who used the nickname, but his parents didn't seem ashamed that their son lit half the town on fire. Running his hand over his forehead and head, he renewed his focus.

"You're a fast runner and can change the switches. We need to make a plan together. Are you going to work with us?" Justin waited.

Without a word, Red went to sit with Nick. Trini was there, but had no cards. So, Red took out his poker deck of cards.

"Texas Holdem. I deal first," he said flatly.

You can tell by the way Nick continued making an incredibly high and perfect rainbow with his cards, Nick's eyes seeking approval from Red, he had his own ideas. Red didn't acknowledge the magician's trick. Nick didn't say a word. They were old friends and I'm sure Nick knew Red's way. Nick resigned himself and set his deck aside. *I guess Nick doesn't have many choices,* Trini thought. *Still, why would he doubt my word about the TV show?*

"Nick, I'll drop it if you tell me your story."

At the age of six, he had already earned the title of Tricky Nicky, a child prodigy. A deck of cards was his only friend. His hands moved so quickly shuffling them, people swore he could perform magic. On Bourbon Street, he set up his table with no help. It often took thirty minutes to walk, falling a few times, to the busy street from his alley way. A boy taken off the streets of New Orleans, but the streets were never taken from the boy. His peers called him a cripple and laughed at him sprawled in the street after another fall. But, when he started his magic card tricks, they stared in wide-eyed awe and amazement. The parents of the kids dropped coins into his can. At least, coins paid for his food. When he was seven, the large crowd that he now drew, included Mr. and Mrs. LeBlanc. They would become his adoptive parents. They owned gaming establishments in New Orleans and New Vegas. So, they could afford to pay for the surgeries on his club feet. But, now seventeen and tomorrow eighteen, his feet have gone back to being crippled.

15

Justin Isn't Playing Games

"HEY, KNOCK THAT off Tricky Nicky," said Red. He scowled at Nick as he moved his hands quickly shuffling the deck on his third deal.

"The hand is quicker than the eye," Nick flashed a dazzling smile bookended with dimples.

"That doesn't work on me. Pretend you're in a tournament and not on Bourbon Street doing your tricks for silver dollars. Come on, stop dealing from the bottom of the deck!" Red said in an angrier and louder voice.

Trini got up and left their table. She bumped into Justin, literally. He remembered she had been in the cabinet after saying something.

"Hey, I didn't give you permission to draw on the map," Justin said, crossing his arms.

"You wouldn't listen to me—"

"I don't give a fig about your excuse. Don't draw on things that don't belong to you." His face was red and hot. He wouldn't be surprised if smoke was coming out of his ears.

"But—"

"There's paper and pencils over there." Justin pointed to the part of the counter next to the wall. He turned his back to her.

She found the paper and a pencil he indicated and sat at an empty booth.

Justin looked up from the map. How could he focus with the ruckus? He casually walked past Trini. She was writing word associations.

Locomotive is to Train as
Horse is to Wagon.

Entrapment is to Insanity as
Freedom is to Sanity.

Justin stood over the map, trying to concentrate. The others were making a ruckus. He could make out Nick's colorful language.

"Red, Red, you are always d' serious one. Bless you and touch you with the fun-loving attitude...you sure need it," Nick laid on his thickest Cajun accent. He deftly shuffled his cards, then dealt off the bottom of the deck, yet again.

"Shut up and deal." Red said.

Justin had circled back to the map. He hoped he would have a fresh perspective. The map took the center of his focus, yet again. After another fifteen minutes, he looked around at the others. Each played his game of choice. He sighed and sat down next to Kofi. Of course, his friend played chess on his handheld. Justin thought back to the old chess set in his wooden ranch house, that his dad had since he was a kid. They would sit at the small card table playing chess for hours. Justin felt an ache in his heart for home and the familiar.

He took out his picture of Vanessa, by this time smudged with grimy fingerprints and dog-eared on all four sides. He sighed. *She's beautiful*, he thought. *No, she's gorgeous!* Vanessa, with her long blonde hair, long eyelashes flashing her baby blues and perfect pearly smile. His mind drifted back to the last time they were together.

It was the evening before he was abducted. They were seated at the ice cream parlor, booth having chocolate shakes, and talking about Justin's new close-cut buzz. She thought it looked more like a football player's haircut and they laughed. He could look at her all evening, but something odd caught his attention.

A man dressed in khaki slacks and a jacket with a Stratton hat on-some kind of uniform- with an insignia on a patch, was leaning on the end of the counter into the workspace of a pretty blonde waitress. She handed him an Apex soda, then he kissed her and turned around. He got weird at that point, looked straight at Justin in recognition. Then the ranger looked to the nearest sconce light, and stood up tall while walking out. Justin still stared at the door that the ranger went out, when all of a sudden, Vanessa leaned over the table, obstructing his view and kissed him full on the lips. He could almost feel her soft wet lips now, but the memory was fading the longer he spent on this train.

She took his hand and led him to the car. It was her suggestion they park at Lavender Fields. It was also her urging them to do more than just a kiss. Justin had said no. They should wait until marriage. It wasn't that he didn't feel the desire. His actions and plead to wait were due to his firm beliefs and would stick to those beliefs. He behaved like a gentleman, taking her home. Still, he couldn't wait to get off of the Beast and back to her.

Kofi continued to push buttons on his game. *He's addicted*, Justin thought. They were confined on this speeding train by metal spidery-like guard dogs and Kofi and the others just lost themselves in their favorite games.

"Kofi," said Justin, "You've been sitting there glued to that game. Your muscles are going to atrophy if you don't get up."

Kofi moved his head around, his neck cracked, then he rose to walk over to the other fourteen-year-old, Tej.

Justin remembered a time two seasons ago, concerned for his team, he told their coach that the players just wanted to play games all day. During the first days of spring training, the players were messing around. Some were playing Hacky Sac, others were wrestling while others sat in their parent's auto pilot cars on some handheld games. Coach Spiker gave him the phrase, *Cast your cares, not your responsibility.* As catcher and team captain, Justin spurred the players on with inspiration from behind and in front of home plate. Justin spoke the phrase out loud this time.

"Cast your cares, not your responsibility."

A sound brought Justin back to his present problem, laughter from Tej's corner of the dining car.

"I'm trying not to," Kofi said in a laughing voice. When Justin turned, he saw the last thing he imagined happening on a train. The backside of Tej, and Kofi holding a lighter up to his backside and the gas of Tej's farts. They laughed again when another fart lit up with a blue flame.

"What in blue blazes are you up to?" Justin asked with utter dismay. The younger boys laugh even harder at that expression. Justin didn't grow up with brothers and didn't see anything funny. "Red, what did you go and give them children a lighter for?"

A reluctant Kofi walked over to Red and gave the lighter back.

Justin pushed the Sudoku puzzle, that he'd been working on, to the middle of the table.

"Here, I got some wintergreen lifesavers in here," Justin reached in his pants pocket and took out the roll, "You can do some sparking. Watch." Justin took one and chewed it with his lips parted. Tiny sparks came from the impact points where his teeth crunched the candy.

"Great!" They both said and held their hands out.

"Here, take the whole roll." Justin said, while handing the lifesavers to them.

Justin's attention turned back to Red.

"You shouldn't be smoking on a train, Clyde." Justin enjoyed chastising him.

"Steam engine, duh." Red said and continued smoking, but took it outside after having enough of Justin giving him the evil eye.

Justin, sickened of immature boys, went to the other side of the car and laid down on the cushion of a booth. He rested five minutes, shifting to his side, the one that didn't have burns, fractured ribs or bruises. Then the pain was too much, with an, "Oof," Justin sat up.

Trini rose from her nap back in the sleeper section of the car, two bunks in front of his. "Hey, are you alright?" She asked.

Justin looked at her sitting at the edge of her sleeper bunk. A spring protruded from the mattress. It seems she was left with the worst mattress to sleep on.

Justin thought, *she's very pretty*. He shook his head and pointed his nose towards his task —the map. "I better get to the map." With no delay, he jumped down from his sleeper bunk and made his way to the map.

Red stood looking at the map as Justin hobbled into the train car.

"You're missing half the map. If you would have opened your eyes while on the roof, you would have something," Red taunted.

"Red, why didn't you inspect the switches while up there?"

"Model train engineering— not my talent. I'm just a card shark. What do I know about railroads?!" Red went to the table in the middle next to the map and continued to play his solitaire game.

After one survey of the partial map, Justin's face lit up as if a switch turned on. Picking up a second color, he drew in the first changed switch that he had seen on the railroad. He was almost finished with it, when he heard a loud *CLICK* coming from outside, then the locomotive lurched. The plates, which the other boys had left on the tables, slid off, the playing card deck slid. The force fanning the cards that were stacked, bodies jolted, everything went to the left. Unfortunately, the windows of the left side were blacked out from the outside with black paint. But Justin knew what this new development meant.

"Keeping us from seeing the rest of the tracks again. The Villains changed the switches, because I saw switches change in the distance, when I was on the roof. Look here," he pointed with his second color. That's all I could see before a hot poker in my side distracted me and the Screakers almost got us." He glowered at Red, who had reentered the dining car.

Red just stood with his hands in his pockets. The boys and Trini looked at Justin expectantly.

"So, what this means is that the Villains are messing with us. Just when we were on the roof "surveying" the tracks." Justin eyes could have been shooting darts at Red.

Bright hair hanging in his eyes, Red ignored him and leaned over the map, studying it. Justin admired his concentration, but the others lost interest and searched for something to eat.

"Get me a po'boy dressed," ordered Nick with that Cajun drawl.

The obliging Kofi answered, "Sure."

"What's a poor boy? food?" asked Justin.

"They really didn't let you go out to eat all those years of competing in tournaments, did they?" Red taunted with a wicked smile.

"So, my parents always ordered room service online from our hotel room. And, I don't have time for your bull, Clyde!" Justin said in exasperation.

"I told you, don't call me that. You Pyro!" Red retorted.

Justin closed his eyes to think, while Nick talked.

"Why, it's lettuce, tomato, pickles, mustard, all the fixin's means dressed. And, a po' boy is a sandwich. We'll teach ya, yet," explained Nick.

Kofi delivered the sandwich to Nick, who said, "Merci," with a bow of his head.

The four boys sat at one booth, while Red studied the map.

Kofi had an open can of black olives, "Hey, eyeballs, catch." The doctor's son threw one towards Tej's mouth. Tej dramatically chewed big and slow saying, "Yummy eye balls."

Justin nibbled at his ham and cheese sandwich. *Stale bread, ham and cheese. It's also tasteless.* He downed his grape Apex soda in a couple gulps. *I'm so tired of grape Apex soda,* even though at home it was his favorite drink. Every thought in his mind turned sour since Red came on the train. The way Leo had helped Red tore at the cowboy. When the bitterness swelled to the point of exploding, he finally went to the Aussie and asked, "Well, MATE, what was that thing with the hot poker? Why was you acting as Red's gopher?"

"Look mate, I don't want to talk about it," Leo turned to hid a blush. Feeling a need to redeem himself to his friend, Leo looked toward the map and changed the subject. "I did look at the new switch directions, which point away from the empty part. We were traveling in this direction, towards the blank part of the map, and then the Villains turned us back to the tracks where we began. What *don't* they want us to see?"

"They are making it near impossible to see anything," Justin scratched his head and said, "But, how did they know?"

"Know what?"

"Know that we had this half surveyed and the other half blank? They can see us and the map!" Justin exclaimed.

Trini had just come into their car. She said, "They can see us and the map, what?"

Tej, after overhearing Justin and Trini's last statement, jumped up and pointed above the map table. The technical whiz exclaimed, "The can light over the table, look." He reached up and unscrewed the bulb. Taking it apart, Tej found a tiny hidden camera with the latest stealth design and wireless technology.

"The Villains can't be more than 105 feet for long-range Wi-Fi to send and receive the Wi-Fi signal. Unless they use satellite," Tej explained.

Justin excitedly agreed, "You're right." He looked at the sconce light cover between the two tables on the clear window side where they always sat.

Leo asked, "What are a steam engine and old passenger cars doing with a surveillance camera?"

"This car is made to look like a 1923 four section heavy weight Pullman passenger combine car from over a hundred years ago.

This," Trini moves her head in a half circle, "Is the lounge section. But it's not, it's a narrow-gauge version. Those gaslight replica wall sconces are run on electricity. Those card tables are made from particle board. Those—"

"I thought you were some inner-city street urchin," Leo said. His brow creased as he stared at the girl.

"Like I started to say," said Trini, "my father started us walking to the tracks to watch the trains go by. And I went to school and libraries." She glared at Leo.

The other boys gathered around Justin. He unscrewed the sconce, took the light out and handed it to Tej. Then he made a gesture towards the light and mouthed, *is there a hidden bug?*

Two seconds later, Tej held up a tiny black dot the side of a pea.

Red grabbed it and smashed it under his foot.

The riders shook their heads at this.

"We could have saved it to trick the Villains with planned dialogue, Clyde!" Justin said in frustration.

"I told you, don't call me that!" He jutted an arm out to slug Justin.

But Justin blocked and deflected Red's arm away.

"We're onto something. We need to work together and we can beat this thing!" Justin looked around.

He searched faces, first Red's, and then to the others.

The biker walked off with the map headed to the passenger car.

With his hands in his pockets, "So much for working together." Leo walked back to where he left his cards, setting up a new solitaire game.

Tej walked back to the booth and picked up his chocolate bar.

Kofi shrugged, patted Justin on the back and took out his hand-held chess game. At first, the chess player rapidly pushed buttons. Then, he slowed in thoughtfulness.

Justin couldn't let go of what they just found and shook his head to clear it. The struggling leader walked around the dining car thinking and searching for clues.

Meanwhile, Nick had lured Tej, with chocolate bar in hand, over to his table. He finished dealing out five cards each for a poker game. On the table lay their day's rations of chocolate.

"I bet you, that you can't …"

Meanwhile, strolling through the baggage section of the Combine, Justin passed a pile of objects. The shiny black nickel of the Saxophone caught his eye. For some unknown reason, he picked it up. He put the strap around his neck and his fingers slid exactly into place. It fit like an old glove. Lips pursed, he blew into the mouthpiece. The cowboy had the embouchure perfect —making an ideal F note. Then he played a Bb scale up and down, then the D minor scale that turned into improvisation. Something warm and tingling flowed through him as he played, spreading through his body and out the instrument. The underlying tune became recognizable. Nick identified the song as a classic Jazz tune.

"Where y'at?" Exclaimed Nick, who pulled something out of his pocket. A harmonica.

Then, inspired by the harmonica, Justin switched to a Delta Blues song.

"Dat's, Baby, Please Don't Go!" exclaimed Nick, catching his breath between blows on his harmonica.

The other boys gathered around.

A third joined them. Kofi sang along to their music:

Now Baby, please don't go.

A fourth joined them. She had been singing since she opened the door to the section.

Baby, please don't go
Baby, please don't go
Down to New Orleans
You know I love you so
Baby, please don't go

Kofi and Trini went on and sang the second verse of the song.

The room was charged. Each of their faces held the wonder of the moment. When he finished playing his harmonica and looked up, Nick exclaimed, "lachez-les!"

Justin agreed, "That was good harmonizing."

Kofi said, "Hey Justin. Wow, I didn't know you were a Jazz saxophonist."

Justin shook his head, as he used his spit rag to clean the instrument.

Leo piped in, "You never mentioned anything about being a genius on the sax." Leo eyed him with amazement.

Still near the door, Trini stared at the saxophone, mouth agape.

"I'm not. I just picked this thing up off the floor just now." He said matter-of-factly.

"What?!" The boys exclaimed. They looked at each other with astonished faces.

Justin shrugged.

Tears were welling up in Trini's eyes as she stood frozen in place.

Kofi said, "My parents played Jazz downloads on their digital device. Man, you were better than any of those cats! Are you sure you haven't been in a Jazz band?"

"No. I never have. I mean, maybe in another life. Oh, I don't know." Justin said, putting the black Cannonball Tenor sax back in its case.

"You got some chops!" Nick said from his table, still with his harmonica in his hand. He went on to solo with an improvised tune of his own.

"Maybe you come from a musical family, huh?" asked Kofi.

No family member that Justin knew of, played any instruments. Another mystery.

Stranger still, tears fell from Trini's eyes.

16

Trini's Flashback

JUSTIN HELD THE tenor saxophone upside down with the mouthpiece off. Trini smelled the sour spit running through the sax and dripped onto the floor. Justin placed it against its case, drew the spit rag and string out and started cleaning it out.

She could still hear the upbeat music still in her ears, bringing her back to when she and her two brothers were little. She closed her eyes and envisioned her younger brother. His lips were tightly pressed on the mouthpiece of a tenor saxophone, which sat in a stand on the floor. As he played their grandpa's instrument, the sun reflected off his copper-hued hair in a dazzling light.

A tan wrinkled-faced man stepped towards them using his cane. His brown eyes projected warmth. "He has the gift," her grandpa exclaimed.

Their dear late grandpa had been the famous one in the family. He used to play at nearby clubs and come home with pockets full of tips. He made more in one night than their dad made in a week. One time, she had seen him dump tons of coins on their old scuff-marked grey coffee table. Her eyes had grown larger than usual. Shiny coins fell like raindrops to the floor. Trini had placed both of her petite hands under to catch them and giggled. Her grandpa straightened to his full height. On his face was a broad smile.

"Grandpa," she said. "You're rich."

"No child, this will only get us through two months." He tilted his head.

She went back to trying to catch coins before they slid off the coffee table and onto the floor. Her two brothers had bumped her out of the way to get to the coins faster than her.

"Hey," the small girl protested.

Tekka caught two, one in each hand.

"Ha, I'm rich," Tekka said. His crooked teeth exposed, he put the coins in his pockets and reached for more.

Ty caught one coin at a time in his right hand, as did Trini. They dropped each coin into the glass jar grandpa had placed on the floor.

On nights grandpa didn't have a gig, he played old Jazz standards for the three siblings. Her older brother snapped his fingers and tapped his foot to the beat. Trini danced. Her parents who couldn't hear would step out on a date. Only when her grandpa came, did her parents have time for each other. The three siblings had held hands and danced until bedtime. Grandpa had tucked them into bed for the last time.

Here in the train car, the teen girl wiped her eyes. She missed having all of them living together, including, her grandpa, her dad, and …her little brother. The lonesome girl took a paper tissue out of her back pocket and blew her nose. Here was her missing younger brother, she was sure of it. They were so young when the men took him. He went by Justin, which confused her. Then Trini figured the men must have given him the new name. She wavered between flinging herself into his arms, or blathering the whole story. Biting her lip, she stepped towards him. She focused her eyes on his hands handling the instrument.

There was no one left in the baggage section except the two of them. Justin placed the Cannonball sax in the case. His right hand was on the lid of the instrument case.

"Wait, don't close it," her voice cracked. "I want to see the sax." Trini sniffled, then forced a half-smile.

"What's wrong?" Justin asked. He shrugged then extended his right hand towards the teary-eyed girl.

As Trini examined the saxophone, she nodded. She knew every lined pattern in them.

"This sax," she said. She ran the fingers of her right hand over the fine cut stone on the buttons. "This is my grandfather's saxophone." She caressed the black metal. Her misty eyes blinked several times. *I cannot believe my eyes. This is the exact Sax. Why is it here? And why did Justin just play it all of a sudden with an embouchure that seemed to sing through the instrument … just like my grandfather's playing. Wait a minute … he also looked like he signed. Let me try something.*

"Tell me what I am saying." Trini started signing.

"You said, Mother is worried," Justin's mouth dropped open.

Too many words threated to choke Trini, "I … You … My brother … Oh my …I've found you, Ty." She held out her two arms, placing them around his shoulders.

17

A Reprieve Under the Lesser Lights

PROBLEMS WEIGHED ON Justin's mind before Trini's epiphany and this musical mystery. Now he had this girl he never met until this week hugging him. He wouldn't have minded if it was to make out, but here was a girl saying she was his sister.

"Look," he said. "I don't have a sister. I'm an only child. My parents are ... well, Mom and Dad, the Waynes. We live in Hidden Valley, Utah. I am sure you ... um ... are confused." Justin looked up while putting her at arms-length so he wouldn't have to look in her misty brown eyes.

"No, I know it, Ty. You're my—"

"I think you, all of us have had a trying time with the kidnappings and dropped here, then crazy monster Screakers and being trapped. I understand, it drives you mad."

"No, that's not it." Trini stands up. Tears flood her eyes. She turned towards the door.

"Trini, don't go like this." Justin tried to grab her right hand as she turned. He wasn't quick enough and the hurt girl ran through the door. "Trini, come back." His voice had a pleading tone in this last imperative. He shook his head, feeling bad for the way he handled that. *Of course, she was confused and maybe too hopeful to find her brother. She was grabbing at straws. The saxophone, the sign language*

*were just coincidences. I could have picked up a little sign language when
I was little. I don't even remember being little. That's all.*

Justin hung his head. His mind filled with depressing thoughts
about their predicament, sank into despair. They had half a map of
the tracks and switches, but it wasn't enough to solve this puzzle.
They rode this prison of a train around in circles, like a carousel ride
with the brass ring out of reach. The solution dangled somewhere
ahead of them. The NFLS kept them in the dark, like a shroud
hiding all from view.

"Aw!!!" He smacked the vinyl seat in the lounge.

"What was that?" Kofi turned to Justin.

"Nothing." Justin paced.

"We're going to watch Nick's magic tricks and then play a round
of Poker. Come on." Kofi gestured for Justin to follow.

"Sorry. I need to take a walk, now that it's dark. I want to see
more tracks before dawn when the Screakers come out." Justin put
his arms though his hoodie.

"You can't see anything in the dark."

"If I can't see anything, at least I'll see the stars."

"Okay. Catch ya later, man," Kofi turned.

Justin walked out onto the dining car platform. In the twenty-
two days they had been on the Beast, the Screakers never appeared at
night. Why would they? The boys couldn't see the switches at dark.

Fresh air. Space. Stars. Justin needed this. He'd always loved
star-gazing. Whenever he felt lost, he loved to look up at the stars.
His favorite had always been Orion with its three bright stars in his
belt. A luminous light grew from behind a grey cloud. Tonight, the
moon waxed, almost a full moon. He turned his face towards the
white dotted black expanse shining like a million points glimmering
on the artificial ceiling in the Capitol. The Plateau, in its isolation
and darkness, made viewing the stars easy. Their twinkling light
held Justin's entire attention. After thirty minutes outside, Justin's
eyes grew accustomed to the dark. He saw constellations of stars and
the planet Venus. Thousands of stars shown clearly. Justin looked

in awe at the shimmering lights. The clarity of the stars on the Colorado Plateau made him feel closer to them. He surveyed the breathtaking beauty of the stars and moon. From his heart flowed a silent song of admiration and peace seeped into him.

Then, he looked towards the heavens.

"God, please help me. We need help getting off this speeding train. Please guide me in leading these whiz kids to find the solution... and get off this beastly train." Then, an idea formed in his mind, like a seed germinating, but without words.

He closed his eyes and let a breath out of his mouth. He started to quiet the troublesome thoughts in his head. He recalled a verse, something like, peace I leave with you. ...Do not let your hearts be troubled and ... do not be afraid. A calm assurance flooded his soul. He silently gave thanks to God.

His eyes once more looked at the twinkling lights.

He let his eye linger on the serene lights as he stood in the fresh breeze and brisk air. He enjoyed this soothing calm, that he couldn't tear himself away, but the seed in his mind grew. He knew it was important, yet he couldn't put it into words. In his head the thought took shape, the moonlight is lighting the rails and switches. He turned towards the tracks. His intelligent eyes studied the tracks and distant switch lit by the moonlight.

Justin could easily see tracks and make out where they were. Just then, a sight struck him, like a meteorite bringing calamity. Justin scrambled up the ladder to get a good look. In the moonlight, he saw the tracks in front of them, and beyond.

Without warning, the wind picked up. He noticed the clouds quickly rolled towards him. The smell of ozone, sweet, pungent electrical smell filled the air. His eyes widen with alarm, the quickness of this storm bespoke an unnatural cause. Now, grey clouds blocked the stars.

Flash. Lightning struck the roof of the dining car only four feet above the space his head occupied, not a minute before. A bright white bolt flashed. *Zing Zap!* The lightning diverted to a lightning rod on the back of the roof, down to the wheels and track and dispersed on the ground.

The cowboy standing on the train platform shook his fist at the clouds and screamed, "Missed me!!!"

♠♣♥♦

"Dude, did you see him duck when I dialed up a lightning bolt?," the first Gamer said in a Bostonian nasal voice. Then, he laughed a nasal laugh.

The second Gamer joined in with his own maniacal laugh. "Yeah man. After Justin found that bug I planted and Tej found the hidden camera that you installed, we had to teach them a lesson."

"That lightning bolt lit up ten miles around their car. Then, they plunged into darkness when it caused a power outage. Guess Tej and Kofi won't be playing on their hand-held games either once their power runs out."

"Man, how long will the cold cuts last in their refrigerator now?

"Can't say. But it would be interesting, if they got food poisoning."

"Yeah. They may puke their guts out."

"That would be funny. Too bad we didn't get a camera in the bathroom. Eat, poop and sleep, that's all these guys do," he says with a devious laugh.

"When do you think they'll find the game box with the game rules?"

"You've seen how Justin has been searching the dining, club car. Ha, ha. Maybe never, or after it's too late. Then, the Wolf will get them. He's not so smart. I would have thought that he would have found it by now. Get a brain Justin, we'll see who the best gamer is yet. Ha, ha."

"Dude, he can't hear you."

"I know. I'm just joking. Of course, I'm the best gamer, and that's no joke!"

"Wrong! You can't beat me."

"That remains to be seen, whether my guys come out on top, or your guys."

"Then let's get the game in full swing."

"You're on!"

"Everything is in place."

Justin's epiphany from the night before, was shattered by the reality the morning brought with it. They were still trapped on this hot, miserable train. Red stole his girl and burned him. He had a weeping girl mad at him. A pop from Justin's neck. Just Nitrogen releasing, he thinks. He cracked his knuckles next, stretched his legs hitting the wall of the sleeping, and bumps his head on the low ceiling. It's been four days and nights sleeping on a little vinyl covered passenger seat. He misses his comfortable bed at home. Sky needs riding and brushing. Shocker, but he even misses his teachers. Then his thoughts turn to Vanessa. He stared out the window, visualizing her sapphire eyes smiling at him when he asked her to the prom. *The prom is tomorrow night*, he remembered. The theme printed on the ticket came from a song, "All of Me Loves Only You." Nodding unconsciously, he thought only of Vanessa, how she is always smiling, is always available when he needs a friend, and always looks at him like he's the only person that matters to her. The teen reached in his back pocket and took out his tan leather wallet. He took out his worn, dog-eared two-by-three picture of her. Looking at her smiling face, he let the tears fall. After putting the picture away, he thought of his second love, baseball. Knowing he already missed four days of Baseball, he gave up hope of joining the team for the state and then national playoffs. He missed everything about his life, playing baseball, lunch with Vanessa, and now ... no, he would not miss the prom. He has to get them off of the Beast, now. With new determination, he stood up.

Justin strode to the passenger car. He looked around for anything helpful. One side of the windows and the sconce covered lights lit the inside of the car. He looked at the four walls, ceiling and floor. Then, he entered the sleeper section. Seeing Tej still sleeping, Justin tiptoed to Tej.

"Mornin' partner. Wake up. I need your help." Justin whispered.

Groaning, Tej stumbles from the passenger bench to the dining car.

Over coffee, Justin explained his plan, "First, we need to do a clean sweep of the dining car. We save the bugs in this can that I found in the kitchen." The cowboy slammed the metal container down harder than he intended.

Tej yelped with a start.

"Can you hack into their signal with the tools and wiring you found on board?" Justin asked the teen with Indian features.

"Whispering secrets?!" Red said loudly as he suddenly appeared at their booth.

Startled, Justin and Tej both let out a breathy, "Man."

"Quit that Red." Justin said. He moved his hand towards a chair near the table. "Now, you're welcome to join us in the plan."

Kofi looked at Justin through one side slanted and shook his head.

Red snarled in disgust, "No thanks. I've got my own plans." He unrolls the map and studies it.

Justin turned back to Tej, "We searched every light fixture, okay? I'll hold the metal box for now."

They found a camera in every other cam light and bugs in every other sconce wall light. Tej took the can of micro cameras and bugs to a corner booth. There the Techie kept his tools, wiring and technology that he stripped off the Beast and got to work. The one thing he didn't strip was the two-way radio in the engine compartment. It didn't work anyway. But he found plenty of hidden wires and lithium batteries.

Justin walked into the lounge part of the car. He saw Nick bent over searching for something in a corner cabinet.

"Mornin' Nick."

Nick jumped, like a kid with his hand caught in the act of stealing money out of his mother's purse.

"What y'at?" Nick said. The Cajun quickly closed the cabinet. Nick limped his way back to his seat. Seated, he reached into his sports coat and exposed a flask. Then the Cajun took a swig.

Wiping his mouth with his arm, he let out an, "Ah."

The cowboy said, "Um…"

Nick's face turned back to Justin. The Cajun said with a shrug, "Today's my birthday. I'm eighteen." Nick gloats. Big smile. Dimples and all.

"Happy Birthday, Nick, and many more," Justin said. "But, do you really think you should-"

"Sure. Why, in New Orleans, I'd be legal today."

Justin heard Leo's heavy footsteps, "Happy birthday, Mate." Leo walked up to Nick. "Now hand 'er over. It's my turn."

"No can do, Bro. I'm the only adult here. So, this lil' dawlin' will stay right here," he said, patting the pocket in his sports jacket.

"Now, wait a minute Nick. That's not very friendly of you Mate," said a disappointed Leo. "And furthermore, the legal age at home is eighteen." Leo smiled and puts out his hand again.

"No, you're not eighteen, yet. When I first got dropped, we had a talk. You said you was seventeen with a birthday in September."

"Only three months away."

"No."

"Aw, you know you're not a rule-follower. You're just being selfish."

"Finders keepers," Nick said with finality.

For someone who skirts the rules whenever it's convenient, he showed great restraint not bringing out the hidden flask until now. Well, it was his birthday after all. Justin went back to his work at the middle table.

The day was a scorcher, and no air conditioning. Sweat dripped from Justin's face as he poured over the map searching for an answer. There was one blank area up ahead to the North on this track and all blank to the east. Eventually they would come out, where? Well ... anywhere. The tracks could go on forever. When he was at home in Hidden Valley, he truly was isolated. The train station sat at the mouth of the valley. That's as close as he ever rode on horseback to the tracks. He thought of one time when Vanessa rode with him. She rode her bay, Prancer, her blonde tresses golden in the sunlight. Then, he reached into the back pocket of his jeans and took out his wallet with the photo of her, a big smile and sapphire blue eyes. That day, he laughed as he stood in his stirrups and rode backwards. She always smiled at him. But that time, the smile reached her eyes. He thought, *I'm so blessed a girl like that loves a cowboy like me. She must be worried sick about him.*

Justin renewed his focus on the map, wiping the sweat with a red handkerchief.

"Rain, we need rain. I can't stand this heat," said Nick looking up from his sticky cards.

Meanwhile, Red slammed, his hand on a section of the map, then took off to the opening to the outside. A brisk early morning with the smell of wet dirt greeting him. The sunlight from the sunrise in his eye, arm up, he looked ahead in a crouched position, only one hand holding onto the handhold. The speeding train passes tall slender orangish pink rock formations. Several used to be arches, but due to The War and due to earthquakes and to nature, only one is left intact. The surreal landscape is a blur to Red as he hung outside the moving locomotive.

Justin walked out behind him, curious to see what the redhead would do considering the force field is four feet out surrounding the train. *He can't run again. Not on those torn up feet. He better not, 'cuz then all of Kofi's first aid was for nothing. If he goes a second time, he's a goner, for sure.* Well, *pride goes before a fall* people say.

All of a sudden, Red jumped straight down to the ground.

"No, you fool!" Justin yelled. Justin leaned forward, then bolted back, holding onto the handhold. *Ugh, how many times do I have to look down and see the ground far below. Not only far, but blurring*

with the speed. I never liked anything higher than the back of a horse.
Justin fights down his nausea.

But, he can't leave Red to die alone. Justin looks at Red, who
is running with the train. *Wow, this kid is lightning fast,* he thinks.
Maybe that is one of the competitions he won, sprinting. Red
keeps pace with the speeding locomotive. Incredibly, he accelerates
ahead. Justin's mouth drops open. Then, Red pulls the next switch
and the train momentarily slows as it curves in the new direction.
Quickly, Red leaps back next to the train and keeps running close.
He lost a little of his pace and got behind the opening. But he again
accelerates. *He's a machine!* Justin thinks. Red reaches. Hands grip
the bar while feet keep running along. Struggling to pull with feet
dangling, swinging towards the wheels. He can't pull himself up.

Justin holds on. Then, the cowboy with his right muscular arm
grabs ahold of Red's belt and pulls him up so that he can put his feet
on the step. At the same time, Red gives one last straining pull and
collapses on the breezeway.

"You aren't hurt, are you?"

Red rises slowly without say a word.

"You're welcome."

Red glowers at him. As he slowly walks towards the entrance
to the dining car, he says over his shoulder, "I still hate you, Pyro."

Shaking his head, Justin followers him. Inside, Justin gets right
in Red's face.

"Red? What do you think you're doing?"

Red yelled back at Justin, "I'm doing *something.* Chill! I can't
keep riding around in circles. I have to switch the direction to see
what else there is on The Plateau. You're welcome."

"What problem do you have with communicating? You're my
barrier to solving this riddle of getting off the train, Red. I wonder
what the Capitol would do with a delinquent like you. Maybe we
should hand you over," Justin said.

"I'd like to see you try." Red said. "And real people call it
Intermountain City, not the Capitol." Red walked up close pushing

his chest against Justin's chest. Suddenly, Red collapsed into a booth and put his feet up.

"That was-," Justin stopped talking when he saw wires sticking out of Red's feet.

♠♣♥♦

"Kofi. Wake up par'ner. I need your help."

"I am awake. I'm just resting my eyes. What's happened?"

"It's Red. Can you come look at his feet, please? Thanks."

Justin punched the seat back that Kofi just vacated.

He had been thwarted by every attempt to do what was right. *Why can't things just fall into place?* He thought. It was something else, something he was missing. There's something familiar, almost like Deja Vu on the Beast, but he's never ridden on a real train before. So, what was it? And, what was he going to do about Red's attitude? Justin needed a plan that required everyone working together as a team to accomplish the daunting task of getting everyone off the Beast alive. Even if he came up with a workable plan, Red was stubbornly set on doing it his own way. What did switching to the other track accomplish, anyway?

Suddenly, they were thrust into darkness. They couldn't see a thing. Shouts. Then, echoes.

"Hey mates?!" Leo shouted.

"Over here, partner," he replied.

"What's going on? Is this a tunnel?" He heard the high-pitched voice of Trini say out of the dark.

"Guys, where are you?" Asked Kofi

"Where y'at?" Nick said. "Follow my voice."

Justin thought, that accounts for everyone except Tej. So, he loudly aked, "Where are you Tej?"

"I'm still sitting in the corner. Do you see the light of my handheld now?" Tej said as he held his handheld outward.

"I see yours. Do you see mine?" Kofi said with his handheld out.

"Yes. Is it a tunnel?" Tej asked. His voice quivered.

"It must be a tunnel through the moun'ain to the North. Don't worry. We'll be out of it soon," Justin said. He kept his voice even and reassuring.

Kofi started singing, Baby, Don't ..." and half way through the song, they were out of the tunnel.

Justin was still standing at the table with his one hand on the map. He focused, like a laser of an engraving machine. The map was filling out now.

Time was wasting. Justin needed to figure out a plan. He understood that they wouldn't be in this tunnel if Red hadn't switched the switch. That's what happens when everyone is a Chief. Everyone goes their own way. He realized that to apply his leadership, he needed followers. He'd rather just tell everyone their job and then get it done. On the bright side, now he knew two things, the northernmost side of the tracks and Red can run like nobody's business. At tournaments, Justin had heard rumors about people with bionic legs. Of course, he thought it was all imagination. Until now. He realized that Red could be useful in running beside the train and pulling a switch without hitting the forcefield. Justin filed that valuable piece of information in the back of his mind for his emerging plan.

18

The Rules of the Game

THE NOON DAY light flooded the car that was the favored hang out spot, the car with food. They were busy putting lunch together. Justin found some jerky, a pickle and a couple cherries. As he holds a cherry by the stem, something else cherry red comes to mind. Justin remembered feeling like the luckiest guy, because of all the sixteen-year-olds in Hidden Valley, his parents were the only ones, not only to give their son a car, they gave him the car of his dreams. On that day, he had taken the keys, thanked his parents and started his red mustang. It had been kept in mint condition and purred like a kitten. He had taken Vanessa for a ride, the first of many. That night they had driven to the point. The advantage of living in such a rural place as the high desert, was the night sky. There were a hundreds of thousands of stars filling their vision. Then they had their first kiss under those stars in his 'stang. He cherished that memory. His life had been idyllic.

A light comes to Justin's mind to use each boy's strengths to get off the train. Obviously, Red is good for more than just a Poker game, seeing that boy run like a cheetah. Tej could try to hack into the NFLS' Wi-Fi. Leo knows railroad engineering. Kofi is good with strategy and medicine. *Well, if we come out of this with some cuts, he can stitch us up again*, Justin thought. Tricky Nick. Got nothin'

111

there. He's a good guy, who entertains. He's good with magic tricks. But, he doesn't even acknowledge there's a problem. No, he's the one We are going to have to save.

As Justin started looking around in the storage closet behind the kitchen, thinking maybe there's something else BBQ and Nick hid that might be useful, he hears the boys are arguing over the unexpected ride through the tunnel. At first their voices are normal.

"I lost one of my cards while it was dark," Nick complained.

"Do you know how much time I wasted, Red. Because of you, I couldn't get satellite connection for two minutes!" Tej scolded.

Trini looks up from writing long enough to shake her head. She's been keeping to herself and just writing since she told Justin her epiphany.

"What is your problem, Red?" Nick asked.

"Slow, you're all slow, the lot of you. I didn't ask to be trapped here," said Red. His voice rose as he spoke.

"Who are you calling slow?!" Nick said.

"You might try listening to us," Leo shouted at Red.

"All I hear from you guys is a lot of noise," Red said. He answered with an even louder voice than Leo.

"No worries. I told ya, my parents will come pick us up in their private helicopter or private plane," said Nick.

"Oh, that's just great. More noise, crazies" shouted Red.

"Hey, don't call us crazy. Jumping off the train, twice, is just, insane. You know what Red? I think you're losing it," shouted Leo.

Pushing aside a menagerie of boxes of plates, plastic utensils, brooms, pails, rags, and a pile of rags, Justin searched in the cabinet near the floor in the combination lounge car. His hand feels until he discovers a box. He lifted it up and out of the closet. He placed the board game kind of box on the counter. On the lid he read the title aloud, "The Game: A Challenge of Whiz Kids Against a Speeding Locomotive."

In the rest of the train car, the other boys' voices rose louder. "Would you two give it a rest? Keep it down," Nick said. He spoke in his familiar deep Cajun voice.

Justin thought, *This box has to be the point of why we Riders are trapped here and all this fuss.* At the same time Justin was thinking about the game box, Red marcheed over to Nick's table in a huff. Red's angry red vein appeared on his neck again. In one swipe, Red sent Nick's cards sailing into the air and on to the floor.

Nick's mouth dropped open. His eyes narrowed. "Red!"

"Hey, fellers! Look what I got here," Justin said. He carried the new-found box out of the supply closet and to the nearest table. He popped up the lid.

Seven pairs of eyes peered in the board game box. Nothing.

Justin turned the lid in his hand over. "Just game instructions," Justin said. Then he read aloud, "The Game: A Challenge of Whiz Kids Against a Speeding Train.

1. **OBJECT**

    The object of this game is to get to Paradise Station first, and choose the right stall, then park your train.

2. **EQUIPMENT**

    You have the train that you are riding.

    You have the use of the switches.

    You will discover a clue by the time you enter the Roundhouse.

3. **PREPARATION**

    Each of the players have been on your train from a day to 20 days. So, you know what you have to work with both mechanical and human.

4. **THE PLAY**

    A team consists of at least five team members. The team work together to navigate the train through the switches to the correct track, to get to Paradise Station.

No team member may go more than eight feet from the exterior of the train in any direction. There is a force field that is kept around the train. To leave your team and your train, beyond the force field results in death. Master the switches and get your train into Paradise Station first.

There are three locomotive stalls. Decide on the one correct stall in which to park your locomotive. You have been given the clues to make the correct decision.

5. **WINNING THE GAME**

Winning the game: A train team must have at least five live players who get to Paradise Station first and park their train in the correct stall in the round house at Paradise Station wins the game.

6. **PRIZE**

Upon successful completion of bringing your train into Paradise Station and parking it in the correct stall in the round house at Paradise station, each person will receive one million dollars.

The odor of unwashed bodies and perspiration reached her nose. Trini winkled up her nose and spread her hands wide. "Okay. It's a game and a challenge," she observed.

"Let me see that!" Red said snatching the box out of Justin's hands.

"It says to work as a team Red. What do you say par'ner? You're a fast runner, you can switch the switches. I have strong arms and legs, I can pull you back in."

Red didn't turn to Justin. He re-read the game Instructions.

Justin let out a sigh, then said, "It says, "at least five *live* players… not a good sign." Justin brushed his left hand like slitting his throat. "Hey, I don't see any clues on the box. And there is nothing in the box, just the lid of the box with the rules printed on it. It looks like the Villains had it made for us, but we have to find our own clues and playing pieces. And make our own map." He turned to Tej and asked, "You got anything on the Wi-Fi yet?"

"Still working on it." Tej answered and walked back to his wires and tools. Justin studied the map.

Kofi put a hand on Justin's bent over frame, "Well, there's good news and there's bad news." He looked at Justin.

Justin gave Kofi, giving his full attention and says, "Good first."

"The good news is that we have seven players,' Kofi grinned at himself, "The bad news... I can predict from the instructions that there is another train."

Now, Red straightened up and swallowed hard. Kofi goes on, "It may look like it is saying, get to Paradise Station first as in first step, but it is under winning. Winning against whom? Okay. Also, it says, the train team to get to Paradise Station first. I REPEAT, there's another train." He looked from face to face.

Red threw the box on the table yelling, "It just gets better and better!"

Justin was the first to address the new revelation, "If there is another train, we have to hurry. And I'm wondering," he has one hand in his belt loop and the right hand pointed toward his head, "what if they get to Paradise Station before us?"

"I don't want to find out, so let's win," Leo stated, stepping forward and putting his finger tracing the instructions on the box.

"Sure, we want to win. But we're not going to win unless we're organized, like a team should be. If we pull our strengths together, we can hit a grand slam and win the whole thing. Now let's see," Justin was deep in concentration. Finally, he said with both hands pointing at Leo, "You're the kid that took first in the railroad engineering contest, where do you think Paradise Station is located?"

Leo shook his head. "The map of the rails isn't finished. I need more information. But, they have us blind in here with the windows on one side of the cars painted black. Let's see more track. Paradise

Station is in one of the blank parts of the map. A station, roundhouse and turntable, plus maybe a train yard requires a large tract of flat land, say averaging about 40 acres for this narrow gauge," he said. He brought the map and lay it on the table. "So, if we look at the map, that could only be in two blank spots, here or here."

Justin saw that the first spot was truly unknown, the southern part. But the most eastern blank spot, he had a feeling that it wasn't going to be right for a roundhouse. He didn't know where this feeling came from. But one thing was for certain, they had to get out in daylight and see more to fill in these two areas of the map.

Justin asked, "Leo, would you try to keep by the clear windows and draw anything you find onto the map?"

"Sure mate!" He responded quickly while bolting for a booth near the clear window.

Most of the boys have tasks that keep them busy, but Kofi stared at Justin, "Hey, you know I'm the wizkid, that for the last six years straight, has held the Chess champion title. So-" Justin tilted his head and his eyes appeared even bigger than they usually looked to Justin.

"Sure, I've been thinking. Mm, I've been thinking that you can keep trying to get into the heads of the enemy. What is their next move, partner?"

"You got it!" Kofi also took a seat and looked out a clear window.

With nothing pressing and no new crisis, Justin went back to his bench seat in the passenger car, and laid down in exhaustion. There is no pillow, his neck is at an uncomfortable angle thinks how he can't wait to be home again. There, his tan suit and bolo are hanging in his closet with his new rattlesnake skin boots on the floor. He wouldn't get to see Vanessa in her red prom dress tailored to her curves. Nothing seems fair, all worms and thorns when you're in pain. Negative thoughts threatened to drown you and pull you down. Down farther and farther, heavy but you couldn't rest and the pain hurt like a thousand needles continuously stabbing you.

No, it wasn't just his raw emotions in pain, Justin's side was throbbing. In a short time, it overwhelmed him with pain. He slowly walked to the passenger car and slumped onto his stuffed vinyl bench. His eyes were downcast. Justin looked up to see Trini standing in the middle of the car, a grimace on her face. She had lifted her shirt an inch looking at the left side under her ribs.

Their eyes met. "Again, I got the pain right here." She lets down her shirt and points at Justin's left side, "You're in pain again." The overwhelmed girl drops into the nearest chair. "I keep getting these pains, right here." She points to her left side, this time without lifting her shirt. It started after I heard you and Red arguing at Hidden Valley Station and you both were at the ladder to the roof. That's when he burned you with a hot poker."

Justin narrowed his eyes at the excited girl.

"It's true," Nick volunteered. "Trini and I were sitting in the dining room. Then, all of a sudden, she screamed. When she lifted the left side of her shirt, there was nothing there." Nick kept an even gaze at Justin.

"What are you talking about?" Justin lifted his hands then threw them on to his thighs.

"You were burned, we both felt the pain. You're hurting now, we both are feeling the pain." Trini moved her torso closer to Justin and waited.

The copper-haired boy shook his head.

Trini bit her lip.

Nick raised his cane. "I have an idea. I lightly hurt Justin," Nick used his cane to walk to Justin. "And ..." Nick gently poked Justin's wound.

Both Justin and Trini screamed in pain.

"That's it," Nick said. "I told you." The Cajun nodded at Trini, then sat down again.

Justin looked directly at Trini. "You could have been acting," he said.

An exasperated Trini charged up to Justin and got in his grill. She opened her mouth and started saying, "You—"

Justin's eyes flashed like a watchful cat. He jumped back.

"There, in your brown eyes. You have gold flakes. You're my brother Ty who has gold flakes in his brown eyes. Our father was the same." Trini grabbed Justin's hand and pulled him to the seat. Sitting next to him. "Don't you see, the NFLS kidnapped you from us in Liberty Alley that day." She waited a moment.

"No, that never happened," said Justin.

"You were a preschooler. I was, like two. Dad had just died in a fire and you were this Whizkid. You could play grandfather's Sax. And you could play the shell game. Tekka had us running a gambling game with you maneuvering the metal cups and oh I—"

"Wait, a fire?" Justin asked.

"I almost forgot." From her back pocket, Trini pulled out a wallet-sized photo. "I want you to look at this picture," said the girl.

Justin's mouth dropped wide open. In the picture was a woman in her 40s, with brown hair who looked like Trini. Something stirred in Justin. After one look, he signed one word. "MOTHER."

"Yes, Ty, you sign and our mother … that's our mother … she's Deaf," Trini said. She glowed like spring budding. Her rose shaped lips spread into a smile.

Justin shook his head. "No," he said. "I have a Mom and a Dad in Hidden Valley. I don't remember anything you're talking about." He threw his hand out at his side. "I'm an only child. I … just made a gesture. It doesn't mean anything." He turned and ran his hand over his face. "These are lies. Why would you—"

"Please listen to me," Trini said.

"I've heard enough. I think you are in on this with them. You're a plant on this train to serve their sinister purposes."

"But—"

Creases appeared on Justin's forehead. He stood up. "No, I won't fall for this." He walked past the slumped girl who was like a wilted flower.

19

Sacrifices on the Tracks

FROM THE WINDOW to the map table, Justin went back and forth. The train was taking them over the empty desert. He drew straight track mile after mile. Like a robot he worked without talking to anyone, least of all Trini. The straight desert area of the map was getting longer. This went on for two hours until his wound started hurting and he sat on one of the bench seats. He put his feet up, sighed, and closed his eyes. Trini sat in the booth next to where he rested. She leaned close to him pleading with him to listen. She relayed her memories of him when she was two.

Justin shook his head, but didn't speak. *No one remembers things from when they were two,* he thought.

All at once, he heard the Riders' shouts, then distant excited talking. "Wow, nice ride!" "Whoa!" "No way!" "I can't believe it!" "Hey, Justin, come look at this."

Justin put his feet back down, got up from the sticky bench, and scratched his backside. He hadn't gotten a nap. Trini had been in the booth next to him talking. He only had a brief time to close his eyes and rest his brain, only to have Trini scramble it again. Justin heard the boys' shouts, but nothing they said made any sense. The teen ran his hand through his copper hair. But their shouts keep him moving forward. They were crowded in the space between the passenger car and the dining car, one hand on the metal bar and leaning outward to see around the engine.

"There's a cherry red mustang on the tracks," Leo said. He spoke to Justin who came up next to him. Leo switched places with Justin so he could have a look. Justin's face went white and his eyes had a look of terror.

"Nooooooooooo!" Justin screamed, "Not my 'stang!" A moment later, Nick shouted out, "Not my 'stang!" Justin leaned out farther as the Beast was thirty yards from a convertible1965 Ford Mustang. The other boys and Trini backed into the dining car preparing for the impact and flying debris.

The train neared to just twenty yards distance from the car. Justin ran through the passenger car out the opening and onto the breezeway, and around the coal car into the Engine. He heard a sound and saw Nick. The Cajun made his way behind him using his arms to swing from handhold to handhold. No time to wonder. The train thundered towards his 'stang.

First, Justin tried the throttle, it was disabled as is the reverse gear. The air brakes wouldn't work. The hand brakes were welded, making it impossible to turn. Fussing, pushing, pulling on levers, but he couldn't get anything to work. He panicked. Fists pounding on the controls, he cried, "Stop! You have to Stop!"

Nick said, "I had one too. I thought this one was mine."

"Is it yours and not mine?" said Justin.

"Mine is not a convertible though," Nick said.

Trini, who is right behind them, asks, "What can we do?"

Justin drew his face into a deeper scowl. He would look out these side windows, but the front and left were blackened. So, he looked out of the windows on the right side. Ten yards until impact. Frantic to do something, Justin continued walking along the catwalk, into the cab of the locomotive. Nick and Trini had followed him to the engine. Clickety clack, clickety clack, the train continued at full speed.

Why was he being punished now? Was no human allowed to

be so blissfully happy? And then he thought, *I didn't earn any of it. I didn't deserve to have wonderful parents, a gorgeous girlfriend, the car of my dreams, an amazing horse, to win the nationals. I didn't deserve anything after what I did. Now, each is being taken away from me. My parents and girlfriend in Hidden Valley were taken away when they dropped me on this insane beast of a train. Second, they have taken my dream car away. In a few seconds it will be junk.* Justin sweated profusely. He griped the metal handhold tighter. He racked his brain for a solution. Nothing came to him. He pounded his head into the palm of his other hand. He tried a second time pushing every button and pulling every switch. It was no good. The train wouldn't stop.

He heard the crash and froze. The locomotive hit the Ford Mustang. Then, the sound of metal against metal reached him. The train pushed it along the tracks. Split. Crumple, crumple. It jostled the cowboy off balance falling against the back of the cab where Trini crouched down. Nick held on with both hands to keep standing. The young man had incredible arm strength and grip holding on to the train. Cherry red pieces flew over and past the train. Justin saw a red piece of the car go by the right window. Nick next walked into the engine compartment. He looked at the tinder box. He noticed something, because his eyes rested on the tinder box and then he leaned towards it.

Trini noticed what drew Nick's attention. A gas line ran to the tinderbox and a blue flame flickered above the opening. So, this locomotive was not really powered by steam, but just made to look that way. They noticed electrical wires. The train was gas and electric powered. *An illusion that this is an old steam engine, but it's not,* Trini thought. She saw Nick pulling his legs up to climb the train. "Wait Nick. You can't." Her heart beat quickly, not for herself.

Another red piece of red metal flew by. A tire rolled away. Nick held on to a higher handle and swung himself on top of the coal. A torn car seat missed Nick by inches.

After the last red piece of the car whiz by, Justin hung his head. Tears fell, hot and angry tears.

Out of his mouth burst a loud, "Aww!" He wiped his tears. Something called his attention, a red glow around the tinderbox. He used the tail of his shirt as a hot pad in his palm and pulled the metal handle. A roaring fire was burning in the tinderbox. This was no place for a firebug. From deep within him, a hunger burned. He grabbed the shovel from the corner and shoveled coal into the furnace.

"Why?!" Ty said. There was no one near enough to hear him. He threw in another shovel full feeling his anger growing. A sinister grin came to his face as he looks into the fire.

"You wrecked my car!" Justin said to no one. He swung the shovel toward the coal in the coal car. Nick has pulled himself on top just in time. Justin shoveled up more coal and threw it into the furnace.

Meanwhile, Trini watched Nick on the top crawling back along the roof. Nick looked at something to his left. Trini looked at the same spot where an almost invisible electric line and pantograph that fed the train electricity sat. Trini thought, *If the train has a pantograph and electric wires, it is run by electricity. This "steam" train is an illusion.* She looked up and saw the wires running miles behind and miles ahead of the train. The wires were suspended. *Just suspended like ...like the hover wires around Intermountain and Old Denver. The NFLS are creating the illusion of an old steam train. But Why? I saw this on TV once in Old Denver. People watch the TVs ... because it entertains. So, there must be cameras.* Trini looked back up to Nick to tell him.

Nick continued to stand on the roof, then raised his hands, like a bird ready to take off in flight.

Trini's heart skipped a beat. She thought how Nick had been lulled into thinking this was a short ride and then his parents would pick him up, that kept him confided to his table and his cards. *Was it that he was a cripple? No. Here he was on the roof of the train car, really riding the train. A cripple didn't do that. A man did. Was it that now he knew the truth and now he was free to be more than a prisoner that was so exhilarating?*

The Cajun yelled, "J'pete le feu."

"No," Trini yelled. There were Cajuns in her neighborhood and she knew he was saying that he was full of energy. "No, Nick. Don't do anything foolish." The wind from the train velocity muted her voice.

Meanwhile, in the engine cab Justin threw another shovel full of coal. "You're keeping me from my girlfriend!" Justin shouted.

Trini turned back down towards the cab. The wind whipped her brown hair like a tempest. Back in the cab, she heard Justin screaming. *Who is Justin talking to?* Trini thought. She remained in the back of the locomotive cab.

Justin kept shoveling. But despite how much coal he shoveled in, the fire remained the same. Kofi and Leo reached their friend in the cab as Trini looked on.

"Mate, stop. Calm down," Leo said.

"What do you care?!" Justin said.

"I care about you, believe me, Mate. I'm sorry for before. Just stop this." Leo reaches for the shovel and gets both hands around the handle, that Justin is gripping. Shove, pull, then Justin shoves hard enough that they both move forward pushing Leo up against the open tinderbox.

"Y-ouch!" Leo yelled. His back side got singed and jeans were smoking. When Leo turned, Kofi used his windbreaker to extinguish the flames and Leo's back side to make sure there were no more cinders.

Leo and Justin were tugging back and forth. Justin had been penned up so long on the Beast. He had to do something. They both were anxious to get off this speeding prison. Leo tried to rip the shovel out of Justin's hands by pulling up, and in the process, knocked Justin in the forehead.

"Ugh." Justin let out with a groan. Justin let go of the shovel to touch his forehead. It was wet. When he took his hand away, he saw how seriously he had been wounded. He had a fierce headache.

"Ew, that's gonna leave a mark," Kofi observed, "Let's get you back to the first aid kit, Justin." Justin, followed by Kofi and Leo, walked out of the cab.

Above, Nick had stomped his club feet on the roof.

Trini thought, *Poor Nick. Why haven't his parents flown to get him in all this time? Something is wrong with Nick up there.* Trini watched him intently. Trini had just gotten a look at the electric wire, when she heard the sound, like fingers on a chalkboard, only these were attached to a buzz saw. Her heart began to race.

She continued to watch Nick on the top of the first train car. Nick started running. He ran right into the pantograph. He had to untangle himself. *Scrrreak, Tap, Tap. Scrrreak, Tap, Tap, Tap.* The sound was growing louder and closer. Finally, the Aussie was around the pantograph. He held his arms out to balance.

Trini was off balanced by the motion of the train. She moved her feet. One foot coming down, now the other. She jumped to the cab floor.

Trini saw the shovel on the floor, right where Leo had dropped it. She stared at it. She looked back up at the top of the train. Her shoulders fell.

She wondered, *Why should I care? It's useless. If I wasn't here, Justin wouldn't have gotten hurt.* Her forehead hurt and she reached to put her hand on the spot. When she drew her hand back, no blood. *Justin,* she remembered. *Justin was bleeding,* she thought.

Nick yelled loud enough for Trini to hear him above the clanking of the wheels. "Trini, do you see? Do you know what this means?"

The girl who can sign read his lips. "What, do I know what?" Trini kept her eyes on Nick walking on the top of the first car. "Careful Nick. I'll come help you. Don't move!" Trini was reaching up but stopped suddenly. She read his lips.

"I can do this-" Nick's foot caught on a ridge in the roof. He balanced on the other club foot. Then he toppled over the car and down. As Justin was running out of the cab, the falling Nick got bumped by Justin. The momentum threw Nick towards the edge of the locomotive. The impact knocked Justin prostrate to the breezeway.

Kofi offered his arm to help Justin up off the breezeway.

"Nick!" Justin shouted.

Kofi handed a gauze to his friend and told him to hold it on his head. He tugged at Justin's arm to follow behind him along the catwalk towards the passenger car.

Trini had been shouting, "Nooooo. Nick. Nooooo." Trini turned away from where Nick fell and hit the forcefield. She cried and her nose ran, but she dare not wipe it. Had to keep holding onto the locomotive. Below was where Nick fell and above and to the front, the Screakers had come out to play.

Scrrreak, Tap, Tap. Scrrreak Tap, Tap.

Justin stopped shouting the Cajun's name. Nick was gone. Then, he turned back where Trini still clutched the side of the locomotive, glued in place by terror. He squeezed by Kofi. They both looked up at the Screaker above her.

Scrrreak, Tap, Tap. Scrrreak, Tap, Tap.

"No, it's too late for her," Kofi shouted.

Ignoring his friend, Justin ran to the frightened girl.

When she saw Justin, Trini fell to her knees and vomited over the side of the locomotive.

Turning around, turned back to look in the cab and her gaze fell on the open firebox. Again, she saw it. A gas line ran to the tinderbox and a blue flame flickered above the opening. *So, this is just made to look like steam. I wonder... but there's no time,* the girl thinks. She rose and ran into the cab.

"Trini, come here!" Justin screamed.

When she was in the cab, she checked the water tank. It was empty. She remembered the wires when she looked up at Nick on the roof. *I do not want to think about ... that.* She figured out that the train was gas and electric powered. Trini had turned that over in her mind. *There must be a generator on board? Where could it be?*

Nothing on this train makes sense, Trini thought. I have to show Leo, since he knows trains and railroad design. Then, she muttered to herself, "This train is crazy."

Scrrreak Tap, Tap. Scrrreak Tap,Tap. The first Screaker tapped its way down to the cab. Trini emerged swinging an iron poker. She smashed the poker into the "head" of the monster, sending it down onto the catwalk.

"Give me," Justin said.

He took the poker and batted the first Screaker into the trucks of the locomotive. Turning on his heel, he pushed Trini behind him and faced the second Screaker. The monster reared back on its three legs and lowered its buzz saw. Justin whipped the poker up to meet the creatures buzz saw. They touched and sparks flew. The Screaker paused, as if confused by metal meeting his metal. As if he mistakenly concluded he had hit the locomotive or another Screaker. This pause gave Justin an opening. The switch hitter reversed directions and hit a homer with the monster as the baseball.

Still holding the surrogate bat in one hand, he walked back to the passenger car protectively with Trini in front of him.

Meanwhile in the cab, there were voices. *Crackle, crackle.* "Dude, I know this is a setback. But let's count my victories over the Whizkids. Did you see that car smash like a soda can, then split in half?"

"Cool! Seeing Justin loose it, like, he was fired up by the fire, ha, ha."

"The Pyro didn't let us down."

"But Nick let them down. I guess he's not lucky Nicky after all." Maniacal laughter.

"Glad our cameras weren't discovered in the cab."

"We're geniuses!"

"Let's see what they do next."

Zzzzzzt. And the speaker turned off in the cab.

20

Leo Faces the Screakers

TRINI TURNED BACK to see Leo now on the second car roof, inspecting the panograph. One screaker was coming up from under the train car's chasse, it's huge ratchet arm extending towards Leo's foot. Justin gasped. Just as the creature's arm reached the soft outer side of his foot, Leo had the shovel lifted over his head and brought it down on the creature's front appendages. Leo winced as the sharp appendage poked and then scraped down his foot. He took a step back with the bleeding foot. Another Screaker came from above over the top of the car. He swatted at it, metal connecting with metal. It landed on top of the first monster, momentarily halting it. A third Screaker was approaching from behind him on the other side of the opening. Would he make it in time? A fourth monster came up from the underside of the chasse on to the breezeway. Leo knew they were on all sides. What could he do against these numbers? Against these monsters of mayhem?

A voice in his head told him what he should do and he followed it.

With all his might, he sprang over the Screaker in front of him. As he did, he hit the monster with a backward swipe of the shovel, like a hockey stick to a puck. The went flying off the breezeway and into the forcefield. It bought him enough time to get to the nearest door, that Red was holding open. One more backwards hit popping the nearest one away from the door and Leo got safely in the door. The remaining Scrrreak approached with one more Scrrreak, Tap, Tap, Tap and halted.

Inside the train car, Leo and Red leaned against the door panting, wondering what the Screakers were doing.

They didn't do anything. They just stayed right outside the door, like guard dogs.

"I guess the NFLS has communicated with the Screakers to keep us inside after all our outside activity just now. See the small radio frequency antenna on the top of each?"

"Yeah," Red said and pounded his fist against the door, "vicious kidnappers and their guard dogs, Screakers!"

Leo limps through the passenger car and into the dining car.

The hot sun, directly above the Beast beat down on it. Luckily, they could open the windows on the right side. A breeze blew into the dining car. Kofi was still stitching up Justin's forehead.

"Yes. The headache has gone down," Justin said to Kofi. They both turn their eyes toward the lone table in the corner.

It's a sober, grieving group Leo returns to. Tej looked up at him, and gives him his bench opposite Justin. Leo limps and then collapses with a moan.

He waved a concerned Kofi away, and instead of tending his wound, explains that Nick was standing on the roof because Nick found something important. His eyes fall on Nick's cane, standing where he left it in *his* corner.

Kofi followed his gaze and sniffled.

Leo walked past Kofi. Kofi could see two bright red patches of skin through two holes in Leo's jeans, one on each cheek. Kofi chuckles and said, looking back at Justin's cut, which he was stitching, "But what about your butt? Do you need me to um - ?"

Leo just said, "No, I'm fine."

"And your foot?"

"It's superficial. I know it looks bad, but it's not deep," says a tired Leo.

He reaches over the table to tap Justin lightly on his hand in solidarity over the loss of Nick.

Leo had been on the Beast with Nick longer than anyone else. He was going to miss his easy fun-loving ways.

Loud enough for everyone in the car to hear, Leo said, "I saw the tinderbox. Then, I briefly went up on the engine's roof and saw that there is also an invisible electrical line system running above the Beast. It feeds it electricity through the pantographs on the roof of the locomotive and the passenger car." Justin added, "And the tinderbox in the locomotive is fed by gas."

Red still stood with his back against the door. He lit something and put it in his mouth.

Justin turned toward him and with his snarkiest voice said, "Gas fed flames, duh. I wouldn't smoke near the locomotive Red."

Kofi's eyes shot open. "That explains how the electrical outlets work, but there must be a generator on board."

"Red ...well," Justin's voice was even.

The biker rolled his eyes then threw his cigarette down and stepped on it. He turned and walked off.

"Kofi, exactly my thoughts," Leo said. "Let's look. You take the cars that we can access."

"What about you?" Tej asked. He tilted his head.

"I'm going to break into that Entry Car!" Leo exclaimed.

The rest of them stopped what they were doing and stared dumbfounded at what he suggested.

"But it's locked up tight." Tej remarked.

"I'm going with you." Red insisted.

"I have the hot poker and shovel." Leo said, raising the tools up.

"Let's do it." Red said.

Kofi's stitches were perfectly done. He had plenty of practice since his parents, doctors in Nairobi, had taught him. Kofi and his mom often went out to help poor Kenyan children who were in need of urgent medical care.

Still turned toward Justin on a folding chair he says, "That shouldn't even leave a scar, or a noticeable one, at least."

Tej adds, "And if it does, you'll have the million bucks to pay a plastic surgeon."

Justin forces a chuckle and a tight smile, but his smile soon turns into a look of terror. Red is bringing his cigarette butt down on Kofi's neck. Justin was too late blocking Red's arm. Jumping up, Justin grabbed Red by the shirt and commanded him,

"Don't hurt my friend. Remember Red, you're a sound sleeper!" Justin said, shoving Red back and getting in a fighting stance.

Leo appeared and said, "Come on Red, or I'm going to have all the fun tearing down the door to the Entry Car." Leo holds the shovel and poker up higher.

Justin doubled over from the pain in his right side.

Red spit on the floor and went towards the Entry Car with Leo.

Kofi said in his most authoritarian voice, "Sit, be still and let me treat that wound." Kofi made a disgusted face, and that was coming from someone who had seen a lot of injuries. He moved with deft hands to clean Justin's wound, apply medicine from the ample medical kit he found on board, and re-bandaged the hot burn wound from the hot poker.

"You know what hurts me more than cuts that need stitching up? Mean people who do stupid things to my friends." Justin looked into Kori's face.

Kofi nodded. "I don't let it eat at me. I know that it's the beast."

"What? This train, the Beast?" Justin frowned.

"No, I'm talking about the beast within. Some people, like Red, aren't very good at restraining the wild thing within and they physically hurt others. Guys like you and I control the beast within. We choose to exercise self-control."

"You think *I'm* good at controlling it?"

"Yeah, of course." Kofi nodded his head.

Justin quietly pondered Kofi's words. He felt ashamed of starting leaf fires and of being a firebug. No, Justin wasn't good enough at controlling the beast within. He needed help resisting the temptation to start fires. But right now, he wanted someone or something to show him how to get them off of this speeding train.

Looking out the window, the cowboy recognized the terrain. Reddish-orange rocks lined both sides of the track. They were coming up on Hidden Valley Station. Justin braced himself for what he would see. He looked through the last window of the dining car. His parents were standing on the platform about two feet apart waving. He waved back.

He quickly walked to where he had cut a hole in the vestibule's plastic. He poked his head through, looking back at the station platform. His parents ran right up to different cars where a person of the opposite sex waiting. He almost fell forward into the hole l with his mouth agape. Shocked. His parents kissed the strangers of the opposite sex. The man opened the passenger door for his mother. This was incredible. His parents had an ideal marriage

Both cars took the frontage road then went in the same direction as the train. He could see in the front car in which the woman was driving his dad. They rubbed up against each other and he kissed her cheek and put his hand on her leg. His parents had always given each other their undivided attention. This couldn't be possible. Justin's head was spinning and not from hanging it outside though the vestibule hole. He pondered this unexpected scene. Are his parents both having affairs? It looked like they both knew. *This is crazy!* Justin thought.

Justin ran to the opening on the other side of the dining car. Through the small window, he could see three Screakers. Should he risk it?

He jumped over each Screaker, like it was a grounded baseball. Without delay, he hopped down and ran alongside the train. He could see their cars driving on the frontage road. Then he saw it. There was a curve that he didn't want to take again, when he got to the switch, he used arm strength alone while zooming by. He got the idea from Red. He did it. The train kept to the right this time. Running, panting, sweating in the hot sun, he realized he was stuck. He didn't have himself to pull him up. He leaped with all his leg strength and grabbed the bar. He didn't know where the first step was, since he was looking at the bar. He swung back and forth searching with his legs. Bam. One of his feet landed on the first step, but the other slipped. The Screakers were coming, *Scrrreack, Tap, Tap, Tap.* At this time, the train was going around the bend. The force spins him to collide into the outer passenger car surface. His right shoulder hit hard and ached. The Screakers had to dig into the metal and wait. After dangling in the air, he got his other foot on the step.

"Oh man," Justin cried out. But he just held on. He didn't trust his tired limbs yet and stayed put. So, he looked around and saw Leo leap over a Screaker moved towards him.

"I'm going to grab your belt," the stocky Leo said. As he reached for Justin's belt they heard, Scrrreak, Tap, Tap, Tap, Scrrreak, Tap, Tap, Tap.

"They're COMINGGGGGGGGGG!" Justin shouted.

Quickly, Leo pulled him onto the walkway.

They looked at each other. Tap, Tap, Tap, Scrrreak. Tap, Tap, Tap, Scrrreak.

Hustling, they got up, ran into the dining car, and shut the door. Slam!

Kofi rushed to help Justin. Justin waved him off, but holds his right shoulder, hurting.

"What did you do THAT for?!" Kofi asked.

"For this." Justin said picking up his pencil at the table with the map lying on it. He proceeded to draw the continuation of the track from the junction going straight south instead of east. They already mapped the east junction. Since Justin pulled the switch, he directed the train on a section they hadn't been over yet. In the five minutes that he was outside, he saw the lower turn, straight track and a junction with another station, Fountain Springs Station the sign read. They were on the track headed north again. But there was a track going south. He couldn't see far enough from the ground. By the time he was back up on the step, they were turning towards the north.

"If those Scrrreakers weren't out there, I cud of climbed on top and seen where the southern track goes." Justin fumed. He threw down his pencil. Hands were in fists at his sides.

Red interrupted, "Don't you want to know what Leo and I found?! We found the compressor in a closet behind a locked door in the Entry Car."

Tej excitedly said, "That's just what I need to divert energy when we need it, and to stop the train when we think we are at the correct stall in the roundhouse. Perfect!"

"Wait a minute! We are coming up on the eastern unmapped portion. Keep an eye out, mates!" Leo exclaimed dashing over to the windows first.

21

The Gamers Over the Trains

"HEY DUDE, ARE you seeing this?" Gamer 1 asked. His voice had a nasal quality.

"Whoo, yeah!" Gamer 2 said. "They got into the red rock area approaching the Arch." Gamer 2 laughed. "Justin should know this area, since Hidden Valley is only what? Less than twelve miles away. But he's too scared."

"Hey. Not true. He was brave enough to face the Screakers. Pretty brave," Gamer 1 said.

"You mean the Ratchets. Are you starting to speak like those Beast Riders? Have you forgotten what the NFLS named their creations?" Gamer 2 said.

"I'm saying from Justin's perspective. He views the Ratchets as Screakers. And, he faced them courageously. I'm still rooting for Justin and his Riders," said Gamer 1.

"Aw, I don't have time for you and your Beast riders. All I can think about is Amy. Her sapphire eyes, tan skin and white smile. Last time she spoke to me she patted me on the back with her delicate hand. She's the most beautiful woman her age," said Gamer 2.

Justin just stood up from the dining table where he grabbed a bite and some peace and quiet. The tall teen had just been looking out of the window on the right side of the car. Tej ran on tiptoes from the generator closet. As he entered the dining car, the short teen didn't slow down, like a truck with its brakes locked up. Tej ran right into Justin and held onto to the tall teen's shoulders. The impact hurt Justin's side. It started up throbbing again, but Justin ignored it.

"Hey Tej. Settle down. You're going to pop a vein or something. So, what is it?" Justin held onto Tej's forearms steading him.

Tej could barely catch his breath let alone talk. "Come," he said while gesturing that Justin should come with him.

In the generator closet, Tej held his right index finger up to his lips. Without speaking, they leaned close to Tej's portable AM radio. They heard a two voices, one nerdy and the other love-sick.

♠♣♥♦

"Man, you would think these whiz kids would have found at least the clue in *the box* by now," said Gamer 1.

"You're just sore that my guys found theirs. I'm going to beat you with my train teens," Gamer 2 said. Then, in a softer voice, "I wish Amy would come visit us."

"As soon as this is over, you'll be with her," Gamer 1 replied, "And don't try to pretend you're not in love with her."

"As long as you know that I spoke for her first," Gamer 2 said.

"No worries buddy," Gamer 1 spoke in his nasal voice. "Oh wow. Look, this is getting good!"

"I know, well, we are glued to our controllers now. Glad we ordered in this pepperoni pizza," said Gamer 2.

♠♣♥♦

"No way, it's got to be the Gamers!" Exclaimed Leo

"The Gamers mentioned the clue "*in the box*." That can help us," said Justin.

135

"Disgusting!" Red said. He threw his ham sandwich down. "Those pigs are eating pizza!"

Meanwhile, Kofi had been keeping an eye on the tracks ahead.

A great red rock cliff lay to the east of the tracks. Justin's chin rose as he strained to see the top. The locomotive started up a steep grade along the base. The teens were forced back, their heads hitting the top of their seats.

"Oh no, we're going straight over that cliff ahead!" Kofi shouted.

"I know a switchback, when I see it. We are going to turn sharply," Leo stated, "Hold on."

The narrow-gauge locomotive and train rounded like a snake sharply around back towards its end.

The boys held on to their table edges while tilting to the right. As the train straightens, the force lessened. They relax a little. As they looked down from where they came, they gasp at how high they have come.

One gentler curve and then the tracks were straight. The train was on top of the mesa. As the locomotive picked up speed, they looked out through the right windows at the sandy desert terrain. The pinkish landscape stretched for at least 40 miles. The locomotive passed through tall red sandstone fins. Each teen tried to look up to the top, then turn around to catch a glimpse as they sped away and the sandstone fins grow small in the distance. Up ahead are several ruins of broken tower rocks and pillar rocks.

"What happened?" Tej asked no one in particular.

"My dad said the Great WWIII War destroyed the natural landmarks, all but one arch in the Colorado Plateau." Justin explained.

"Which arch?" Kofi asked.

"Folks now call it Massive Arch," Justin said.

They survey the odd variety of rock formations.

"Wow! There it is! Yippee! We're going through it!!!" Justin hollered.

The Beast chugged over a trestle built to take the train up

through the uneven terrain and level again. Then they saw the arch ahead with its pink tint. The locomotive picked up speed.

Whoosh! The locomotive sped through the center of the arch. They boys cheered.

"Yippee!"

"Cool!"

"Cool!"

"Very cool!"

"I want to do that again!"

They turned to look backwards to make the moment last longer. Then the last car passed through the arch. Again, the locomotive traveled on a trestle going back to the smooth even ground.

Orangish red rocks can be seen. The red comes from a change in the iron in the rock. When it is in contact with the air, it turns the reddish color. They pass double O arch, now a tall U shape from breaking in the middle.

The tracks continue around counter clockwise.

Finally, a long, but broken arch. A somber mood pervades the car as the locomotive sped away from that last broken and tumbled down arch. They are taken on trestles another route to smooth even ground and another switch back and they are off the mesa. The colorful mesa receded from their view.

After forty-five minutes and miles of seeing flat desert, they start to recognize that they have been over this stretch going north. The northern beginning of the Wasatch Range is coming into sight where the tunnel waits for them.

With his railroad design experience, Leo says, "That eastern section straightened out and is taking us north. We just passed the previous switch; which Red switched the last pass we had made. You know what that means?!" He had his hands extended out in a meaningful gesture then walked to the map. Drawing in the unknown region where the map was blank to the east with an arch and tracks going through it.

Grinning widely, he said, "Mates, we now have the eastern part. That leaves only the mysterious south past the junction."

"Yes, south of Foun'ain Springs Station across the Colorado River we'll find Paradise Station and Roundhouse, yahoo!" Justin added.

"Yeah!" The teens shout collectively.

On the back side of the map, Justin drew more of the locomotive. A black steam locomotive with an Art Deco front and all black. And on the number plate, 674. Their locomotive, engine number 674, had a bullet shape with a barely visible smoke stack. He already had everyone's attention.

"This is what I remember from when I was last on the locomotive."

Leo spoke up first, "Justin, do you know what this looks like? Of course, you know."

Justin nodded his head.

"They were made like the 4-6-4 Hudson J-3a steam locomotives, also called 'Dreyfuss' steam locomotives," said the intelligent Trini. "Isn't it ironic?" She looked at the two, model railroading engineering whizkids.

Leo said, "We've been taken for a ride. We're too smart to have missed this. What's wrong with us!" The only thing he could do was facepalm, and he did. It left a light pink outline of his hand on the upper part of his face.

"Right. I put my foot though a wall and so did Red. They're made of plastic." Justin rubbed his chin.

"With metal roof, trucks and wheels," Trini added.

Leo balled up his fists and screwed up his face.

Kofi and Tej looked at each other.

Noticing their confusion, Justin said, "I'm sure you guys have played with toy trains in your countries, right?"

"Sure," they answered.

"Leo and I played with toy trains," said Justin. He ignored Trini. "When I was twelve, I used to have a Bornel streamline J-3a

"Dreyfuss" Hudson engine but standard gauge, 4-6-4 engine 674 toy locomotive with die cast metal trucks. I didn't stay with model railroading long enough for my parents to buy me the higher end Lionel LionChief Plus Hudson steam engine."

"I have a LionChief Plus Hudson locomotive No. 674 at home. It's the best, and more historically accurate and totally fun! This locomotive that we are on; however, is a replica of the Dreyfuss J-3a Justin owns, a Bornel toy locomotive engine No. 674, made of plastic except for the metal trucks. Anyway, the train that we are trapped on is actually a narrow gauge. So, the NFLS took the toy Bornel train and made a life size one, but not as big as regular tracks. They made it narrow gauge, you see how it turned around the curves up the mesa and through the arch?" He looked at their nodding heads, "Well, this is the same design as the Bornel toy train version.

Red loudly said from his corner, "I knew it all the time you losers!"

Ignoring his belligerence, Justin picked up his train of thought, saying, "Playing with a model train is a game. It seems we are in the game here on this speeding locomotive. Just like the game box." Justin scanned the teens. "From our model railroading, we are familiar with building an environment, putting stations down, STATIONS, those exact ones Bornel had, Fountain Springs Station and Paradise Station and roundhouse. So, the locomotive is run by one player, or as you say," Justin said. At the same time, he looked at Leo, "uh,-Gamer. So, remember how we think there maybe another train? Well, one gamer running our electric train, and another running another electric train. The one who gets his "toy" train into the station and Roundhouse first wins, sound familiar?"

"Yeah," Leo agreed.

Tej and Kofi nodded in comprehension.

"Gamers? Trini asked, "Who are these Gamers?"

Justin looked at her, but didn't want to talk to her.

Tej explained, "When we went to the locomotive a few minutes ago, we heard the Gamers mocking us over the two-way radio." Tej put his hand on his belly, "And they were eating pizza."

"Okay," Trini crossed her arms.

"I noticed the exact locomotive as one that I used to have," said Justin. "This dining car and passenger car, just like the train I had. But I didn't expect it on a narrow gauge. I probably didn't recognize it, FROM THE INSIDE OF THE TINY TRAIN!!! THEY ARE CRAZY!" Justin shook his fist in the air.

The other riders just let him get it out of his system, but they stared with furtive glances at the light sconces.

Oh no, Justin thought, *they all could be pumping their fists at The NFLS right now.*

"We tried the Engine, somehow the Gamers run it automatically and remotely. The question is, how does this information help us?" Leo asked.

Kofi, after a long pause, stepped forward, "If I were the Gamers, I would start helping my train to win. So, they control the tracks and switches, but haven't blocked us from running and manually switching them. That's good."

"I can try to break into their frequency. Better, what if I can remotely operate the switches. Then if they work, Red won't have to risk so much."

"Are you saying I'm weak? Or going to fail?" Red stood up and walked over towering over Kofi.

"Just saying that we can have a play and a back-up play." Kofi had stepped back and was keeping his eye on Red's fists.

"Thank you, Kofi, I like that. Red, you are strong and have incredible stamina. But, Kofi thinks about moves and having a back-up move to play. It's a good strategy."

"Whoa, dude. You mean they shrunk us and put us in a toy train?!" Tej exclaimed.

"Really? He's genius, and he says something like that," Red said to Leo.

Fortunately, they were walking to the map table and Tej didn't hear Red, or presented not to hear him.

With patient attention, Justin said, "The NFLS designed these narrow-gauge scale toy cars and locomotive based on the Bornel midrange toy trains. They built toys to be life-size to set up this twisted game of theirs. Understand?" Justin looked at Tej, who nodded his head, "Okay, go work on the electronics of triggering the signals."

Then, a not too high female voice from the map table was saying, "If Red can do his trick again at this switch," Trini pointed at the map, "The train will go east around Old Denver. Paradise Station is that way." The city girl kept her chin high.

Justin shook his head. *I can't count on Red ... or Trini, if that is her real name.*

Next, he looked at Leo and Kofi, "We need the two of you to look at the map and predict any surprises we may need to anticipate. I don't like ugly surprises."

Trini turned abruptly with her brunette hair flying behind her and stormed out of the train car.

Justin neither bothered with Trini nor Red. Justin couldn't trust the liar Trini and he knew Red would be doing his own thing. The cowboy noticed Red. True to his selfish nature, Red was playing a game of Solitaire and eating peanuts and pretzels while guzzling down soda. Justin watched to see the biker drink his second soda. *Good thing there is a small restroom as we enter the passenger car. It has become Red's second home.*

22

Trini Learns of the Pyro

"Pyro, I hate you!" Red said as he walked past Justin in the dining car on his way to pick out some food.

Justin shook his head, "Red-"

"You and I have nothing to talk about," Red said without looking at Justin.

They both know they have to pass Hidden Valley Station one last time before they get to the switch and then to the junction to the end of the line. Each hope Vanessa will be there with a sign of love for himself. Justin decided to choose self-control instead of feeding his bitterness.

Justin has had his share of difficult teammates as captain of the baseball team over the years, like Randy Cole. Rockin' Randy would be at second base dancing to the music on his headphones. Justin was constantly telling him "Heads Up Randy!" "Pay Attention!" and "Hey, are you in the game?!" Randy would respond by bending his knees, putting his glove out and eyes watching the ball only until Justin stopped looking at him. Justin knew he would slip back into his music and dancing around second base. But trying to get Red on his team was a nearly impossible task. Red was the most hateful person Justin had known. True, the Pyro stuff, Justin thought. But that was in the past, or was it?

Red saw Tej staring at him. Red pointed at Tej's Mahjong handheld game and asked, "Is it true you change your underwear right after losing a game?" Red asked smiling.

"I don't change *my* underwear!" Tej said lifting his chin.

Red, Leo and Kofi bust up laughing at Tej's gaff.

Justin stands just out of the door of the car looking out from between the train cars.

Sitting at the booth next to them, Trini watched Justin, but listened to the boys to learn more. Since Justin walked into the next car, the other boys looked at Red waiting eagerly. Finally, Tej asked, "So, tell me, why do you call Justin Pyro?"

"Cuz he is," Red responded curtly.

"Mate, mind if I tell the boys the story?" Leo asked while bending over in his booth. The other boys scooted closer to Leo.

Trini opened her mouth, then decided to be invisible to them. That way, she could hear what they had to say.

"I ain't stopping you," said the red-head.

"Okay. So, Red told me that Vanessa showed him an old article about Justin when he was eight years old." Leo said. His eyes gazed off sideways, like he was trying to remember something.

"Vanessa is such a two-faced two-timing, uh—" Tej cut off his comment as Red looked at him with daggers in his eyes. Tej shrunk into his bench and looked down at the table.

Red "Okay, so, Justin was eight and in the small town of Hidden Valley…."

The boy was bored. It was another dry hot day in the high desert. The town of Hidden Valley looked like something out of an old magazine, one main street, wooden boardwalks on each side, hitching posts, all wooden. He wandered behind the shops on Main

Street. Behind the butcher's shop, used butcher paper stained red with coagulated fat stuck to it lay in a heap. On the other side of the path stood a large cottonwood tree, three feet in diameter. It was said that this tree had lasted through the Civil War and three world wars. Just being near the tree soothed a weary soul. The boy didn't stay too long near the tree. He was just interested in the dry leaves at its base.

Picking up a handful of the leaves and "cotton" from a nearby cottonwood tree, he walked over to the pile of butcher paper. Taking out his magnifying glass, the boy place the first dry leaf and some "cotton" on the butcher paper, then moved the magnifying glass over it. The sun shone through the glass, but it only shown on the leaf. The leaf just have been too wet. The boy searched through his handful of leaves and found a leaf so brittle he had to be careful not to crumple it into pieces. He put the dry brittle leaf on the paper. This time, the leaf started to smoke from a black home at the center of the beam of sunlight concentrated at the spot. When a flame started, the boy was wild with excitement. He fanned the flame with one hand while putting more leaves near the flame with the other hand. The flame turned into a fire. It burned into the butcher paper. He could hear a crackling and pop from the grease on the paper. Whoosh. Blaze of fire shot up. The boy stepped back, dropping his magnifying glass on the dry leaves. He just stared into the fire, like he was mesmerized. After the boy had been staring a minute at the fire, it turned into a blaze. The blaze leaped up. The butcher, Mr. Woodburn, looked through the back door and saw the boy and the fire.

"Hey, boy, come here!" Mr. Woodburn shouted.

The boy came out of his hypnotic state and ran in the other direction. He ran past the tree and out of sight. When the local sheriff caught up with him, the sheriff took him home. The whole town burned down. His parents would have to pay $10 million dollars in damages. No one died in the fire, but Mr. Woodburn had second and third degree burns all over his body. Justin remembered the last sight of Mr. Woodburn. Justin's parents told him that the butcher would never walk again.

"The newspaper article gave the basics of who, when, what, how and why," Leo continued.

"Justin went pyro," Red said. The redhead walked to a far table and set up his cards for a solitaire game.

"That's how Vanessa knew. The article named Justin Wayne as the fire starter. The article said that he had a long history of lighting small backyard fires, they found his magnifying glass at the scene. His parents reported that he started his first fire at the age of five years old with leaves and a magnifying glass. I guess since his parents are loaded, they just paid for everything and life went on as if nothing had ever happened."

Kofi said, "Still, why did Vanessa show Red that article, unless Vanessa *wanted* Red to be mad at Justin? That girl is causing trouble."

Tej added in a quiet but opinionated voice, "That girl IS trouble!"

Leo had the final word, "All girls *are* trouble! You don't see me lovesick, making myself a fool over one." They all nodded their heads in agreement, except Trini. She was thinking about another fire.

23

Justin's Misery

THE SUNSET CAST red fingers into the sky. The bone white disk had been rising a half hour already. The almost full moon shone brighter and brighter as darkness fell. Justin loved the night sky and went out between the cars to look at the moon and stars. Not surprisingly, he could see outside as the train sped along. The tops of the reddish-pink desert hills were illuminated on their east sides. The boys wouldn't focus. Red was selfish and Trini ... well, she was lying. Maybe the NFLS told her to tell him a story about being his sister. Justin turned his face towards the stars. He found the big and little dippers. Now, the cares of the day seemed a distant memory.

The tall teen thrashed in his sleeper bed. He was ten-years-old watching butcher paper catch on fire behind a wooden building. The butcher shop, suddenly was engulfed in tall flames licking the posts and porch like a lollipop. A severely burned man with red marks on his skin walked with his mouth gapping and hands raised like a zombie coming towards the frightened boy. The boy stepped backwards into a deep dark hole. He fell farther and farther until he came out the other side of a tunnel between sooty brick buildings. He was now a preschooler who threw down the matches he had been playing with into the burning pile of trash in the alley next to the apartment building. Suddenly, the building was all aflame. It looked like a huge fireball. He opened his mouth to scream, but no sound proceeded from the chasm. His front side felt hot and burning, but he was frozen in place. Then, a figure all a blaze walked out of the fire towards him. The man was a black shadow with the red glow of fire all around him. He walked nearer to the frightened boy. Finally, the preschool boy felt on fire. Hot flames were all around him.

Justin suddenly woke up, soaking wet in sweat. He thought about the nightmare. *No, it was real. It happened. Both Mr. Woodburn and the man at the apartments were real.* Ever since the fire in Hidden Valley City and what Justin's parents told him about the poor man's fate, he felt guilt stricken and had the nightmares. The ten-year old boy turned into a pleaser. He did everything his parents asked him to do; whether it was to wear a certain clothing to competing in certain events. He helped his neighbors with recovering lost animals and repairing fences. All of Hidden Valley knew that he wanted to redeem himself.

His parents always seemed to have plenty of money. The Waynes had the most prosperous ranch around. When they said they would pay to rebuild the town, people believed them. But the boy was less concerned about the monetary side. The butcher's injuries bothered the boy. At night, he would wake up from a reoccurring nightmare always with the same theme, the butcher burning in the fire. In his nightmare, the butcher's apron first catches on fire and he drops the water bucket trying to untie the apron. Flames spread to his other clothing. He morphs into a giant cow with Mr. Woodburn's face, roasting in a huge fire. He runs to the shop next to him screaming fire, fire, fanning the flames as he runs. The flames burn his clothes, his flesh, his hair. Screams that sound nothing like a human terrorize the boy's nightmare. Then, the boy wakes with a scream. Sweating and panting, he lays back down, but can't sleep. He stares up at his dome glass over light bulb on the ceiling. Reoccurring nightmares like this haunted Justin.

24

Justin's Horse in Jeopardy

A BLAZE OF white followed the yellow light just over the horizon. The tracks reflecting the bright sunlight shown like gold bars. Right at the cutoff behind the switch was a large creature. Its shiny coat shown in contrast with the shadows. The train sped east along the tracks. Looking into the sunrise, Justin strained to see. The animal moved its head. The sunlight reflected off its white mane. *What! Is that a horse?! What would a h- oh no, Sky!* Justin thought.

He scrambled down and bumped into Red, who had also seen the poor creature stuck on the tracks. The horse seemed to have a device on its hoof. The frantic animal tugged whining, nostrils flared.

Before Justin could jump, Red was already down and running. The moonlight brightly illuminated Red's moving figure. Sky was directly ahead. It's whining could be heard. It is a heart-wrenching sound touched him. Tears were in Justin's eyes as he watched his doomed Palomino. The train was quickly closing the distance to Sky.

Red strained hard at running. How could he switch the lever if he was just even with the train? Then, with what seemed like superhuman ability, Red sprinted and leaped on the switch lever, just in time for the Beast to divert to the short cut. As the train overtook Red, he again was running hard. It was impossible for any human to run that fast. Justin reached with both hands as, Leo held Justin by the belt, and Kofi and Tej each had one hand on Leo's belt and one on the bar. Justin lifted Red under his armpits, until Red could grab the bar. Then finally, Red lifted himself up with his legs against the step, as they pulled him in. They all fell like dominos back onto the breezeway as the train turned east. A minute later the train turned northeast. Finally, they stood up.

"The Scrrreak don't come out in moonlight," Justin observed.

"Yea," Tej repeated, "not in moonlight."

Justin looked at Red and said, "Thank you for saving my horse."

Red shrugged, "I didn't do it for you. I just don't like to see a good horse wasted. It's just that I can't stand the Villains." Red kicked at the wall, which busted with plastic pieces falling to the floor.

Justin looked into Red's face nodding, "Let's beat the Villains. Let's beat them together."

Red nodded and walked into the dining car.

Justin explained, "The plan is set. There is one more shortcut coming up. Until Tej breaks into the electric switches, Red will switch them manually."

Kofi had a look of concern on his face, "But,-"

Red spoke loudly, "That last switch was a close one. After the next two for the second short cut, I hope Tej did the electrical switching." He looked at Tej sternly.

Kofi spoke, in his usual mild voice, "I have -"

Tej exclaimed, "I got it! Let me test it on the next switch."

Kofi, with less confidence, "Well, -"

Red said, "I'll be ready to switch it. I'll wait until the last moment, if you don't succeed, I will switch it." This time no arrogance, just facts.

Tej nodded. Kofi is back at the map engrossed in his own thoughts with his finger on Hidden Valley station.

Red had to manually switch the shortcut switches. Tej dropped his chin, since he was back to the drawing board. Since it was still dark with moonlight, he moved outside to the pantograph electrical connector for the passenger car. He had room in the passenger car and had a table set up in the middle of the car. He came back down from the room, stood on a small table and opened the ceiling up. Kofi handed him a meter.

Remembering there was a camera or two that they had left in the passenger car, Kofi started acting, "So, I know the plan is for all of us to sleep, when we pass Hidden Valley Station." Tej looked down at him. Kofi winked.

"What-" Tej said still confused.

"Boy, I'm tired. I can't wait until we finish this night light you're rigging, so we can all sleep soundly," said Kofi.

When Tej looked at him, Kofi winked and nodded.

"Oh yes. I am so tired. I am almost done with this night light. I will sleep very soon." Tej tried to say his line with sincerity.

Terrible acting, Justin thought.

They estimated the time until the junction at the south and set a timer.

When the other boys come into the passenger car, Kofi whispered, "We have a timer set, so we can sleep until right before the junction." Kofi lay down, exhausted. Sleep sounded really good to all of them and they all hit the sack in their sleeper beds. Justin may have been closing his eyes, but his mind was racing. Thoughts of what they needed to do filled Justin's night. Hoping they can get to the junction and Paradise Station before daylight, Justin worried about missing the switch. *Then, even if we make it south, what if we can't stop the train? What if it's farther than I thought to the station and the sun rises and the Scrrreak come out? While we try to switch it and stop the train he Scrrreak could maim us or worse. Too much could go wrong.*

Suddenly, out of the silence in the passenger car, "Zzz," Kofi snored. "Zzzz." Justin couldn't lay down with his mind choked with worry. He looked at his friend Kofi and whispered, "Sleep while you can, friend."

Justin marched to the map. He wondered how far it was from the junction to the station. After more than a half hour of worrying, Justin looked up with a line between his brows. Leo was standing in front of him.

"I've been concerned too," Leo said, "If I were to build a station and roundhouse, it would be on flat land." He points to where the Colorado river is on the map. "The river would have carved through rock and the canyon have steep sides. So, it has to be a little more south."

"But how far south? 5 miles? 40 miles? 50 miles?"

"That I can't tell. We just need to be prepared that it might be farther than we'd like. It might be daylight by then. You know what that means!"

Justin put his hand to his side where he fell. It was a little sore. He didn't think about it until now. It was nothing compared to what that buzz saw could do."

The more they studied the distances, the more worried they became.

Something peaked Justin's curiosity. He went to the window, then went to the opening to the outside. He tried to see ahead, but the train blocked his view of the track ahead. He was hoping to see Hidden Valley Station.

After waiting a long while outside, he heard someone come up behind him just as he recognized the terrain for Hidden Valley Station on the right. The first thing he saw on the platform was Vanessa, dressed in her prom dress. He puts up his hand making the I-L-Y sign. She blew him a kiss and waved. On the south side of the platform, he saw his mother, and Vanessa faded from view, just as he heard a voice behind him say, "Girl, you look great!"

Justin was too focused on his mother. Her face was contorted in anguish.

Mrs. Wayne waved at him.

Bang, bang! Suddenly, she crumpled to the platform holding her hands over her abdomen.

"Nooooo!" Justin shouted. He saw his father standing next to his car with a pistol still aimed at his mother. Mr. Wayne put the pistol back in his jacket, got in the car and backed it up.

Justin looked as long as he could, even after his father's car was out of sign. He no longer saw the Station or Vanessa. Justin put his hands over his face and cries. After a minute, the shocked son sensed something, hairs rising on the back of his neck. Someone or something was right behind him. He turns and the yellow sunlight was on Red's face. He had a dreamy expression of someone in love. Justin remembered how Vanessa had blown a kiss. *Could it have been meant for Red who was standing behind him? What was that he had heard? Red saying, "Girl, you look fine!"*

Wild with emotions spinning inside him, Justin grabbed Red by the shirt with both hands and slammed him against the wall of the outside of the car.

"Clyde, you no good rascal, stealing my girl!" Justin gritted his teeth.

Mock laughter shown in the Biker's eyes. "She love me!" Red socked Justin in his hurt side. Justin doubled over grabbing his side. Leo ran up in between them, forcing them apart.

"Stop this! We have to focus on the plan, mates!" Leo looked from one to the other.

Red and Justin panted and circled around Leo like two mountain lions waiting to pounce.

Leo continued to separate them with his arms out wide.

Kofi ran up to them, "I knew this would happen, "yawning, and explained more, "I predicted the the Villains would do something with Vanessa at the Hidden Valley station to set you two against each other. Don't give in to their prank. They are playing you two by using Vanessa. Don't you see?!" Kofi looked desperate to make himself heard while standing between them, but behind the taller Leo.

Leo still had a hand up blocking each. Justin seemed to

understand and closed his eyes. He took a deep breath and exhales out of his mouth, as if he is exhaling his anger.

The cowboy nods briefly. "Okay," Justin said, "let's get off of the Beast. Back to the plan." He started walking to the car with the map.

Red combed his fingers through his long red hair in front and swooped it to the side. As the walk behind Justin, the biker turns his face to Leo and said, "What are you lookin' at?" I know my part. I'm staying right here!"

Leo nodded then caught up with Justin and went into the car where the map was waiting.

Trini stood nearest them, turning to face them.

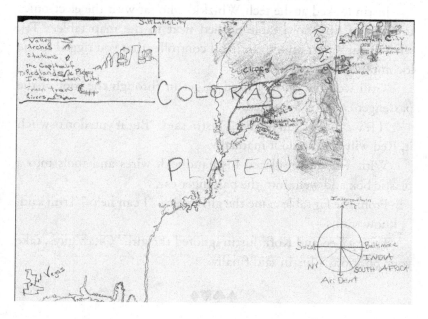

"I heard all that," the girl said. "I've studied the map and the game box instructions. I think—"

"No, Justin said. "I don't trust you." He glared at her.

"That's not fair. I—"

"What's this?" Leo asked.

"She lied to me," Justin said. His eyes scanned the map.

"I did not," Trini said. Her forehead wrinkled, she spread out her arms.

"Stop picking on her, Justin," Nick said. His eyes narrowed at Justin.

Justin gestured with his hand outstretched towards the eastern side of the map. "We're almost to the junction," Justin said. The cowboy still looked at the map, ignoring Trini's stare.

Trini let out a great sigh and stomped over to sit with Nick.

Although the smiling Nick brought out his cards saying something to her, Trini kept her attention on what Justin and the others were saying around the map.

Justin looked at the tech Whizkid who sat with the electronics in front of him on a table pushed next to the map table. "Tej, what's your report on the electrical controller that you rigged to the locomotive electrical lines?"

"Still working on it. I need to get in through the roof of the passenger car," Tej answered.

"I leave that to you par'ner," Justin said, "But if you don't switch it, Red will have to do it manually.

With a nod, Tej placed his handheld, wires and tools into a plastic box and went into the passenger car.

From the far table came the girl's voice. "I can help," Trini said. "I know trains—"

Facing Leo and Kofi, Justin ignored the girl. "Okay, guys, take your positions," Justin said finally.

The sky turned pale with an orangish-pink hue in the east over the distant mountains. As the junction came into sight, Red jumped down and ran alongside the train. He knew to be careful and less than eight feet from the forcefield. From inside the passenger car Justin turned from the right window where he watched Red. Justin and Tej were at the table in the center of the train car. Tej, touched the screen of his handheld. His program should work. Justin went between checking on Tej's progress and watching Red.

Outside the sky turned azure with more orange streaks. On the ground, the athletic Red panted. The switch hadn't moved. The runner squatted and pounced on the lever, throwing his weight on it. The lever went down under his muscle and weight. The switch turned just in time and the locomotive curved south. The train sped on. Red was running along the second to last train car now. He had to run faster to make up for his switching.

On the outside platform, the turning movement had Justin off balance to the left. He gripped the train rail, then hand over hand made his way back to the right side of the train. He kept his eye on Red and one arm extended at the ready.

Red evened out his running with the stairs near where Justin bent over. The tall boy reached down and hefted Red up onto the first step. With the speed of a tiger, Red grabbed the rail up high and leapt to the top. Their eyes met.

Justin nodded in admiration. *Finally, we're working as a team.*

Inside the passenger car, they found Kofi and Tej watching the Techie's handheld screen. Leo stood with his head over the middle table, glancing at the map and then up. He looked out the clear window. Leo drew the train bridge they crossed over the Colorado river onto the map. Leo steadily moved the pencil forward, drawing the track, mile after mile.

"It's too many miles. Look, dawn is here." Leo shouted to the boys and Trini.

Then, the Beast lurched on the new track,

The Beast straightened and it gave the riders a clear view ahead at the curving track belting around the old city.

"This is Old Denver," Trini pressed her face to the glass of the window.

Slowing, the train curved and then setting on a straight track east at the southern end of the train beltway.

"Look at that switch," Trini said. She pointed forward on the right. The teen girl spotted it first and held her head up higher.

Justin now saw the switch. His mouth was agape as he stared at the girl. *Whoever she is, she has an eagle eye, that's for sure.*

The train kept speeding. About two miles ahead they could see the junction. The switch ahead looked like a "T." The train slowed.

Jumping on her toes, Trini said, "There it is, the Station, at last!" She pointed at the end of the "T" where the tracks went behind trees and then extended to a building.

From the main line, they saw a single-story passenger station looked like it had a fresh coat of pastel green paint in the distance. Slightly behind the station was a large brick roundhouse.

"I see it!" Justin exclaimed with a finger pointing ahead while leaning out the opening between the cars. The white wood trim didn't have a spot or stain on it either. As they neared the junction into Paradise Station, the hidden end of the line they all went onto the platform between the cars. Justin held on above to the roof. Trini's small hand grasped the hand rail. Justin looked at her, eyes wide, smiling in admiration.

"And there's the other train!" Red shouted.

A mile south of the junction sped a thundering locomotive headed straight for them.

25

The Wolf Approaches

JUSTIN RAN INTO the car where Tej was working on intercepting Wi-Fi. He took the wiring and intercom from the engine and set it up in this car.

"Tej, tell me you broke into their Wi-Fi." Justin pleaded.

Tej dipped his head close to the speaker on his table. "Listen. . ."

Over the two-way radio the teens hear two voices in conversation.

"Dude, check out my team on the Beast. They don't get better than this. Did I, or did I not pick the smartest team!"

"Peons. Man, I'm telling you, my guys on the Wolf got this. Gary and Dylan know what they're doing. They are going to trounce on your team. Game over!" He laughed.

"You think you're witty. Humph."

"Here they come! End of the Line for the peons," He laughed a maniacal laugh.

Still near the radio, Justin drew his mouth to a line. He thought he knew those voices. Then he said, "The Wolf, that's the other train with the other team of boys on it. They said Gary and Dylan."

Leo looked up, "What?!" He walked to the space between cars to get a better look.

Justin and Leo were thinking the same thing, *Could it be our model railroading friends on the Wolf?* They looked at each other. The cowboy saw the concern in his friend's eyes.

"Oh man!" Koji said. "We're going to collide!"

"Tej! Get that electrical device of yours working and switch our switch, hurry.

Tej focused on the Pantograph connection wires. He untwisted another wire when he heard, *Tap, Tap, Tap, Scrrreak.*

Red bounded out off the train and barely touched the ground. Running and panting, Red was a yard ahead of the Beast.

Justin steadied himself on the outside platform. *Apparently, Kofi and Tej did a good job putting the wires of Red's bionic feet back in the right places,* Justin thought.

Half a mile coming straight at them, they see the other train. The first part of the Wolf that they saw was its large circular front and Art Deco circular light in the center. The aerodynamic streamline shape of the sleek silver and black locomotive with red trim comes into view eliciting gasps from the boys on the Beast. It's too far to see the boys on the train, but no one would be in the locomotive driving it anyway.

So, the NFLS were letting the two trains speed towards each other. Now what? Justin thought.

26

Paradise Station

THE WOLF AT full speed crashed into the dining car of the Beast smashing the entire car. From inside of the passenger car, Justin looked with a terrified expression at the splintering car behind and at Leo just this side of the door who made it out of the dining car and into the passenger car, slamming the door behind him in the nick of time. He bent over, hands on knees panting.

Looking up at Justin, he said, "Never liked the food anyway."

Justin smiled and looked for Tej.

Above on the train car, Tej concentrated on his electronics, pliers in hand. An opening in the roof below him had wires and gadgets coming out, laying on the roof. An exposed mother board connected to wires lay in front of his right knee. He looked at it as he attached the wires to the connectors.

All of a sudden, he and Justin hear a tapping sound coming from the front of the car Tej is on. Justin hung on to a built-in ladder at the back of the car. A black metal monster tapped and screaked up to the Tech Whizkid. *Tap, Tap, Scrrreak,* a second Screaker was on the roof. The first black metal monster to reach Tej lifted one of its spiky legs.

"Tej, watch out!" Justin screamed.

Tej continued working, not hearing Justin over the noise of the wind over the roof. He secured the last wire, automatically switching the coupler with a broad smile pins his leg with one of its knife like "legs." A second later, the Screaker stabbed the boy's big toe. Tej screamed and dropped his pliers.

Buzz. The buzz saw of the first Screaker flashed down on the same toe and sawed it. He looked at the red wound. Tej held his foot, screaming.

Justin was screaming Tej's name when Screakers came over the next train car to Justin's rear.

The second Screaker reached Tej and stabbed a pointy leg into his other foot. Tej rocked back and forth, screaming. His eyes were wide with terror. It seems the more he screamed, the more Screakers surrounded Tej.

A dozen or so black metal Screakers engulfed Tej like a swarm of tarantulas, blocking Justin's view of his friend. Something red trickled back over roof of the passenger car.

Justin sadly shook his head. He looked down at Leo on the platform. The leader slowly shook his head. Justin then descended to the catwalk. He hurried to the next opening near the Engine with Leo behind him.

While he scurried along the catwalk, Justin saw that Red, after switching the junction switch, ran ahead on the track and to the end at the turntable and roundhouse. Red waited at the turn table switch. Tej had done it. He managed to turn off the forcefield after all. It was too high a price. Justin's chest tightened as did his throat. He let out one last, "Teeeej!"

Leo was now right behind him followed by Kofi and Trini. The girl had picked up two brooms, one she kept the Screakers off with. Leo had the other broom, defending them from Screakers coming from the roof. "When the Wolf hit the back end of the Beast, the compressor stopped, all power stopped. But it was Tej who unhooked the coupler and electrical connection to the engine that stopped the train."

A deep grief passed over their faces at the mention of Tej, but they couldn't afford to lose themselves in grief.

"Right," Leo said. He batted at a dangerously close Screaker. It slid. With one more whack, Leo sent the Screaker soaring away.

The remaining riders set their gaze on the roundhouse, which they neared.

As Justin leaned over the catwalk on the locomotive, he spotted Red at the turntable switch.

Detached from the overhead wires, the train ran out of power. The Beast stopped on the turntable.

Standing slightly behind and next to Justin, Leo said, "We don't know which train stall to go in." He pointed at the round house then turned to poke back a Screaker.

Justin screamed down to Red, "Ready?"

Red nodded and grabbed the switch. "Well?" he asked. His eyes were wide as he leaned forward. Waiting at the turntable controls, Red spit, "Come on. Which bay?"

Trini poked with the broom at a Screaker behind her while speaking.

"There's only three opening, but one chance according to the game rules," Trini said. A round saw slices the end of her broom. The Screaker had brought down its buzz saw. Now it was raising it to slice another piece of the broom. "Hurry!"

Justin sprinted into the cab and emerged with the poker. He batted the nearest Screaker off the locomotive with one swing.

The three of them studied the three stalls in front of them. Justin scratched his head and asked Red, "Three Card Poker?"

"Not a chance. There are no choices of cards," Red said.

"Right. So, we have to think of things that have threes. I know Kofi plays Mahjong with three dragons, red, green and white. But that is no clue to which stall." Justin rubbed his chin.

"No way that it has anything to do with chess." Kofi volunteered.

"Hurry!" Leo shouted. One Screaker sliced down with its buzz saw again and again at Leo's broom. With only the bristles left, he threw it at the monster.

Looking back toward the passenger car, Justin tried to remember all the games and the game box. There had to be a clue or a connection. It wasn't a shell game, there was nothing in those three stalls. He leaned on the engine for support while poking the steel rod at the Screakers. His eyes rest on the engine number.

"Whoa!" Justin exclaimed, turning to look at the stalls, "It's the middle one." He pointed as sure as a hunting dog with the location of the downed duck.

In a blink of an eye, Red had the Beast pointed in the direction of stall 2.

"Man!" Red exclaimed.

Justin realizes it at the same time. As Justin looked around for a solution, he said, "What will push this disabled train into the stall?"

"The diesel," Trini pointed with her button nose towards the diesel engine, hitting the arm of the Screaker on the catwalk with her.

"Trini," Justin said.

She looked up just in time to see the poker being tossed up to her. She swung it around as the Screaker's buzz saw came down. Sparks flew as it made contact with the steel poker.

Chee, wu, wu, wu. Someone had started the diesel engine. Its noxious exhaust smell assaulted their noses. Then they saw Leo leaning out of the diesel engine coming out of the yard behind them.

"Whoot hoo!" Justin, Kofi and even Red shout as they saw Leo slowly coming up behind them.

Leo's diesel engine easily pushed the Beast. Then, Red, Justin jumped up with Trini. Leo runs along still on the ground.

"The rules of the game," Trini exclaimed. "We all must be riding."

Justin positioned himself at the railing. Leo jumps, with Justin and Red catching him beneath his arm pits and hauled him up.

Red scrunched up his nose. "Man, you need a bath." Red wiped his hands against his jeans.

Justin laughed.

While the Locomotive passed into the opening of stall two, they gathered in the passenger car, bracing themselves.

Leo asked, "Why the center stall mate?" He looked at Justin with a look of amazement and curiosity.

"Sudoku." Justin stated. He squared his shoulders and raised his chin, looking like the cat that just swallowed the mouse.

The other boys look at each other not seeing the connection.

"Justin played Sudoku all the time," Trini said.

Smiling at the girl, Justin said, "Yes, all the Sudoku puzzles in the passenger car that I worked on, the center three numbers were always 674."

"The engine number of the Beast." Trini said excitedly.

"I know the engine number is 674," Leo said. He looked sideways at Trini.

Justin continued. "Well, it was staring me in the face. That's how I knew the engine goes in the center space. So, I told Red to point us in the direction of-"

"Stall 2, the middle stall." Red said. The biker finishing Justin's train of thought. Then added, "I knew it."

Kofi shook his head.

Trini rolled her eyes.

Justin shouted, "Heads up."

Inside Stall 2, The Locomotive crashed through the bricks in the back wall. The Beast was finally stopped.

Only the sound of crumpled bricks falling could be heard. The silent teens watched the wall, mouths open. Then, they looked at each other. Justin counted the losses, nine days, (for Leo, the first on the Beast 21 days), losing BBQ to the Scrrreak, Nick's death falling and ricocheting into the forcefield, the discovery that it was not a steam engine, the game box, the loss of Justin's mother, and probably Tej, the loss of Justin's Ford mustang, and almost losing a horse. It seemed like half a life time that they'd been trapped, no, not just trapped, tortured and some killed. Now, Justin felt paralyzed, unable to take the next step.

Finally, Red said, "I'm free of this thing!" He ran and leapt off the train. Justin thought, *He's going to get to Vanessa before I do.* Justin jumped to the ground and ran after Red. The others followed, each jumping off and passing more than eight feet from the train. Nothing happened. No spark or jolt. It could have been disabled by any number of things. Red and Justin resumed running with the others trying to catch up. They ran right into the red ribbon across the back entrance to the station where a pale thin man with an official looking hat and railroad uniform stood with a clipboard and a copy of the game lid with rules. Bursting through the tape together, they stop in front of the pale thin man.

"Hold on there." The pale thin man said.

"Who is this bloke?" Leo asked incredulously.

"I am the Train Master, or you could say, the Game Master. I officiate the rules of the game." He held himself stiff and tapped his finger on the game box lid.

The boys looked to each other with confused looks. Justin wondered what now. They got off the speeding locomotive and the riders stood at the finish line. Red contracted his fists into balls, letting out puffs of air through his mouth. Leo and Kofi, narrowed their eyes, each deep in thought, wheels turning.

"The rules state, and I quote from the game box, "Winning the game: A train team must have at least five live players who get to Paradise Station first and park their train in the correct stall in the round house at Paradise Station wins the game."

Leo says what both he and Kofi have realized, "Tej is not with us. Now there are only four of us."

"This is jacked up! Tej gave his life to make it possible for the Beast to get to Paradise Station first." Justin said angered at this pencil neck man and his rules.

Grumbling, the boys stepped towards the Game Master. Six-armed National Film Location Service (NFLS) rangers approach the corner of the station and surround the boys their hand guns pointed at them.

Holding up a hand, the Game Master said calmly, "However, Tej had a heartbeat when the Beast rolled into its stall in the Roundhouse. What I was getting around to, is that you have won. Congratulations!"

Justin thought how surreal this whole game was and still is. It was one nightmare after another, with them surrounded by six guns and now knowing the worst horror. Their friend didn't just die quickly. It was too much. Justin surveyed the surroundings, looking for an attack plan, but stopped. Two handguns poked into his sides. He wiped the tears for Tej from his eyes, ignored the pain of his sore side and crossed his arms and looked stared with daggers into the Game Master.

"I only wrote the rules, I assure you. I was doing what the producer wanted. And your friend is receiving medical care at this moment." The Game Master said.

Just then, a medic approached Justin, setting him down on a bench. He gave him a shot and a medicated salve on his wound. "That will start your real healing, until you get to the doctor at Headquarters this afternoon." With that he left and the Game Master waved to an approaching female medic. Two medics were behind this female one. Between them they helped a boy with black hair.

"Tej!" Exclaimed Justin and Kofi.

The Game Master looked at Justin. The man said, "Come, come and meet the rest of the team, the producer, the director, the gamers and the actors." He gestured for them to walk around the station to the front side.

Pokes from the NFLS rangers' guns, further hurting his wounds, got him walking. Then, they all walked around on the wooden boards under the porch to the front.

A red 1965 Ford convertible mustang drove up to the front of

Paradise Station. Justin's jaw dropped open. Could it be? Impossible. From the train, he saw it smashed by the Beast.

He looked to the driver. What he saw paralyzed him with shock. He could hardly breath. There she was, getting out of the back door in a black short dress. *Vanessa*, he mouthed the name with his lips. She looked dolled up to go to somewhere fancy. They all did. His pa and his... it couldn't be! But she's stiff with a fake smile plastered on her face, like a doll that is just for show. Justin is confused. Why isn't she hurrying over?

Justin's ma, Mrs. Wayne, stepped out of the passenger side of the mustang wearing a long black sequin dress and waving to the audience.

Justin scanned the crowd of people, all slicked up. He wondered who all these people were. There was a crowd of people in black and white. *These people looked as out of place here as penguins in the desert*, he thought. The other boys recognized their parents in black formal attire getting out of limousines. Formal was not a word that went with the Colorado Plateau. The boys were dirty, still dressed in the clothes they wore the first day they "entered" the Beast.

Seeing his ma, alive, signaled a red flag in Justin that kept him from running to Vanessa and his parents. He shouted her name,

"Vanessa! Over here. I'm *over* here!" Justin shouted. She didn't look his way. Suddenly, Red shoved him back,

"Hey, doll face! . . . Vanessa! . . . Vanessa!" Red shouted as he tried to run towards her but was stopped by armed NFLS rangers. She didn't look at Red either. Eventually Red stopped struggling with the ranger.

With two rangers blocking Justin and Red, Justin spoke to Vanessa, saying, "So is it true, you're an actress?"

Vanessa, with no 1950s Utah country accent, but in a self-confident un-affected voice she said, "I'm an actress. My name is Candy Cook." She kept her same fake smile the whole time.

Justin shook his head. He knew that was a stage name. But after the way she played him and Red, it suited her. She cooked their bacon alright.

Red again shoved his way in front of Justin, asking, "Candy, you meant it that you-"

"You deserve each other!" Justin said interrupting. Then walked off. He felt sorry for Red, since Red said he did more than kiss her. Justin thought how Red deserved to suffer, although he knew he should forgive the biker. As for Justin, he was raised with old fashioned values. Enduring values. Justin was actually glad of his abstinence. He could walk away from "Vanessa," still holding his head high. She didn't make a complete love-sick fool out of him, as she did Red.

Then, Justin spotted *the butcher*, Mr. Woodburn, standing a little ways from his parents. Justin's first response was to go up to the butcher and apologize; however, there were no scars from burns. Mr. Woodburn's skin was as smooth as his. What is going on? This has to be a dream. No, it's another nightmare!

Everywhere Justin looked, he could see cameras and camera men. Is this, because they won the game? Are they going to be on television receiving their million dollars? His mind was spinning. Everything happened so fast. They got to the end of the line ALIVE. That was what ultimately mattered. Then his thought had been to get off the Beast After that, he had to admit that the thought of revenge against the kidnappers and the Gamers was growing in his mind. He did not expect this. This was, was... Hollywood. The next thing he saw was too much. A red carpet was rolled out from a makeshift stage to the right of the station. This nightmare was getting more and more surreal.

"What in the blue blazes is going on!" He said loudly to no one in particular.

Trini spoke from his side. "I've never seen anything like it."

Justin put his hand on her shoulder. Then, he looked at the other boys, they were just as astonished as he was. He motioned for them to group up.

"Partners, no matter what the money or fame offers me, I'm not going to change. I'm still the Justin that went through the game on the Beast with you. Thank you for your teamwork. I really mean it." He swallowed hard. He had grown fond of his *"friends," no, not just friends, they were brothers, even Red and especially Tej.* He would never forget Tej and his sacrifice.

Leo shook Justin's hand with a big grin. "Can we forget about the worst of it and start over, mate?"

Justin swallowed again and just nodded his head, shaking Leo's hand vigorously. After swallowing hard, Justin nodded back.

A charging Kofi ran into Justin giving him a big hug around his middle. Then the hug got uncomfortable with others watching and they stepped back. After shaking each other's hands, they turned, looked toward the group of actors and saw *him.*

The man was tall handsome man in a new tailored tuxedo strutted to the microphone on the makeshift stage platform. Nick appeared from behind the opposite red curtains. He easily strode to the center of the platform to stand to the announcer's left.

He didn't limp or trip. He wasn't crippled. In fact, he wasn't even dead. This can't be real, Justin thought. He now knew he was stuck in some surreal dream.

"You're supposed to be dead!" Red shouted, balling up his fists.

"I saw you fall into the forcefield and .... Burn," Leo choked out the words.

Kofi straightened to his full height and declared, "You fell to the ground, but I didn't hear the zap of the forcefield behind the train. You were in on it. In on everything! You're an actor. Traitor!"

They stared at Kofi. He wasn't just a kid any longer. And, he was right.

I couldn't believe what came out of Nick's mouth next, "Check mate," he said and smiled with those big beguiling dimples. "I'm an entertainer, what can I say?!"

Tricky Nicky, so true to his title. But he was so likable. I even shed a tear at his "death," Justin thought.

Justin knew. They all knew that Nick was never one of them. He played the pity card well. They felt sorry for him. So, they never questioned what he did or didn't do. They were brothers, but he was a Judas. Then, as if they had talked about it, they turned together with their backs to Nick, the actor, the traitor.

"Gentlemen," the man gestured to the Riders of the Beast, "please join me on this stage. For a second, he wondered about the Riders of the Wolf, when he saw ambulances at the junction. A handful of medics were helping the few survivors. From where Justin stood, he could see to his left behind Paradise Station ambulances with severely hurt boys and several body bags being wheeled away. It made him sick to see boys, including Gary and Dylan...gone. There was no excuse for it. Not the money. Not winning. Of course, they didn't choose this. But Dylan and Gary and other boys still died on the Wolf. BBQ had really died. It was a bitter victory, and no cause for celebration to be freed from one's own captivity by causing injury to other boys. No. Justin knew this was wrong and he stomped his foot. He wanted to rebel against this televised show of theirs. Then, he saw the NFLS guards lift their rifles. Now was not the time to make waves. Rebelling now would be crazy.

So, they strode to the red carpet. Each winning Rider walked on the red carpet, looking to the left and right where the people were gathered. Each boy gave a wave in return to his parents waving. Something was odd. *Why didn't they run to hug us, their lost boys who have returned?* Justin felt like he was numbly going along with a dream because none of this felt real.

A sharply dressed woman in a dark green suit on the stage greeted each boy as they stepped up. She pointed where each should stand with Justin in the middle. Justin felt uncomfortable about the extra attention that she was giving him.

"Justin, you will be presented with your winnings last. We are saving the best for last," the woman said.

He wondered how she knew his name. She talked to him like she knew him. He didn't have time to ponder it long, since the man started the ceremony surrounded by huge expensive looking video cameras surrounding the front, audience and the platform.

Articulate and with a clear voice, "Ladies and Gentlemen, I'm Harlan Frost, your host and MC for this TV show "Rail Way to Riches!" He says it with a dynamic crescendo holding the "s" longer at the end. "For the last 23 days you have been watching our Whiz kids on what they named, the Beast. It has become the number 1 TV show in the country!"

27

Justin Learns the Truth

"IT HAS BECOME the top-rated show for the last year!" Harlan Frost had just said.

What is he talking about? We weren't on the Beast a whole year. We were home with our parents. But this isn't a surreal dream, it's a nightmare. He pinched himself, but he was still standing on the platform with a couple hundred people looking at him.

After the applause died down, Harlan Frost continued, "We've accomplished what we set out to do. We're number one! It wouldn't have been possible without our sponsor, Moon Drilling for alternative energy." Applause. "We owe gratitude to our brilliant Producer Edwin Shart." Applause. "Let me thank our show manager, Amy Foxglove." Applause. She had her ash-blonde hair teased and poofed around her head, like a fountain. The woman who directed them on stage waved, a big white smile across her tan face. *So, her name is Amy. She knows something,* Justin thought.

"I would also like to thank the NFLS, the National Film Location Services for giving us the use of this beautiful location and Hidden Valley where Justin was raised."

Justin ignored the stares from the other boys and looked at Amy. She just smiled sweetly, tilting her head. He couldn't believe what he was hearing. *What does this mean? Who can I trust?* Questions were swirling in his head, like a tornado threatening to set him off.

"Speaking of which, we have to thank the actors who were the parents of each Whizkid. Would you please stand so we can acknowledge your contribution to the show." Seven sets of parents of different nationalities stood and waved with big smiles. Each boy on stage had an expression of shock while looking from the different parents to each other on stage.

When am I going to wake up from this dream? Justin wondered.

Justin whispered to Kofi next to him, "Those are your parents there, the Africans, right?"

"Of course, their my parents; they're not actors. Silly! My parents are nurses."

All the boys whispered to each other until they heard Harlan Frost say, "And, here are the Gamers, Jack O'Neill, and Kio Mineta. This is the first time the boys of the Beast will see them." He turned and gestured to a screen to his right.

An enormous flat screen the size of a billboard flashed on. In larger than life, were two boys only a year or so older than us. The first one spoke in a Boston accent.

"It was dicey at first," Jack O'Neill said. "But I knew I could operate the best train of riders. That was one wicked ride."

"That's Jack! No way!" Justin exclaimed.

"And Akio! The blighter!" Leo said.

"I still win. And I am rich," the second gamer said in a nasal voice. Then, he laughed his maniacal laugh.

The teens had heard the same two on the radio Tej had fixed up. It was Jack and Akio. Listening to Akio now, they knew they'd never get that laugh out of their heads.

Both Gamers waved with smug, self-satisfied expressions on their faces.

Next, the producers played back the last video footage of the two Gamers at the moment they were running their trains towards each other. Then the cameras cut to the Beast. They saw themselves and Tej on the roof. The cameras cut to the boys on the Wolf, they had competed in Chess, Maj Jong, Card games and even baseball against most of them.

Each of the Beast's teens whispered a name on his lips. The name of his game rival and friend on the other train. What were the odds of that? They knew they all had been used as pawns in this game. The two Gamers came back on the screen and said together, "Thank you for watching, "Riding for Riches.""

The boys knew they were not riding for riches. This was for entertainment. Pain, horror and death for entertainment. And this was the number one show?! People enjoyed watching a reality show where the participants are kept in the dark. They want to see our raw unpracticed reactions. That's why the cameras were on their faces half the time. *That's why they put Red on the train,* Justin thought, *to cause more drama. He was a pawn, just like me.* The dumbfounded faces of the boys of the Beast were being televised now on the screen.

Harlan Frost thanked the Gamers, one more time and went on, "This show was so successful, because we and all the world were watching these four young men, the other three from their train and the seven young men on the losing train, grow up. Every milestone, developing their gifts and their intelligence, winning competitions, learning to drive a car, having their first date and first kiss. Then, finally, we enjoyed seeing them solve the challenge of the game that we placed them in. We watched knowing that for them, it was a reality show. They reacted in real life, although we put them in an NFLS set with actors. The boys on the Beast particularly entertained us. They had challenges and injuries, and we hurt for them. We cheered for them, especially the cowboy on the Beast, Justin...."

Justin didn't listen to any more. Actors. Harlan Frost said "actors." Were they all actors, his parents, his late grandparents, Joe who took care of their horses, Miss Stinson, his favorite teacher and ... Vanessa? No, not Vanessa. She could not have been acting. He loved her and he knew that when they were together, she love him. She said that she loved him. He shook his head, trying to clear it.

Justin looked at his new brothers. The other boys looked just as disturbed. A line formed on Red's brow and he started for the steps. Amy blocked his path.

Harlan Frost addressed their concern, "I know this must be a shock." He looked to the cameras and nodded at Justin. Frost seemed to signal to the cameramen to get close ups of their faces. *This is a circus. How could people be entertained by our pain? Our pain is our; it's private.*

"Listen young gentlemen, you each are being awarded one million dollars." He nodded to the woman in the dark green dress, who gave each boy a monetary chip for 1 million dollars, called a Millichip. "Let's hear it for our winners!"

The audience broke into wild applause.

"We need you to stand close together and hold your monetary chip out in front of you," the woman said. She pretended to hold one in front of her in her delicate hand. They weren't two-years-old. *Why does she treat us like we're toddlers,* Justin thought.

Red bluntly said, "Why should we?!"

Justin said, "Amy, will you explain things to us, if we do?" He held the gaze of her sapphire eyes.

"Please just pose for the cameras, they're watching us."

"No, not until you tell us what happened to us and our real families!" Justin asserted.

"Alright, alright." The nervous administrative assistant looked between the audience and the boys a couple times.

"Do you promise?" Justin held out his hand.

Amy considered it a moment, then shook his hand saying, "Right after the ceremony, meet me in the train station, okay?"

The boys nodded their heads in agreement and lined up with their Millichips in hand.

The first to jump down from the stage, before the last word was spoken, was Red. He raced to Vanessa. She was smiling, but looked stiff and cold, distant as the cold moon but more radiant. Red yelled her name. She just smiled that big toothy smile with blank eyes. Justin shook his head. He should have known when he saw her poster for Red that they were both being played. Well, he had to admit that abstinence saved him from the hurt and humiliation that Red was going through right now.

Justin closed his eyes and forgot about Red and Vanessa. He forgot about the kidnappers and the NFLS guards. As he quieted his spirit, Justin had a vision of a little brown-haired sister with large brown eyes and an older brother standing with him in front of a little table with three metal cups on it from his earliest memories. He wondered if that was real or from a dream. Well, they would find out during their clandestine talk in Paradise Station. *Paradise. What a joke, Justin thought. This is no paradise for the winners. Fools station was more like it. Fools who were played, while the world watched.*

Amy was standing at the back wall in the station. *Was she the enemy? Were the kidnappers the enemy? The ones who did this to us?*

When all the boys arrived, she said, "Lock the door, Trini."

The girl narrowed her eyes and stared at the woman.

I need to know what this woman has to say, Justin thought. Trini, please lock the door."

Trini nodded towards Justin. Then, she pressed in the key pad to lock it.

"You all will be debriefed at HQ, but I promised to tell you personally what happened. Before the legal formalities and signing your names to documents, let me speak to you privately."

Trini crossed her arms.

Amy added, "Just the truth."

"Ha!" Leo scoffed.

Red, with his hands on his hips, said, "More like a pack of lies."

Justin said, "I'm angry too. Guys, let's just hear what she has to say. After that, we can ask questions."

Amy nodded gratefully to Justin and said, "You all came from tragic homes. Some orphaned, some homeless on the streets, some fatherless, but you all showed brilliant genius from a young age. Your guardians sold you to the producer of this show. There are records from whom you were purchased. When we get to HQ, I will show them to each of you. You will be emancipated at that time. What are your questions?"

"You say the world was watching us all these years? Can we see the TV show? Tej asked.

"Yes, that is in the separation papers. You have free access to watch the streamed show up to a year. Okay. When you're done here, I'll meet you at HQ," She paused her explanation, scanning their faces. "There's one more thing. You will all be offered a contract to appear in the sequel TV series, another high-speed locomotive reality show. You're all celebrities, you know. Your fans are dying to watch the next show."

"You can take that offer and," Justin bit his lip.

"Shove it where the sun don't shine!" Leo said with his arms crossed.

"A second time?! No!" Red exclaimed.

Brown eyes narrowed, Trini turned her back to Amy and unlocked the door.

The other two boys were airing their complaints along the same lines.

"Hey lady, are you done with us?" Red asked.

"Yes. See you at HQs." She said in a dejected tone.

Trini was already out the door with the boys following.

To Justin she said, "I know you're smart enough to know there's more explaining that I need to do for you.

"Just tell me. I want to know where my family lives now."

"Justin, what I want to tell you starts with how the producers found you. You were only four years old, very bright. You had this … inner light that shined from your brilliant eyes. The scout saw you on the street with your older brother and Trini."

Amy nodded towards the exit door.

Justin drew his lips tight and balled up his fists.

"When you played the "shell game," no one could beat you. The scout saw your potential to be our star of the show."

"But my parents-"

"I'm getting to that. The scout carried you with your brother and sister escorted through the alley of the tenements. He saw the squalor your family lived in." Amy swallowed.

Justin dropped his eyes and didn't raise them until she was done with her explanation.

"Three Deaf couples and children, dividing up a three-bedroom apartment in the poorest inner-city tenement building in Old Denver. Your ribs showed from lack of food. Your father died and your mother was worried about how she could support the family. The producers of the show gave your mother cash, credits for ten year's worth of food and rent paid on her own apartment for ten years. So, you see, you saved your family from starvation. It was the least the scout could do for your poor grieving mother - Anyway, um, you were cute. When the headquarters groomers had you bathed and hair trimmed, you had people turning their heads and saying, "Ah, what a darling boy!""

Justin thrust his cleft chin up and stared at the woman. "Okay, I get why you kidnapped me-"

"Kidnapped?" She said with disgust in her voice, "The producers didn't-"

"Right, you say they bought me and I saved my family, but then I was kidnapped from my fami-, the actor-, The Waynes." The exasperated teen grabbed two handfuls of his auburn hair. "Augh!" He let go and slapped his hands against his thighs. "I was kept on the Beast. All of us boys were kidnapped from the only families we knew. That's not right!" The gold flakes in Justin's brown eyes seem to blaze. He gritted his teeth.

"Listen, you don't know the world. You've been isolated in Hidden Valley most of your life. Our way of life is media. You haven't been allowed to see what a big city is really like. There are cameras everywhere. Televisions in the public places. And screens for you to view programs 24/7."

"It just isn't right. People making money off of watching us suffer and at least four died. People entertained by viewing us making fools of ourselves." He threw his hand out as he spoke.

"You'll learn that when you have money, and now you do, you can do whatever you want. Have a TV screen to watch a different program in each of your rooms. Carry a personal entertainment center in the palm of your hand. It's wonderful!"

He ran his fingers through his reddish-brown hair. "Tell me, is my name Justin? Who is my mother and where is she?"

"Your name is Tyson, Ty for short. Her name is Saunia Wayfield. Her last known residence was in Old Denver."

Ty strutted to the exit door.

In the middle of the group of actors, Ty lunged at Mr. Wayne. The fuming teen grabbed the lapel of the man he used to call "Dad." He let go when over the man's shoulder, Ty saw Trini's face. A single tear ran down her cheek.

"Trini," Justin stammered. "You're my sister." His eyebrows slanted and his mouth turned down as he walked around Mr. Wayne and straight to his sister. "I am so sorry that I doubted." Ty reached his hands out to her and drew her into a hug.

"Ty," the sister said, "I tried to tell you."

He nodded. "Okay. Ty is not so bad of a name. But that woman said I came from a place called, Old Denver? Never heard of it."

"You know the capital, Intermountain? Okay, the capital is a huge modern metropolis. Old Denver is the old city center close to where the mountains start. It's not far."

His eyes softened as he looked into her face. "Just a moment. Stay here."

Ty felt betrayed, abandoned and alone. His stomach ached as he looked at the Waynes. He was revolted by the actor family. How could they do that, for years? He remembered that he had to get his Mustang back. When he approached the Waynes, he kept his face a mask. He simply jutted his hand out for the key.

The Waynes both said, "Good luck."

The teen kept his eyes straight towards the vehicle. Ty carried his key to his mustang. On its keychain, a brass letter J on a leather background, in his hand. It reminded him of his fake name and how he had been deceived. He slid the key off the keychain and chucked the thing at the ground in front of the Waynes. He didn't bother to look for their reaction, but took his sister's hand and walked towards his car.

Some of the boys were still talking to the actors, their teeth gritted. In Red's case, screaming at his "parents." Justin looked his car over. He let go of Trini's hand and ran his fingers over the hood. A dent that he put in the left front bumper when drag racing was still visible. He thought of all the dates he had gone on with Vanessa in his red-hot car. Now that was over. He caressed the door. *Well, it's just you and me baby,* he thought. Justin finished walking around his car, remembering every detail.

A minute later, Kofi stood next to him on his other side, waiting patiently. The shorter boy frowned. His shoulders sagged.

"Hey. Everything alright?" Justin asked.

"I have nobody," Kofi said flatly.

"I'm very sorry. But you have us." Justin gestured from himself to Trini.

The corners of Kofi's mouth rose and he hugged Justin.

After Kofi let go, Justin asked, "Have you thought about what you're going to do with your money?"

"I'm going to travel … with you. If that's alright."

"Fine with me. I'm going to Old Denver."

"Where?"

"Not far from here. I've got to find my real mother and brother, um…" Ty looked to his sister for help.

"Tekka," Trini said. She smiled up at Ty.

Ty was already feeling like he belonged to his birth family. He was one of the three siblings whose names started with the same letter.

He put his arm around his sister's shoulders. Then, she put her arm around his waist.

Kofi started to cry. Justin put an arm around his friend too.

Kofi said, "My parents are dead. So, I'm an orphan. I'm alone."

"No, we're family now."

Trini nodded

Kofi wiped his last tear and smiled.

Leo joined them. Red took a step nearer, but was still a few feet behind Ty and Leo.

Ty turned and lifted his eyebrows, perplexed by Red's standoffishness.

Red eyes narrow as his gaze followed the people. He watched the last of the adults leaving Paradise Station. The teen turned to face his fellow riders.

"Since my parents are dead, I'm free to ride, not trains but Harleys. Red and me are riding the highways together.

"So, Justin, I mean Ty, what are you going to do with your million bucks, Mate?

What would he spend the money on? Ty couldn't help thinking how he and Leo had braved a rocky trial on the Beast. He had forgiven Leo just as he decided that he is going to forgive Red. How could he feel anything but pity for the guy? Vanessa played him worse. Justin thought how he even planned to forgive Vanessa. He didn't feel like forgiving her. But he just said it in his head each time the bitterness welled up. He rather think about his real family, his mother, his brother and Trini. At least he got to know her a little. So, he felt less nervous about meeting the other part of his family. If there's one thing Ty knew for sure, it was that people are more important than money. He raised his face to Red.

"I have a mother and siblings in poverty," Ty said. "I plan on making a new life for us with my winnings. I'll find a nice valley where we can raise cattle, and be self-sufficient." Looking at Trini, he squeezed her tighter.

Trini's eyes glistened. She didn't speak, but nodded.

"Hey, our first step can be to help you and Trini find your family. Is that alright with you, Mate?" Leo's eyebrows were raised.

Ty's mouth was drawn in a line. After what seemed like a very awkward lacuna, the cowboy put out his hand. The two Whizkids shook hands. They were like brothers after all they'd been through.

"Pyro," Red smiled. He nodded toward Paradise Station.

Justin scowled at the offensive name.

"Mate, he's smiling," Leo said.

"Red, I said don't call me that-"

"Ty, peace. What do you say we light a fire tonight?" Red nodded again towards Paradise Station.

Ty, the other boys and Trini smiled mischievous Cheshire Cat smiles.

Darkness fell over the Colorado Plateau. This night, the darkness closed in with grey clouds. The teens stood without even so much as a shiver. The moon waned as had the boys' childhood. Since their captivity on the Beast, and recent events, they knew too much about the dark side of the world.

The clouds moved slowly over the heavenly body. In the fading moonlight, the little station is barely visible. There were no lights. From a distance, an auburn-haired teen with the smell of natural gas and liquid gas on him, hurled something, a baseball? No. A grenade into a garbage can sitting in gasoline that led into Paradise station. The same teen ran up the hill. Suddenly, the garbage can exploded. The fire continued along the gasoline into the station. The vile station exploded.

"Kaboom!" Ty lifted his hands.

A great explosion sent pieces of painted board in all directions. Then a second explosion demolished the round house with the Beast in it and what was left of the Wolf. The film set was gone, engulfed in flames.

On a hill in the distance, a red mustang sat with its engine running. Justin put a saxophone case into his trunk, making more sitting room. He plopped into the driver's seat in the vehicle with his four passengers. He pulled onto the road. The driver enjoyed watching the flames, his biggest and final fire.

As he drove away, lost in his own thoughts, as each mile passed, his anger slowly melted away, mile by mile. Here he was, not alone, but with his brothers and a real sister, forged in the crucible of challenges beyond human comprehension. They weren't perfect, he learned to forgive them, but they were his brothers. He loved them and Trini, just because they were his.

His thoughts turn to his biological family. At HQ, Amy shared all the information she had on his family. He thought of his biological mother. Ty was not looking forward to their meeting. He thought how he could never exchange his own child, or any child for money. His stomach tightened as he felt the bitterness of having been rejected. How could a mother sell her child, no matter how poor the family? Justin ached when in his mind a memory flashed of him as a four-year-old, being carried away by a stranger, a man in an odd uniform. The more Ty entertained negative thoughts, the more depressed he became. Then, he pictured his nightmare and the man in the fire. Was it his real father? He was dreading that the man in his fire dream was his father. Could he stand the truth? Could he forgive himself, if the worst was true? His head shook. Behind his eyes the turmoil spun until he felt dizzy. The thought of how he didn't play with his brother and sister growing up stung. Tekka will be a stranger to him. And, Amy told him of his late maternal grandfather, who had been a Jazz musician. A longing for the grandpa that he never saw or heard play on his tenor sax left his heart aching. Ty remembered how easily he played the instrument. He thought of how his grandfather's gift for Jazz music lived on in him. *How life would have been filled with real family love and daily affection, if I had not been ripped from them.*

He felt a deep hole, a space that needed to be filled. The cowboy fretted about what would fill it. He knew that seeing his mother, sister and brother again would not bring back his childhood. Ty looked up at the stars and waning moon. Was his mother looking at this same moon even now? He didn't want to be sad and bitter. At that moment, he made up his mind to say no to bitterness. Justin decided to say yes to forgiving his mother. He whispered, "I choose joy." A satisfied smile crossed his lips.

"What was that?" Trini asked from the passenger seat.

"Nothing."

"You obviously didn't forget how to drive," Leo said from the back seat.

"You know driving is like magic," Ty grinned.

"Say what?"

"Driving is like magic. It's all about the mirrors."

They guffawed. Ty thought how good it felt to laugh.

Ty reached the highway and looked into his mirrors. the blinker of his right signal indicator, shown through the dark night. He turned his Mustang's steering wheel hand over hand towards the left. The vehicle continued to the right.

"What?!"

"What's going on mate?"

"I have no idea."

Surprisingly, the Mustang turned right, back towards Paradise Station. Justin frantically tried to put the vehicle in neutral with no effect. Next, he tried to turn the car off, but the car accelerated to 30 mph in the opposite direction of where they want to go. The boys tried the doors. *Locked. Won't open.*

Just when Ty thought he was getting his life and his 'stang back. If it's too good to be true, it's too good to be true.

28

Justin Feels Trapped

THE RED MUSTANG was programmed. It was taking them to the west, towards the HQ of this NFLS operation.

"No, I'm not going back!" Justin said with determination. He was determined to keep trying. He had a pocket knife. What could he do with that?

Red shouted, "No way. I'm not going back!"

"Me neither," agreed Kofi.

"I'm not going to be trapped again!" Leo exclaimed.

In the back seat, Red and Leo put their feet up to the back window and on the count of three, kicked against it. Nothing happened.

"Crazy," Red exclaimed.

"There's got to be a way," Leo said.

"Can anyone get their window to roll down?" Kofi asked.

They tried, but the handle busted off.

Justin lay across the middle looking under the dash. He cut the wires to the engine. The car slowed.

Kofi said to Justin, help me with this convertible top. Of course, the automatic switch would have been disabled. But they tried to manually open it. It was welded shut. Leo opened the pocket knife once more.

"Wait!" Shouted Justin, "Don't damage my vehicle." He held both hands up in front of Leo.

"Listen, Justin, I understand. But, they will spot us in this red car in a minute. We're going to have to find new wheels, if we want to get away," Leo said.

Of course, he was right. He was always right, except that one time when he brought Red the hot poker. Anyway, he was right about this.

"Okay," Justin said through gritted teeth.

They cut their way out of the mustang. Justin ran his hand over the car's lines.

"Goodbye ol' buddy," he whispered.

While Justin said goodbye to his red Mustang, it started up, the engine humming. Justin jumped back just in time. The empty red Mustang peeled out and sped to the left. It crashed in a stack of haybales next to a barn. The barn was half a mile west of Paradise Station. As the teens walked towards the barn, they could see in the distance the stands, large speakers and jumbo screen between where they stood and Paradise Station. Ty made sure everyone was alright as they stood in the rays of the sunrise. Ty and Trini were arm in arm.

Ty said, "Don't worry. We're alright."

Just then, an image came on the screen from the ceremony grounds at Paradise Station. The footage was of Ty and Trini, arm in arm near the haybales. This was live. The captions said, "LIVE EPILOGUE." The screen flashed to a new image. A woman with brown hair and salt and pepper roots and a young man who looked like Trini stood behind a metal barrier about 20 meters to the north of the train tracks with two armed NFLS guards at their elbows.

"Mother, Tekka!" Trini screamed.

On the screen, Tekka's face, framed by wild brown hair, was scrunched up in anger as he pulled against the guard's grip. Tears ran down his mother's face. An interpreter stood next to a reporter and a mic hung from a metal extension pole. Through the interpreter the reporter asked her, "How do you feel about seeing your son on TV for the first time since you sold him?"

In live streaming larger than life, his mother shook her head defiantly.

On the screen, the bubbly reporter turned to Tekka. "How do you-"

"Trini, Ty, I've been looking for you. Meet us at mother's lot." Tekka spat on the ground in front of the guard holding him. The image changed to the rolling credits to the theme song of the show.

Ty stood still staring at the screen, his mouth dropped open. He balled up his fists. He turned to his right. "I need to go to Old Denver," Ty told Leo.

"Mate, Old Denver is about four miles across the train tracks. Leo pointed a half a mile north.

"Five miles," Trini said, "I can show you where Mother works." Her hands rested on her brother's arm, urgently pulling at it. "It will take a while, so let's start walking."

Justin saw the dirty brick apartment buildings crowded together to the north. He nodded.

Red's cell phone rang. He had gained reception. "My buddies are coming," Red curtly stated and walked into the barn.

Ty thought, *Great. Red's motorcycle ... "friends".... buddies... gang will be our ride.* Then the cowboy settled in some hay, pulling his hat over his eyes. He wondered if he would like his mother. Amy told him that she was Deaf. How would he communicate with her?

He turned to his sister, "Would you teach me some sign language?"

The corners of Trini's mouth rose and the smile shown in her eyes.

After a five-minute wait, they heard a loud sound in the distance.

Ty got to his feet.

"I think it's thunder," Kofi sat up straight.

"That's not thunder. It's the roar of motorcycles, lots of them!"

An excited Leo practically hopped all the way up the ladder to the loft.

Red just crossed his legs, chewing on a piece of straw, "Told ya."

The rolling sound grew. Leo finally shouted, "Mate, I see them. Oh, that front bike's a beauty! Black Harley Road King with chrome. The Harley rolls on 19" chrome decked out rims and black and studded saddlebags."

Red replied, "That would be Bart on his hog." He straightened his motorcycle jacket, took out a silver and black bandana and put it on his head. Red strutted to the barn door.

Bart and his gang rode up on their Harley's to meet them in front of the barn. There were eight bikers, not counting Red. Eight road bike rolled up. The Harleys had their travel boxes and saddlebags. Good for hitting the road, and staying on it. There wasn't a gal among them.

"Thanks for coming Bart!" Red reached out his right hand to the broad-shouldered man with the ash colored hair and handlebar mustache. The leader clasped his right hand around Red's forearm. After the gang handshake, Red swept his hand towards the other Whizkids.

"Bart, these are my brothers from the Beast. Justin, -"

"I know Justin and the others," he looked back and forth. "We all do. Remember, we watched your TV show. So, you guys are millionaires!" A greedy smile spread across his lips.

"Now hold on," Red held up an index finger, "the government took their share in taxes."

Raucous laughter from the biker gang as they moved away from their parked bikes and surrounded the four boys.

Red might have been friends with these bikers, but Justin and the boys felt nervous about their grins and laughter. They reminded Justin of a pack of wolves before the kill.

Red's voiced boomed, "Okay. You transport us to our hideout. I pick up my Harleys for Leo and me," he and Leo exchanged fraternal looks, "Then we ride to Mammoth's Biker Stop, and these two guys can buy their bikes at his dealership."

"No thanks. I'll get another 'stang."

"For your information, cowboy," Brute Bart gestured at Justin's hat, "you're not getting through Old Denver in a car. The streets are littered. You'll be grateful you bought a hog."

"You told him where we're going?" Ty walked up to Red, "How can I trust them?"

"Tell me who you can trust?" Red said, "Can you trust your ACTOR parents? Can you trust your GIRL FRIEND VANESSA?" Red rolled his eyes.

Justin stepped back shaking his head in defeat.

"Wait a minute. I don't have a license," Kofi pointed at himself with his right hand.

"No problem," he patted a lanky young man on the back, "Bones here can get that for you, fellow, for a price." Bart smiled a toothy smile. More raucous laughter.

"Bart, we want fair prices. We suffered and won fair and square and our winnings are our winnings." Red boomed louder.

"Bro, I'm hurt," Bart spread his arms wide, "Of course, we're fair. And, you want a ride there, with your friends. Don't forget us, brother."

"Don't forget, I could have called anyone, my parents, my agent, but I let you pick us up. Just remember that, brother!" Although his voice kept even, Red's face flashed crimson.

"Chill. Save your temper for the cheats that will come your way. Before long, you'll be grateful for the Silver Thunder. Believe me, you need us to protect you."

"Protect us from who?" Ty stuck out his muscular chest.

"Everyone that owns a TV set knows what you guys look like. Every citizen of The Redlands only need look up at Triumph Square at the Capitol or any major square to see your faces plastered any one of twenty jumbo screens playing your TV show," the leader raised his voice, "Since you were pronounced the winners of a million each, you're each a target. Understand?"

Ty understood, but he didn't have to like it. Justin stood on the edge of this new life totally unprepared for the real world. He thought, *It's not my fault!* He balled up his hands into fists. Letting out one big breath, Justin kept his cool now faced with this biker gang. His "fake" life kept him sheltered, like a patient in a padded room. But once released, he's clueless.

Ty, Leo and Kofi looked at each other and moved together. Leo spoke what they were all thinking, "The NFLS ruined our lives. We didn't get the real-world knowledge that we need. I say we accept the Silver Thunder as our body guards." Leo's eyes looked to Ty in expectation.

First Justin nodded.

"But we could walk," Trini said. Her arms were crossed and she stood her ground, feet apart.

"Who is this street urchin?" Bart said. He kept staring at Trini. "Listen sister, now that you've been in a TV show, your enemies will be after you."

Trini shoved her hands in her pockets in resignation.

"That's what I thought," Bart said.

Kofi nodded next.

Red took the boys nods as a good sign and continued, "Our goal is to get to the capital. Justin has to find his real mother. Then, we hit the talk shows and talk up our experience. We're celebrities. That'll give us power."

"And, why do we want power?" Ty faced Red.

Red put a hand on his shoulder, "So, we can hold on to our winnings and our freedom. Don't forget that the NFLS still controlled your car to bring us back."

Justin nodded, "Yup."

"First lesson on the outside, only the strong hold onto what they have," turning to Bart, "You have four new members of your gang."

29

Members of the Silver Thunder

IT WAS A five minutes ride to the biker gang's lair where they picked up Red's two Harleys and sleeveless Silver Thunder jackets for the new comers. Next, they rolled up to Mammoth's. This biker's oasis sat on I-70, a mile from their lair. In front of the shopping square two-story brick and steel store with a corrugated tin roof, an old flag, the stars and stripes flew on a flagpole. *Well, at least that wasn't a lie. We still live in a place that flies the stars and stripes,* Justin thought. The building housed a dealership, gas station, biker stop and cafe. In the back, stood a special shop where Mammoth sold weapons: guns, knives and salvaged military weapons.

They parked their bikes along with less than a half dozen other hogs in the grease stained parking lot and the gang made their way in through the double glass doors. A thundering voice welcomed the gang.

"Howdy! Welcome. It's been awhile Silver Thunder." A giant of a man stood greeting them in the entry.

"You must be Mammoth," Justin stuck out his right hand and arm.

Rick clasped his thick hand around Justin's forearm in their gang's own hand shake. The owner knew each biker gang's handshake. Before Justin could give his name, Rick expectantly looked at Brute Bart.

Did he know Red called him Pyro? The seventeen-year-old, almost eighteen-year-old bristled at being ordered around by this biker leader barely in his twenties. But, Justin knew he was a greenhorn in this gang. So, he bit his lip and did what he did best, observe, learn and adapt. Red wanted a turn and quickly named the others.

Pointing at Leo, he said, "Rider."

Leo made a motion with his right hand, like revving a motorcycle gas.

"And you're Doc," Red patted Kofi on the shoulder.

"What's your name?" Kofi inquired.

"Red, duh"

He should have known.

Mammoth pushed Kofi on his butt, "Stupid kid."

Ty held out his hand to help Kofi up. While he was doing that, Mammoth had his arms around Trini.

In a flash, Ty had Mammoth by the shirt against the wall behind him. All eyes turned to Ty, who was still pressing Mammoth.

"Leave the kid and my sister alone. Or you have me to answer to," Ty said through clenched teeth. Shoulders squared, Ty didn't back down. After a couple minutes, Mammoth went over and put his hand out to shake hands with Kofi. When he approached Trini, she crossed her arms in defiance.

They all sat in the café and ate chicken wraps and of course drank Apex soda. But this time it wasn't grape. They had raspberry. Leo piped up, "When do we get our Silver Thunder tats?"

"What?!" Ty exclaimed, flinging out his hands in disgust.

Red gave Leo an approving sock in the shoulder, "That's what I'm talking 'bout! Don't be a crybaby, Smokey. Get your tat like a man."

"I thought we were just joining this gang, you know, temporarily?"

Ty said. He didn't like the nickname, Smokey, nor the idea of a tattoo.

"Oh, so you just want to live temporarily, then die alone without your gang to protect you."

"No, I mean -"

"Get this, your life will never be the same again. The sooner you accept our Silver Thunder Gang way of life, the better your chances of staying alive."

Justin didn't like change. He grew up as a cowboy. But, he saw the reasoning. A millionaire needed bodyguards. Well, just until he found his mother and brother, which they should be on their way. "Come on, we're burning daylight."

He interrupted Leo and Red's exchange about tattoos. Red had pulled up his right t-shirt sleeve to show the Silver Thunder Gang tattoo just under his right shoulder on his arm. The tat sported a lightning bolt with silver lines coming from it in a shield shape with wings at the top and in silver 3D lettering the words, Silver Thunder. His biker men friends all showed off their identical tats.

Justin drew his mouth into a line in consternation. He raised his hand, but Red put his arm around him and said, "Come on. Leo is excited about this, aren't ya?" Red looked back to make sure Leo and especially Kofi were following.

Leo said, "You better believe it, mate!" He took long strides to catch up with Red and walk alongside him, chest out in pride.

"No," Justin said. "Not now. You can do that later. I'm going now. Are you coming with me?" Justin looked from Red to Leo.

"Sure, Smokey," Red sneered. "You're the boss."

"Why do you call me, Smokey?" Justin asked.

Justin felt exposed. Why was everyone looking at him? He drew his hand across his eyes. This newest gang member boiled to one degree below rocket launch. Ty had had it. He threw his right hand out and snarled through clenched teeth. "Why did ya hafta pick Smokey?"

Then a young feminine voice called out, "Because that's what you are, smokin'!"

It couldn't be. That beautiful sultry voice that drove him crazy. Before he turned, he knew what he could see, Vanessa. But nothing prepared him for the transformation. She had a few inches cut off her hair, dyed red and wore it up in two ponytails. Her clothes were foreign to him as well, black leather biker chick jacket and tight black denim pants that she filled out just right. She stood with the biker chick gang, Denim Angels.

"Hi boys. Call me Lashes," she said. "It's my biker name." Vanessa, or Lashes batted her long full lashes.

Ty's mouth dropped open in total surprise. Vanessa was the last person she expected and the last person he wanted to see. With his finger pointed at her, he asked, "What are you doing here?"

"Same thing as you, love." Vanessa put her hand on his chest.

He knew the actress was after something. His eyes blazed like lightning. He picked her hand off of his chest and flung it away from him. "Whatever you want, the answer is NO!" He glared at the tricky ex-girlfriend. "And I am in a hurry to get to my mother and brother. My REAL mother." When he shook his head, his copper bangs whipped his eyes. He pushed them back with a sigh.

"Now, Justin. We were good together." She batted her eyelashes. "We could ride together." She formed her lips into a rosebud.

Ty shook his head, averting his eyes from her lovely face.

Red stepped up to her with his fist extended at her and through clenched teeth said, "You dirty traitor. I would trust a rattler before I listened to you. Get out!"

Vanessa poised with her hands on her hips, an evil grin on her face, *like a villain in a comic book*, Ty thought. *What role was she playing now?*

She pointed towards herself, "Lashes." She batted her eyelashes while pointing her index finger at Ty. "and the Denim Angels challenge your gang. The gang with the best time through the obstacle course wins. We win ten grand for each of us from each of you. For your biker gang reputations, you'll do it"

Red kept his smoldering under control, but focused eyes on "Lashes," and walked past her, bumping her shoulder. One by one, Ty and his friends filed out the front door. The boys and Trini walked to their bikes and rode towards Lib square.

Ty hoped that was the last he would see of the treacherous Vanessa. Thinking about all her deception, his head ached. He felt like he would explode with anger. He squeezed the handles tightly, white knuckled one after the other. The NFLS were bad enough. They kidnapped him, killed Tej, stole his childhood. They were despicable, but she had kissed him and told him that she loved him. The memory stabbed his head like a knife. Vanessa . . . There were no words for her kind of low, debase behavior. Then, he focused on the highway that would take him to his mother and siblings. Maybe he would then find out why he had the nightmares.

30

The Place Nightmares were Born

OLD DENVER WAS a maze of high-rise crowded inner-city tenements. Towers, like jungle trees, competed for sunlight above the canopy. The brown sky blocked all but the brightest lights, unlike the oxygen producing jungle. The distance from the outskirts of Old Denver to the new capital of Intermountain is Twenty miles of the poorest people in the new republic. They rode east on 14th, down to 13th and then went west a block. Ty blew air out of his mouth. He wasn't used to these one-way streets. His jaw dropped as he passed the run-down businesses. It felt as if he swallowed a rock, which was sinking into his stomach and weighing him down.

They hung a left on Sherman Street, on which sat some of the oldest apartments still standing in Old Denver. Ty turned into an alleyway with the apartment building on the right.

"Stop!" Ty shouted. On the first block was a three-story brick apartment building surrounded by a mixture of debris. Pieces of bricks, small concrete chunks and asphalt lay in heaps on what used to be a lawn. The war-ravaged Old Denver. The people of The Redlands and The Plateau united to fight the different factions on the continent. The Redlands also known as The Plateau, prevailed. They joined in a treaty with the wealthy and powerful in the other factions. They formed the North American Union Republic

(NAUR) government. The Naur government promised prosperity for all. However, only those with contracts with NAUR became wealthy. The poor, only got poorer with no farmable land, no assets and no marketable skills.

Ty wondered about how all these people earned money, grew food, or even shopped. Mostly, he wondered, *How could this be the home where I spent the first three years of my life?*

They looked up at the brick building with yesterday's wash hanging from a clothes line connected to the next building on the other side. As Ty surveyed the facade, he saw faded white numbers, 1265 and looked again at his paper that Amy had given him. The address and note were in the administrative assistant's handwriting, *Go to 1265 Sherman Street. Last known address of Saunia Wayfield.* "This dump?" As Ty surveyed, the alley and corner of the building to his left felt oddly familiar. He suddenly stopped. For the first time, he noticed the papers discarded and piled high next to the building. Jutting out of the papers, a blackened 2020 Ford F-155 truck. *This truck, no, it couldn't be real. And that! It's not real either.* At least, he hoped it wasn't. He looked up and saw the fire escape on the side of the building. Someone had made an attempt to clean them, but still bore the discoloring of a fire. The building was brick with a metal roof, which meant it could withstand... fire.

He feared the nightmare had really happened. Had he killed his real father in the fire?

"Ty, what's the matter?" Trini looked concerned.

"Nothing," Ty hung his head.

"Something is the matter. Let me help you." Trini put her hand on his shoulder.

"I always have this dream, no, a nightmare," Ty said. He described the nightmare.

"It's just a nightmare because of the fire Mother told us about."

Then it was true. His worst anxiety had come back. His face paled.

"Ty, it's only a nightmare. It never really happened. I mean, you did not cause the fire that took our father."

Ty's head shot forward, "Seriously, I didn't cause it?"

"No. An electrical wire to the heater shorted."

Ty kept repeating this in his head. He had worried for months since this nightmare had started that he had killed the man from the brick apartment. It turns out, it was his real father, but he didn't start the fire. *What tricks the sleeping mind plays on a guy,* he thought.

A stooped unshaven man walked out of the building towards the garbage cans with a small plastic bag in his hand. *Maybe HE knows Saunia.* The man glanced from side to side without raising his eyes to Ty. The copper-haired teen decided to ask the poor soul.

"Howdy mister. I'm looking for . . . well, Saunia Wayfield. Can you show me which apartment she lives in?" Ty inquired. The man didn't respond. He continued placing the trash bag into the garbage can.

"What are you doing? I know where we live. I know where mother is now," Trini said. She made a gesture to her brother next to her head in a circle. No translation needed. She rolled her eyes at him.

"I want to know where the first apartment was where we lived with dad."

"Oh," Trini whispered. Her shoulders drooped.

All of a sudden, a mangy mutt ran between Ty and the man. The man in the street looked up and looked into Ty's face with a start. The man could see Ty's lips moving. The man gestures towards his ear with his index finger while shaking his head. The man was Deaf. His mother was also Deaf.

"I told you that our mother is Deaf and the neighbors are almost all Deaf," Trini said. She had both hands on her hips as she stared at him.

"Sister, would you interpret to the man that I want to see the apartment we used to live in," Ty said.

"No," Trini said, "I am sick of always interpreting. And, … I do not want to go back there." She crossed her arms.

Undaunted, Ty searched his memory. From somewhere in his past muscle memory, his hands drew out the sign, MOTHER.

The man's eyes grew and then he signed with his hands flying. Now Ty's eyes grew large and he shook his head with negation. An idea came to Ty, taking a pen out and the paper with the address, he wrote, "Where did Saunia Wayfield live with her husband Mr. Wayfield, please?" The Whizkid held the note towards the poor man, noting the man's empty smile. *Would the man know his mother? Was this a dead end? Maybe I'll have to search for days, or weeks to find this missing hole … and answer to my nightmares.*

Excitedly, the man nodded his head, pointing to the paper and then down the street to the right. It seemed that he knew both his parents and where they used to live. A toothless smile and he motioned down and to the right.

"We'll stay here and look out." Red's eyes darted from side to side. "I don't like the looks of this place."

"Hey," Trini stared daggers at Red. Then, turning to Ty, she said, "What in the world are you up to?" She moved her face closer to Ty.

"Come with me," Ty said to her.

Leo stood back to back with Red, eyes searching the other side of the street.

"I hate to say it man, but how can your mother live here?" Kofi stood close to the tall teens.

"Remember, I told you. I'm going to take my mother, brother and Trini away from here. I'm going to buy a ranch for us." Ty held his head high, set his jaw and looked toward the entrance of the apartment building.

"She's at work in the Lib," Trini said.

"Lib like library?" Leo asked.

"No, as in Liberty Square," Trini smiled at Leo. "Will we see you later?" Her eyes fluttered.

Leo's cheeks turned red. He shrugged. "I guess."

As Ty and Trini turned to follow the hunched over Deaf man, Kofi called out, "We'll all go to the ranch."

"Yup." Ty looked back at the building, which had been his home. Why couldn't he remember it? The NFLS kidnappers must have given him something to forget his life before he was five years old.

When they reached the corner, the man pointed to the right. Trini strutted ahead of the man ignoring him. She had walked this way thousands of times.

The man smiled and signed, "MOTHER, FATHER, (point)." The man was pointing to the number on the door. He turned, ready to walk back down the hallway.

Ty held out his hand to shake the man's hand. The man readily stuck his hand in Ty's hand. When the man withdrew his hand, he found a pre-paid credit card for $500 lying in his palm. The man's eyes went wide like he's seen a treasure chest. Well, to him, it would be a treasure chest, but to Ty, it was just one his currency as a millionaire.

The man shook his head and tried to hand it back. Ty looked the Deaf man in the eyes and signed, "PLEASE." And then, "THANKS." Excitedly, the copper-haired teen looked at the door and around it trying to find a doorbell. He paused, wondering how his mother would know he was ringing the bell if she couldn't hear. There were two doorbell looking little boxes. One was a rectangle in a larger off-white rectangular little box on the wall. Over this on the wall, he saw a button in a small box on the wall. The Deaf man pointed to the button on the upper little box on the wall. *Oh, a special doorbell. Cool!* Ty rang it. This doorbell made no sound. Then, he heard heavy footsteps inside approaching the door.

Oh no, he thought, *this is where they used to live. What do I do?*

He glanced at Trini, who was doing the gesture for crazy at him again. Ty moved his hand dismissively towards her, but her heard her say, "I told you to follow me."

In front of Ty, the door opened. A black woman answered the door.

"I'm sorry ma'am," Ty started to say.

The woman looked at Ty and then at Trini. Her eyes widened as she recognized Trini. She signed asking Trini who this teen boy was and what he wanted.

Trini nodded.

Ty did a palm plant on his perspiring forehead.

The siblings looked around with Mrs. Jefferson's permission. When they went through the back door in to the back yard, they saw two young men, one of African American descent and the other a young man with brown complexion. They were crouched down like they had just jumped over the fence. Their eyes turned towards the siblings as they heard the screen door squeak. The two young men's mouths made an O shape in surprise.

In characteristic curiosity, Ty looked from one to the other. His gaze rested on the one with brown skin, copper hair with a beard to match and brown eyes ... with gold flakes in them. He had the same Roman nose as Ty's. It was like looking at a tanner version of how he looked in a mirror.

31

Ty Comes Face to Face

IN THE NEXT minute, Ty was standing face to face with the young man with the scraggly brown hair. Ty's jaw dropped as he recognized the heart-shaped face, wavy dark brown hair, and brown eyes. The young man looked just like the face of the middle-aged man walking in fire in his nightmare. Speechless, Ty stumbled back against the screen door.

The young man looked at the teen with a puzzled look then at Trini. He ran three-quarters of the way across the back yard until Trini started running.

"Tekka!" Trini's voice sounded a pitch higher.

The first thing Tekka did was to scoop up his sister. Trini buried her face in his beard.

Despite his racing heart and frozen feet, Ty lifted his right arm, like it was the weight of lead. Still, Tekka reached out, pointing his hand at the teen. First, Tekka stared at the copper-haired boy, then looked at him from head to foot. Next, Tekka was gasping. Then, he shook his head. When he looked into the teen's eyes, recognition came to Tekka, who placed his hand over his mouth.

The former neighbor walked over and stood next to Tekka.

"What's the matter Tekka? Who is this?" The neighbor looked at the copper-haired teen curiously.

Tekka stammered, "Ty, is that you?" He stared at his little brother.

Ty's stare was fixed on the young man's face and he couldn't speak or move at all.

It seemed like an eternity until any of them moved.

"Well ..." Trini said.

Then, Tekka spoke, "Trini, I believe this is our lost brother Ty. Am I right?"

"Your lost brother, Ty?" The neighbor asked.

Tekka turned towards the copper-haired teen. "Ah, . . . so, you're my . . . brother? I thought you looked like, um."

"You thought I looked like who?" Tekka tilted his head and leaned forward in confusion.

"Never mind. Um, ask me later." Justin stood silently for a couple seconds. Then, suddenly his face lit up, "Wow. I have a brother!" Ty sprang forward to hug his brother. "Trini told me about you."

"I can't believe it's really you. I dreamed of the day you would come back." Tekka said. His eyes, mouth and chin lifted.

"Come in. I have a gazillion questions to ask you." Tekka patted his brother's shoulder. "First, why are you two dressed in biker clothes? Do you have a bike outside? Can I have a ride?"

Ty looked from one to the other and then inside the apartment through the open door, "Is mother here?" He asked in a desperate pleading voice.

Tekka shook his head, "No. She stepped out to find something to eat."

At this moment, Ty noticed Tekka's thin frame and tattered clothes.

"Oh, I won ... did you see me on TV?" Ty awkwardly said. He leaned and tilted his head.

"No," Tekka shrugged. "We don't own a TV. We passed one once or twice."

Trini screwed up her lip. "Yeah. I tried to tell him." She nudged Ty. Then, she put her hands on her hips.

"We have pre-paid credit cards. We won. So, Trini and I have money for us," Ty said.

Ty and Trini smiled encouragingly at Tekka.

At this Tekka's eyes widened.

Ty and Trini held out a couple $500 pre-paid cards. Tekka stared at the cards their hands like a kids in a candy store. He was almost drooling.

Ty took out one of his $500 money cards and held it out for his brother to look at.

Since Ty showed Tekka one first, Trini put her cards in her jacket pocket. She pressed the Velcro tightly together.

"Can I touch it?" Tekka asked. He looked up sheepishly for permission.

"Of course." Ty drew the corners of his mouth up. After Tekka touched it with one finger and stared at it for a full minute, Ty couldn't stand waiting any longer.

"Let's go." He moved both his hands towards the stairs. "Take me to where mother shops for food."

Five minutes later, in front of the first of the food booths, stood the boy. Ty stopped. Tables with old rusted legs filled this booth. Dirty and broken PVC pipes served as makeshift racks where cloth, old wire, and mugs were hung.

"What?! I thought you'd take me to a restaurant or a supermarket.

His siblings looked at him out of the corner of their eye.

"What? No, we barter and trade," Tekka said.

"Do you mean they don't take VISA here?" Ty asked.

"Don't you remember Lib Square?" Tekka screwed up his face. "And, no one we know has a VISA card. Those are for the Rich." Tekka leaned away from him.

Just when Ty was feeling good about winning the money to help his family, his brother was become more distant. "Listen. Let's find mother, and I'll take you to a restaurant." Ty quickly shoved his pre-paid card into the pocket of his leather pants.

"Let me use one of my cards to buy us lunch," Trini said.

"No, please, let me. It —" Ty got a lump in his throat and swallowed.

Trini was going to argue, but stopped. She studied his face. "Sure," Trini squeezed his arm.

"Let's go," Tekka said. He led the way to the booth where his mother shopped.

A nearby trader in a Star Wars shirt under a black blazer looked at Ty squinting his eyes. Ty recognized that look. He knew they had to keep moving.

Ty hurried them along walking through the milling shoppers down another aisle of stands. Ty looked for their mother at stand after stand. Finally, at a stand on the outside of the bend, Trini and Tekka saw their mother.

Ty followed their eyes to a woman dressed in a tattered grey blouse and faded jeans, facing the grains and beans stand.

As they approached, Ty's siblings each waved their right hands out towards the woman to get her attention. She turned holding a bag of pinto beans.

"WHAT'S-WRONG," she signed. She was still turned toward Tekka and hadn't yet seen Trini and Ty yet. Ty was standing back.

"LOOK, (pointing) T-Y." Tekka signed to their mother at the same time that Trini wrapped her arms around her mother.

Their mother turned her gaze to the tall copper-haired teen. At first, she didn't recognize him. It had been thirteen years.

Ty saw a woman who was an older version of Trini and knew. "MOTHER," he signed.

Her eyes widened and she dropped her bag, pinto beans spilling on the asphalt. She covered her mouth with her right hand, and sunlight sparkled off the tears filling her eyes, like two diamonds.

Ty threw his arms around his mother. His mother hugged him tightly and cried.

Just then, the trader with the Star Wars shirt reached into Ty's pant pocket and yanked out Ty's prepaid cards. Tekka lunged at the figure who pushed him back. The thief ran through the opening at the next curve of stands. The siblings ran after him chasing him down the street. They passed rundown buildings and the intersection.

At the entrance to the overpass, there was the figure of a young woman in a trench coat and hat with her bottle red hair pulled up in a bun at the top of the catwalk. The thief handed one prepaid card to the woman.

Ty was the first to cross the intersection and caught up to the thief on the top of the catwalk over the freeway. Ty grabbed the thief by the lapels of his blazer and spun him around, shoving him into the chain linked fence of the catwalk. The thief twisted free, grabbed and pinned Ty to the chain linked fence. The slender man was surprisingly strong. Ty, filled with adrenaline and something new, his mother's love, pushed the thief with all his might. The thief fell to the concrete with an exhale of breath. Before he could get away, Ty held him, putting all his weight on top of the man. They were in the middle of the catwalk and the woman backed away towards the other end. The thief looked around then bared his teeth. With a grunt, he shoved Ty in a new direction, towards a hole in the fence.

The thief pushed Ty, who saw one edge of the hole in the fence behind him. Thrown off balance, Ty fell back towards the hole 80 feet above the speeding traffic below. Panicked, his stomach lurched. With deft hands he grabbed the sides of the fence, stopping his fall. Holding on white knuckled for all he was worth, he looked down with eyes bulging in terror. He breathed heavily. His biceps twitched. Three fingers released their grip on one hand. He stared at them with frightened eyes. His other hand slipped completely. Then, he swung his left hand up again, catching two fingers on the cold metal of the fencing. He still hung suspended over the hole high in the air above the speeding cars on the highway below. His terror of heights froze him now. He couldn't jump up onto the concrete footbridge if he tried. He closed his eyes and screamed, "Help me!" He couldn't hold on much longer. Ty thought of how his body would splat on the freeway and he would die. It wasn't fair. He didn't even get to talk to his mother. Ty wished he could say goodbye to the mother he just found not ten minutes ago.

32

Ty and His Mother Together Finally

HE OPENED HIS eyes and saw his mother and siblings running up the catwalk.

"Mother," he screamed. Simultaneously, he realized she couldn't hear him. Hot tears ran down his face, two silver tracks, like the train tracks. "Awwwww!" Ty felt trapped, like when he was on the speeding locomotive. So, this was the end. He found his mother only to be killed by a thief. What good was the million dollars?

The thief had run the opposite direction of his family. But, at the end of the pedestrian overpass. It was a footbridge above the freeway for pedestrians. The pedestrian bridge a chain linked hurricane fence on both sides and curved inward at the top, leaving four feet of open sky at the top. Three Harley's and their riders drove up the pedestrian bridge. They stopped, blocking the thief and the woman in the trench coat and hat. The thief couldn't go left or right, so he started climbing the fence. The woman took off her hat and trench coat revealing a curvy figure in a tight black dress. Red ran to the thief and yanked him down, then knocked him out with a right cross. Then, he turned with his right fist ready. He stopped short. The girl was batting her long eyelashes at him.

"Hi Red. It's been a while, hasn't it?" The woman's sultry voice was familiar.

Vanessa, or Candy, or whatever her real name is, Justin thought momentarily. His heart raced, but not at Vanessa's voice. He was slipping through the hole. He told himself to hold on.

Leo and Kofi ran to help Ty's family pull him out of the fence hole. They laid him on the concrete footbridge with his head in his mother's lap.

"Whew, good thing we rode past this footbridge." Leo patted him on the back.

Ty blinked, trying to control his breathing. He managed to whisper, "Thanks."

Kofi smiled down at his friend, "Just like old times saving your bacon when you tried to get back on the train."

Red joined Kofi in a chuckle.

Saunia signed to Ty, "MY BOY. YOU'VE COME-BACK. I LOVE YOU." She smoothed his sweaty hair back and kissed his forehead.

When Ty had recovered, he sat up. He was relieved that he was alive. He decided not to let angry words get between him and his mother.

"MOTHER." He signed, "I LOVE YOU."

She signed the same back to Ty.

"I DON'T-CARE . . ." Ty stopped signing. He didn't know the rest of the signs. It had been too many years and he was only three when he had been sold away.

"Brother, would you interpret?"

Tekka nodded and moved next to his brother across from his mother.

All of a sudden, his mother grabbed his face in both of her hands. She looked into Ty's eyes.

"FORGIVE-ME," his mother signed.

The copper-haired son inhaled deeply. Ever since that NFLS woman told him that his mother sold him to the NFLS, he had been bitter. He chewed on his lip. He saw Trini chewing on her lip too. And when he looked at his mother, she was chewing on hers. They were connected … a family. Before any explanation was given, Ty had already decided he would forgive his mother. He nodded.

He found out that his father had just died, she didn't have a job and she was pregnant and later had a miscarriage. Ty was a child prodigy. The NFLS men said that he would be a whiz kid and a TV star. In exchange, the NFLS would give them enough for rent and food for ten years. She asked him, "PLEASE, FORGIVE ME? I'M SORRY. I—" Those diamond eyes glistened filled with tears.

Ty saw the poverty that his family lived in Old Denver and his heart ached. So, he held her hand and interrupted her, saying, "Mother, I forgive you. Back in Moab, I decided to forgive you." He swallowed. Then, he closed and opened his eyes. "I've been having a nightmare. Maybe you can help me."

"TELL-ME YOUR DREAM," she signed.

Ty told her about the alley, his playing with matches, lighting paper and a leaf on fire. How the old truck, the ally even the apartment building all lit on fire. At last, he told her about the man walking in the flames.

His throat constricted in fear and dread. He looked down and took her hand. When he looked up, he used his right hand to sign, "FATHER?" He lifted both his eyebrows in a questioning expression.

Put her petite hand on the side of his face and nodded. His suspicion was confirmed. His worst nightmare was that he lit a fire and his father had burned in the blaze. He now knew his worst nightmare was true. He had killed his father with the fire he had lit. Distraught with grief, shame and relief, he collapsed into his mother's loving arms.

After all the tears were expelled, like a cloud drained of its moisture, he sat back with his eyes downcast. Suddenly, Ty gritted his teeth and took the W branded lighter out of his pocket. He gave it one last look. The lighter with the symbol of the Wayne's ranch was the last thing from his fake life. He held it in a throwing position, and with the precision of a ball player, threw the fire starter thru an opening in the chain-linked fence. It soared out of sight. Slowly, he looked up and asked, "MOTHER, FORGIVE ME."

His brother put his hand on his shoulder. "Ty, you misunderstand. There were two fires. When you were a little tike, you lit a leaf fire in the ally. Father found you and stomped the fire out. It was eight or nine months after that the apartment caught on fire," Tekka swallowed. "Father made sure we were out on the sidewalk, then ran back in." Tekka swallowed again.

Tears that were a trickled now flowed down their mother's face like a dam had burst. Ty felt moisture on his cheeks as well.

"We saw him scoot a family out the door to us. But they said one child was missing," Tekka said. "Their family and mother held a taut blanket over an old mattress in the alley when they appeared in the upstairs window on the alley side. The girl jumped in time. But … not our Father." Tekka looked at his feet. All were silent with shiny cheeks.

As the night fell, Ty sat with his mother's hand in his looking up at the moon and stars while Tekka and Trini spoke softly to each other. They sat like that silently for a few minutes, both looking up. Ty always felt at peace looking at the stars. He remembered a signed phrase, then signed and said, "The stars show God's handiwork."

Everyone's eyes turned up to star gaze with Ty as they stood on the catwalk overpass.

His mother waved her hand in front of Ty to get his attention. She signed, "YOU REMEMBERED." His mother was nodding her head eyes smiling.

"YES." Ty smiled widely.

She stood up and pointed at the moon, "AND I THOUGHT-of YOU WHEN I LOOKED-AT the MOON."

Ty inhaled, "I LOOKED-at the MOON EVERY-NIGHT SINCE THEY TOLD ME ABOUT YOU and WONDERED IF YOU were LOOKING at THAT SAME MOON."

His mother's face beamed with happiness. She placed her hand on Ty's shoulder. Ty looked at his mother when suddenly, her face twisted in horror.

Vanessa ran on the catwalk at them. Her full force slammed into Ty, whose body knocked into his mother. His mother flew backwards. Vanessa's momentum carried her forward and she couldn't stop. She fell through the hole. Before the stunned Ty could react, he watched his mother and Vanessa falling through the hole. A hole that looked to Ty to be an opening between life and death. A hole that looked like a huge laughing mouth, mocking his fate. He stood, holding on to the cold hurricane fence with one hand, the other hand reaching downward towards his mother.

"Mother!" He screamed. He watched Vanessa falling. His mother had managed to grab on to the fencing edge with her quick reflexes. He couldn't lose his mother, he frantically reached at the fence edge and grabbed his mother's arm. He heaved with all his might. Other hands came to help him pull his mother up to safety.

Meanwhile, Vanessa was falling straight down where the middle of the freeway was outfitted with modern mass transit.

Ty closed his eyes and saw Vanessa slam into the roof of the light rail car.

He opened his eyes and saw a streak with red hair. In a second, Red was on top of the train car with his arms extended.

Vanessa kicked her feet as she fell, screaming.

She fell into Red's outstretched arms.

They and the train sped down the tracks.

Ty collapsed onto the concrete in a lump, like a balloon with all its air let out. He covered his head, rocked back and forth, screaming, "The Beast. The Beast. The Beast."

Kofi put a hand on his shoulder, "Remember, we defeated the Beast."

Ty sat up. He drew his hand over his face, as if erasing a white board. He focused his eyes on his trusted friend.

Kofi smiled at Ty.

"That train," Trini pointed after the commuter train, "will stop at New Liberty Station. Red and Vanessa will disembark and go off with each other."

The copper-haired teen was relieved. He had forgiven both Vanessa and Red and didn't wish them harm. There was one more whom he overlooked.

Ty took Trini's hands in his while saying, "Um, … Trini."

"Yes," Trini said. She looked at him, studying his gold flecked brown eyes. They were sad and glistened.

"I'm sorry," he said. "I'll just say it. I was wrong. And, thank you. Thank you for not giving up on me." His eyebrows dipped and he looked from under them.

Trini kissed his cheek and said, "Welcome home, bro!"

Then, Ty nodded to Kofi and Leo. He put his arm around his mother. She exhaled and smiled at her teen son. Tekka and Trini stood arm in arm next to them.

The police shoved the thief's head down into the police vehicle parked at the end of the catwalk bridge. Pedestrian traffic on the bridge went back to normal. The gawkers walked on. A grey cat bounded by with a small child chasing the pet. A middle-aged woman pulled a small tow box of groceries behind her. The sun cast its golden glow on the west side of the bridge.

Ty and his Wayfield family hugged.

The sun seemed to float over the mountain peaks. It was the golden hour. Ty shaded his eyes with a hand. He Kofi and Leo. The three friends shook hands, patted backs, and laughed. Ty said, "Thank you, partners."

"Mates," Leo said, "It's thank you, Mates." Leo broke into a monkey smile.

Leo and Ty laughed.

"Whizkids, we're finally free," Kofi said. He looked from Ty to Leo putting his hand in the middle as a team, waiting for the other two. Leo placed his hand in the middle and nodded.

To their dismay, Ty stepped back. Kofi and Leo wrinkled their brows. Ty turned to his left. Trini stood there, eyes wide. Golden light reflected off her intelligent brown eyes.

"Whizkid," Ty said. He picked up his sister's hand and placed it on Kofi and Leo's hands.

Trini smiled.

Ty completed the Whizkid team by placing his tan hand on the other three.

About the Author

I have extensive training. My first Master's degree is in Education. I have held secondary teaching credentials in Social Studies. I am working on a second Masters in History and plan to create an exhibit on Patience Loader Rozsa's Utah Territory. I will graduate in June 2020. I have taught English to Deaf youth, homeschooled and continue to work with youth. I started writing young adult fiction while teaching high school American Sign Language and raising two teens. I want to pass on my love for learning and reading to the young adults who read my books. I love fiction books of the genres of Dystopia and Historical Fiction. I live in Lehi, Utah with a daughter, son, and husband. In my free time, I dress in period attire for historical reenactments.

Printed in the United States
By Bookmasters